Echoes *of the* Red Earth

Cornelius van Dijk

 FriesenPress

One Printers Way
Altona, MB R0G 0B0
Canada

www.friesenpress.com

Copyright © 2024 by Cornelius van Dijk
First Edition — 2024

All rights reserved.

No part of this publication may be reproduced in any form, or by any means, electronic or mechanical, including photocopying, recording, or any information browsing, storage, or retrieval system, without permission in writing from FriesenPress.

ISBN
978-1-03-919629-2 (Hardcover)
978-1-03-919628-5 (Paperback)
978-1-03-919630-8 (eBook)

1. FICTION, SCIENCE FICTION, APOCALYPTIC & POST-APOCALYPTIC

Distributed to the trade by The Ingram Book Company

Echoes *of the* Red Earth

PROLOGUE

Generations have come and gone, disasters have struck, sicknesses and starvation have wiped out clans and villages.

These are the stories of the survivors, the Adams and Eves, nameless, faceless, new beginnings after the floods.

The stories may shock you; they may bore you, and they may be repetitive.

THE PAST IS
THE FUTURE

I am a child of the future, but I live in the present, and I have also been in the past. I live fourteen generations from the present, so as yet I have no name. My skin is red in colour, and my hair is long and black. My hair is a sign of my strength; I am told to keep it long.

I am never to drink the fermented juice that drips from the pile of grapes that Uncle keeps in the vessel that he made from the red clay. I am never to touch a corpse.

Father says I get my red skin from the red cliffs. He says I am created from the red clay that is in those cliffs.

Uncle uses the red clay to make pottery for cooking and tablets for writing. He says it is pure and virgin earth, the best to be used for moulding pottery.

Father shows me the patterns of lights in the sky at night. He says they are stars. A group of seven stars in a pattern resemble a pot that Uncle made from the red clay. The two stars at the end point to a star that is always in the same position. All other stars revolve around it.

Father says to never lose sight of this star. It is the star that will save us when we are lost. My sister calls it the "Saviour." This star is the last star on the end of the handle of the Small Dipper. Like the Big Dipper, it also has seven stars in the pattern, resembling a ladle.

Father has named each star in the pattern for the seven of us that are in our group. We are a small tribe. Everyone else has disappeared, some by fire, some by flood, and many by famine and disease.

I often wonder why it is just us who are left. It is my father and his brother, my brother and his wife, my sister, my uncle's daughter, and me. My cousin, his wife, and their two daughters were with us for a while, but they left to go to the other side of the river. I heard that his wife died on the way and became a petrified rock.

Travelling with us is an orphan pup from one of the fanged creatures. It has adopted us like its family. I think the offspring of this fanged creature will be man's best friend for many years to come, forsaking its original family.

I have become proficient with the use of the bow and arrow, and when I shoot, it is like I have become one in spirit with the bow. There is no thought anymore, just one fluid motion, and the beast I hunt for food drops in front of me. They say it is because I am gifted, and the spirit of the bow is in me also.

I have seen the seven colours of the bow in the sky after a rain: red, orange, yellow, green, blue, indigo, and violet. They say the great creator placed the bow in the sky, which appears after a storm as a sign.

They tell me that my mind is sharp, and my eyes are like that of an eagle. My right eye is blue, and my left eye is green. I can see things others cannot, for I easily see a division in the colours of the rainbow, whereas the others only see a blurred distinction between the colours.

I have searched for wood with these colours and made a bow compounded with these seven different woods, layering them like the colours of the bow in the sky. It is a superb bow, as if crafted by a god.

Ahead of us in the distance are many towers that appear to be made of stone. Some have fallen, and all are crumbling. Inside these towers are many white boxes with black screens for faces. They have small squares with figures on a tablet before them, connected by a thin vine, braided in three. They are like the tablets that Uncle moulds from the red clay, but they contain no knowledge, just empty faces, like the long-tailed creatures that walk like us but have no knowledge.

The people who used to live there disappeared generations ago. Farther in the distance are more towers. They are in the shape of a pyramid. These towers are few in number, but although thousands of years older, they are in far better shape than the newer towers. If I look hard, I can find some tablets of stone with figures on them. I am told they contain knowledge. Pictures of people on those tablets show that they were people like us.

Father says I am to repopulate the earth and pass on the knowledge that I have learned from him. I do not remember my mother. I am sure I had one, even though I was told I was created from the red clay, and my sister was created from my rib.

I am told that there is a great creator who created everything. He set everything in motion, and the stars all point to him. He created a set of laws for everything to follow.

Tonight the moon is very bright, its light reflecting off the snow. It is the last full moon before the days get warmer. Uncle calls it the "Snow Moon."

Soon a red-breasted avian, as red as I am, will appear in the area. I wonder if it was created from the same red clay as I was. It follows me as it picks up the wriggling creatures to feed its young. It is as if the red-breasted avian knows me. I am not sure how it knows when to leave before the cold weather comes or how it knows when to return. The red-breasted avian must visit my mother when it leaves.

There is another bright light in the sky tonight. It has a tail on the end of it. I have seen a picture of it on a tablet, but no one has seen it before. I think it comes once every hundred revolutions of the sun.

Tonight I am out hunting for food. In front of me is a beast like what I have seen on the carvings among the ruins, but it is more like a cross between a couple of the beasts pictured. Instead of two horns on each side of its head, this beast has one horn coming straight out of its forehead. It also has wings on its shoulders, but I think it is too heavy to fly.

Far in the distance is a huge desert. That is the end of the world; nothing can live in that heat. On the other side of us is a huge body of water. It is the other end of the world. Uncle says that nothing can live on the other side of the body of water. They will drown before they get there.

I can see the stars clearly tonight, the seven-star pattern of the Big Dipper is shining brightly. Nothing can inhabit those stars because, like the great beast that I am about to shoot with my bow, we are unable to fly a few feet above ourselves.

There is a great tree in the distance. It is the largest tree around. Father says it contains knowledge because it has been here since the beginning of the world.

My sister found a branch that is hollow. With some shaping using a sharp stone, she has carved an end that she places in her mouth. As she blows into this branch, the most beautiful music comes out of it. It is as if her spirit is coming out of her and singing through the branch. Her and the branch become as one, as I have become one with my bow.

One day she is with me as I hunt. The rain has stopped, and all is still as the bow in the sky appears to span the whole earth. We see the one-horned beast lift its head. With a quick draw, I lift my bow, letting an arrow fly. It is the bow with the wood of the seven colours of the rainbow. With a sharp twang, the bowstring releases, and the arrow flies straight and true.

She listens to the sound, then fashions a bow of the seven pieces of wood, compounded like the colours of the rainbow. She curves the bow a little differently, then she takes seven strings, like the seven stars in a row, and fastens them to the bow. When everything is taut, she strums it with her fingers. It is like the bow sings a beautiful melody.

Sometimes a foul spirit enters Uncle after he has drunk the juice from the fermented grapes. When the spirit enters him, my sister plays for him. The soothing music drives the foul spirit away, and Uncle starts making marks on his tablets again. He is trying to make a sequence of designs to put in order, so he can remember how things are done.

My cousin has also become one with a couple of sticks and sharp rocks. She rubs the two sticks together rapidly over a bundle of dry grass. The heat ignites the dry grass, and she blows into it to create a fire. At times when the sticks are damp, she will strike two stones together. They will make a spark, and soon the dried grass is burning with a sweet odour. It is a pleasing smell for Father.

Father puts the beast that I shot into the red dipper that Uncle made. It resembles the seven-star pattern in the sky. As the meat is cooking with a sweet, savoury smell, the fanged creatures and the long-tailed creatures that walk like us gather around. We throw the bones to the fanged creatures, and they eat them. The long-tailed creatures that walk like us chatter incessantly.

I tease my cousin that we look like the long-tailed creatures that walk like us, but they are like the boxes I have seen in the ruins, empty screens with no knowledge. I will marry my cousin because I am told it is wrong to marry my sister. We will have children, and they will have stories to tell.

I look at the seven stars and think, seven things are easy to remember. We are seven in our family, like the seven stars. Three is an easier number to remember, as in the three parts of the egg, which we eat often.

Uncle tells me that he will stop the number of different symbols on the tablets at thirty because he does not believe people will be able to remember things past thirty. He says the symbols will be like numbers; you will always be able to switch them around, to change the tales being told. Most arrangements will have between three and seven symbols, making a word.

He also says the moon is full every twenty-eight days, but thirty is easier to remember, so he has created a month of thirty days and a week of seven days. A full rotation of the four seasons around the sun is three hundred and sixty-five days, so he has divided what he calls a year into twelve months, with each of them having four weeks. He has named each month after the twelve patterns of stars he believes are in the sky.

Of course, one item is the easiest to remember, like the one creator who created the seven stars and the three parts that make the egg.

With my eyes I see thousands upon thousands of stars, but I always look to the seven stars and the two on the end that point to the saving star or fixed star. The fixed star is called the Saviour because all the stars revolve around it, and it does not move. My sister thinks it is the god star, the maker of all stars.

I think that if I can travel to the star as fast as the light travels from the star, I can go to a different era and watch the pyramids being built. I do not believe there is no one else but the seven of us. It is like the seven stars. There are multitudes of stars, but we only see what is around us.

I will travel across the desert with my wife, and we will return one day with knowledge. Our children will tell the stories over time. Their stories will be the same, but different, depending on which child tells the story.

THE BLUE HILLS

The red-breasted avian chirps early in the morning, searching for the wriggling creatures crawling in the wet earth. I awaken, watching her flit around as she pulls the wriggling creatures from the dirt. I smile as she pulls on one end while the other end tries to re-enter the earth. Sometimes the wriggling creature snaps in half, both halves wriggling, one half in the red-breasted avian's orange beak, and the other half disappearing into the ground.

A brilliant reddish hue covers the clouds as the morning sun rises over the red cliffs. I and the red-breasted avian are one, created from the red clay of these cliffs. On the other side of the great water, the moon dips below the horizon as it prepares to sleep for the day. This morning the moon is full and round, a vivid orange colour emitting from her. I refer to the moon as a "she" because it has the same face as Sis when she sleeps.

The water before me is as smooth as glass. Small specks of white float on its blue-green surface. Ice; some white, some blue-green, some soft, some hard, float upon the water, bobbing in the waves. The green ice is hard, as hard as the sparkling rock that Sis found in the soft black rock last summer.

"Look at this!" She had smiled at me, her eyes shiny.

"Feel it," She had urged, placing it in my fingers. The rock was hard and lustrous, sparkling in the sunlight like the ice upon the water; green, blue, violet, and other brilliant colours reflecting in the sun.

"How can something so hard come from something so soft?" She had turned her face to me, her eyes twinkling.

"Look what Uncle has created." She had held her finger up to me, showing me a yellow band circling it, a diamond-shape embedded in it, sparkling in the sun.

Uncle had created the metal band from the pure soft metal he dredged from the bottom of the river. Melting the yellow ore, he placed the sparkling rock in it, creating a symbol that will last for eternity. He placed it on Sis's finger, telling her that their bond will last forever.

I rise from the soft moss. The moss is cool, wet, tickling my arches, but when it is dry, it is a soft mat to lie on. Steam rises around me as the sun's rays warm the earth. I stretch, facing the sun, feeling its warmth on my body. I walk toward the water's edge, crossing a muddy depression in the ground, cool mud squishing between my toes, my six toes embedding their imprint into the soft ground. I walk across the soft mud, marvelling at how the mud turns to soft sand as I near the rocky shore. I look back at my tracks, seeing my imprints change from firm indentations to obscure prints as I walk through the white sand.

The mud is red, the sand is white, and the rock ledge is black. The sea beyond me appears blue. I wonder how this can be.

I stand on the rock ledge, its base firm under my feet, hard, my feet leaving no imprint. It is as if I leave no trace as I stand upon it. The sound of the water lapping against the rock ledge entices me. I yearn to dip into the water, to cleanse myself. I kneel, lowering my hand into the water, then reach out to grab a speck of pale green ice rising and falling in the waves. The water is ice cold, and my fingers turn white, tingling. I grab a large chunk of the pale green ice, gripping it in my hand. My hand becomes numb, turning blue. I toss the ice from hand to hand. I cover the ice with moss, anxious to show it to Sis and tell her how it matches her special rock, the rock she says will last for eternity.

"Where were you?" Sis beams at me as I near the camp, running to greet me. She leaps on me, her legs encircling my waist and her head thrown back as she wraps her arms around my neck.

"Look what I found!" I show her the ice wrapped in moss.

She releases my neck, balancing on me, her legs gripping tighter. She reaches for the moss, her eyes glowing. I watch excitedly as she opens it. The ice has melted. Only bits of wet moss fall from her hand, dripping wet, the cool water running down her belly. The coloured ice, as hard as rock, has turned into a clear, cold liquid, dripping from the green moss.

"Where is your rock?" She giggles, lifting her finger to me, showing me the diamond embedded in the soft gold band. "Although some things appear the same, they are quite different at times."

Her eyes are alluring as she speaks.

"I will wear the ring on my finger for years to come, a symbol to last for eternity." She kisses the ring, then leaps down from me.

"Don't worry," she says, smiling at me. "You will find another." Wet moss clings to her body, green against her red skin. She wipes it off, her nipples puckering from the coolness. I look into her eyes, blue-green like the ice but warm.

"Where do you think the blue-green ice comes from?" Cous asks, looking up at me.

"I will look for the source," I say. I have no idea where the ice comes from or where the sparkling rock that is the same colour as the ice originated from. Both are hard, but one will melt, and the other will last for eternity.

"When all the snow is gone from the hills, I will search for the beginnings of the ice," I say as I look wistfully at the hills. "Last summer I climbed the great hill and looked beyond the red cliffs, which we are told is the end of the world. In the far distance, I saw a wisp of smoke rising from a fire, much like the smoke rising from the fire beside our tents, the tents we make from the skins of the beasts we slay."

"I wonder if there is other life on this earth," Cous says, looking at the sky. "I believe there is life among the seven stars in the pattern that Father makes his pottery in."

"This is the third full moon since the days have been getting longer," Sis says. "During the second full moon, it appeared that a dark hand passed over the moon for a portion of the night, causing blackness in the sky." She holds up the stick she uses to mark the moon cycles, pointing to the last remaining star in the morning sky.

"It was during this time that the moon turned a deep red colour, darker than the red cliffs, emitting no light at all," Cous reminds us. "After that, until the next full moon, the air was icy cold, the ground was white with snow, and the nights were freezing."

"And we spent most of our days looking for trees and branches to throw on the fire," I reply, chuckling as I remember gathering wood for the fire. "It was hard work to gather the wood in the deep snow and the cold weather."

"But now the weather is warm." Sis says, beaming. "We no longer need to wear heavy skins to keep us warm." She stands in front of us, her hands on her hips, her head tossed to the side.

Honk! Honk! A long-necked feathered creature flies overhead, flying toward the source of the floating icebergs.

"It is alone," Cous says, looking up.

"Others will follow her," Sis replies. "She is the leader. The female is always in front." I chuckle. "Don't laugh!" She leaps on me and tosses me to the ground. She pins my arms down, her pelvis pushing my pelvis into the sand.

Honk! Honk! Other long-necked feathered creatures follow the leader, flying in a vee formation. "See, more are coming." She rolls off me, sitting in the sand.

"Why do they fly in a vee?" Cous asks.

"This is the feathered creature that the others follow." Sis sits in the sand with her legs outward in the shape of a vee. She touches the feathery folds between her legs.

"The other feathered creatures follow her. The strongest is in the front, and the two lines each angle away from the one that leads, then each one rotates through the line from front to back and then from back to front again." She moves her hands up and down her legs, indicating the movements of the long-necked feathered creatures.

"I think this is to conserve energy. Each one shares its wings so as not to tire the next one in line. I will make a mark like this formation and call it a vee," she says, drawing a vee in the sand and angling it toward herself. "I will show it to Uncle, who is trying to match the letters to words spoken." She glances at Uncle as he struggles to make symbols on a tablet of soft clay. Unconsciously, she crosses her legs and leans forward.

"I will follow the long-necked feathered creatures to find where they go, and they will show me their secrets," I say as I look at Cous and Sis as they sit across from me. "Last summer I saw enormous winged creatures with no feathers on them. These winged creatures could no longer fly and were sitting disarrayed together in a meadow, like corpses in a graveyard. Their skin was hard and grey, and instead of eyes, they had a clear substance, easy to look through. I tapped on it, feeling its hardness. I could easily see the emptiness inside their heads as I looked through the clear substance. Their feet were round with a soft black layer on the outside and a hard, smooth grey disc in the centre. As I looked into the winged creatures' heads, I saw bones sitting on a seat made from the skins of the beasts. These bones were like those of the long-tailed creatures that live in the forest. But like us, they had no tail. I have never seen any other substance in the forest or cliffs like what these large winged creatures are composed of, or creatures with feet as round as theirs. These winged creatures do not decompose like the feathered creatures. They seem to last for eternity, but they never fly. They must have been used to transplant the gods in the past, gods long since dead."

"Do you think there are others like us?" Cous asks, looking at me.

"Of course!" Sis jumps up. She erases the imprint of the vee her body made in the sand, sweeping her feet across it, her toes curling to scoop sand into the impressions of her bum, the balls of her feet levelling it out. "I will go with you," she says, looking into my eyes.

"The fanged creature that followed me during the last full moon will come with me, I say to her. The disappointment in her face clearly shows.

"It has a white star like a cross on its forehead, and like you, its one eye is blue, and the other eye is green." Cous reaches over and pets the young orphan. "And it's red like us."

"He follows you wherever you go. You have become its master." Sis kneels in front of the fanged pup, letting it sniff her as she pets it.

A red-breasted avian chirps at us, skipping across the meadow as it searches for the wriggling creatures. It stops at a small puddle, tugs on one of the wriggling creatures, then pulls it from the damp earth.

"Look at the red-breasted avian," Sis puts her hands on her breasts, cupping them as she lifts them. "Her chest is red like mine. I am the red-breasted feathered creature."

"But you have no feathers." I run my hands across her smooth breasts. She giggles, smiling coyly, her nipples hard and erect. Cous smiles shyly at her.

We watch the red-breasted avian as it searches for the wriggling creatures emerging from the ground. When it finds one, it plucks it from the earth before flying to its nest, the wriggling creature dangling from its beak.

"Let's catch the finned creatures that swim in the water." Sis leaps up, pulling a wriggling creature from the ground. It stretches three times its length before releasing itself, wriggling around her finger.

"Ew!" She scrunches her nose. I poke a thorn through its middle, embedding it on the hook. The wriggling creature curls around, trying to free itself from the thorn.

"Let me try to catch the finned creature," Cous pleads. I tie a tiny vine to the thorn, looping the other end through a hole at the end of a flexible yet strong branch. Then I hand it to Cous, the hook dangling from it.

Cous smiles at me, then stands on the ledge, dropping the hook into the water, letting the wriggling creature skip along the ripples. A large finned creature with scales lunges for it, its sleek body surging through the water, swallowing the wriggling creature, thorn, and all.

"You got one." Sis leaps with excitement, her bare feet planted firmly on the rock. She grabs the rod, helping Cous draw the finned creature in.

"Quick!" They yell at me. They both struggle, hanging onto the rod and groaning as it curves. The finned creature thrashes vigorously, the thorn embedded through its lip. I reach around them, grab the string, and pull the finned creature onto the rock beside me, kicking it away from the water. The slits behind its mouth open and close as the finned creature struggles to breathe.

"It's one third my length." Sis gushes as she unhooks the thorn from its lip. She touches its slimy scales, hooking her fingers beneath the gills as she lifts the finned creature up.

"You will be delicious roasted." She giggles, lifting it to her mouth and kissing its nose. Cous smiles, feeling elated from catching the finned creature with scales.

"I will carry the scaled creature." Sis leans over, kissing me, touching me. She beams as she holds the finned creature. I smell her excitement as she stands next to me, her musky odour.

"Your skin is smooth; you have no scales." She rubs her hands along my body, her hands soft. She grabs my hand as we walk back to our tent.

"Will you roast it for us?" She asks Uncle as he sits by his tent, his flask in his hand. "It's a beauty." She holds the finned creature up with one hand, her other hand on her hip, her legs bent as she poses for him. The sun shines behind her, her hair flowing wildly. I look at Uncle as he stares at her, his eyes bleary.

Cous blows on the coals, then wraps the finned creature in wet leaves. I place the bundle over the coals, and then put more coals on top of the wet leaves. The meat sizzles, steam rises from it and goes between the coals, popping the cool ones as the steam heats them. The smell is tantalizing, and our stomachs growl.

"It will be so good," Sis says, her face beaming.

Father walks toward us with a sack of grain in his hands. I help him pound the grain into a fine powder as Cous prepares the hot coals to bake the flat bread. Sis breaks an egg, then drops it onto the crushed grains and scoops water into the mixture. She kneads the dough to a proper consistency, rolling it into a ball, then spreads it out into a flat cake. She drops the cake onto the hot stone, watching as tiny bumps appear across it. She turns the flat bread over, revealing its golden-brown colour, the colour of her nipples. When both sides are a golden brown, she divides it into seven and passes us each a piece.

Cous removes the finned creature from the coals, pulling the leaves from it and separating the rainbow-coloured skin from the pink flesh inside. I pass each person a piece, and we eat the flatbread and the finned creature together until our bellies are sated.

"Tomorrow I will search for the source of the ice," I say. "I want to see where it comes from."

"Why?" Sis asks, tears sparkling in her eyes. "We cannot go." She stands beside Cous, giving me a beguiling look. I gaze at her standing before me, her body full and flushed, remembering the musky scent as she stood beside me, the aroma of the finned creature emitting from her body.

"I will come back." I bite into the pink flesh of the finned creature, looking at her, desiring her.

"Take the dried meat, it will sustain you." Our brother's wife hands me a satchel of the dried pink flesh. She has learned to hang the finned creatures over tree branches, letting them dry out in the hot sun. She has found that it will last a long time like this, and we can eat the dried meat any time we like. It will also provide food for us this coming cold season.

I feel sad to leave, but I am excited to explore. I roll my mat out across the tent floor. "I will leave early in the morning," I whisper.

"We will lie with you." Cous and Sis lie on each side of me, our bare skin against each other's. I lie awake, listening to their soft snores, my mind preparing for the journey. Sis snuggles against me, her breasts pushing against my face. I suckle on her nipples, feeling their tiny bumps becoming hard in my mouth. She puts an arm around me, holding me close. She wraps her legs around me. I fall asleep in her arms, dreaming wonderful dreams.

The fanged pup licks my nose, waking me. Sis's right hand is on my loins, her other hand is against her face, her thumb in her mouth. She opens her eyes, giving me a shy look. "Come back safely," she whispers, leaning over me, her blue-green eyes peering into mine.

I crawl from between the two, then go outside to relieve myself. A flock of the long-necked feathered creatures flies overhead, honking loudly. I crawl back inside and roll my belongings inside my mat, then tie a string around it. "I will leave today," I say, staring at Sis as she leans on her elbow, her body stretched out. "I will look for the wisp of smoke I saw last summer on the other side of the red cliffs."

Cous rises from the mat, grumbling.

I whistle for the fanged pup. The warm rains have made the ground soft and spongy. The morning dew is heavy and wet on the newly growing green grass.

Sis sits on the mat, rubbing tallow on the leather moccasins she made for me. "These will keep your feet warm and dry." Her eyes smile at me.

"Thanks." I grin at her. "When I return, I will make you a pair. I will find the beast with the strongest hide for them." I look at her slender feet, her toes flexing as she stretches. She leans forward, touching her toes, her body lithe and trim, her long black hair flowing across her back.

"Here, take the rest of the tallow." She passes me a small piece, her fingers shiny from rubbing it on my moccasins. "It will also keep your skin smooth." She winks at me, rubbing the tallow on her body until her skin glistens.

Cous packs some dried meat mixed with berries for my trip, passing me a leather pouch filled with it.

Sis rises and hugs me, tears flowing down her face. "I will miss you," she whispers, nuzzling my neck. "Come back safely to us."

"I will be careful." I hug her, tasting the saltiness of her tears as I kiss her. She clings to me, sobbing.

"Don't fall off the edge of the earth," Uncle warns me. "Remember, the earth is flat. If you stumble at the edge of the red cliffs, you will fall down forever. Your arms and legs will keep flailing in the empty air for eternity, never reaching the bottom."

Father gives me his blessing. "Here, take my bow made of the seven woods." He gives me his bow he made as a child. I carry the bow in my left hand, putting the sheath of arrows over my right shoulder.

"I will walk with you to the end of the meadow." Cous picks up a hollow instrument and blows into it, creating a beautiful melody as we walk. We walk through the meadow, picking flowers and smelling them. A yellow insect with black stripes and a fuzzy body lands on my bow, crawling on the bow string, its legs laden with yellow pollen. I laugh and then flick it off, watching it fly to another flower.

Screech! Overhead, a red feathered creature with a hooked beak and sharp talons soars through the sky, its wings outstretched. Suddenly, it tucks its wings in, swooping down. With its sharp talons, it grabs a furry rodent, then flies to the top of the cliffs. Far up in the cliffs, I see a nest. Five babies are inside, their mouths open. The red feathered creature swallows the rodent, then regurgitates it into her young's gaping mouths.

A flock of the long-necked feathered creatures fly over us, honking loudly as they fly in a vee formation. We stop, looking up at them as they honk. "I will follow them, but I will come back," I say as I put my arm around Cous and Sis.

"Take these leaves and remember me." Cous passes me a sachet of dried leaves. "At the end of the day, drink the leaves with hot water, sweeten it with the golden liquid from the fuzzy yellow insects' hive, and dream of me. We are the six sides that are left, and you are the seventh in the centre, binding us together, the sweet nectar inside."

We lie down together on the moss, feeling its softness on our bare skin. We watch the long-necked feathered creatures land in the water by the falls, their long necks bobbing under the water to get the fresh shoots growing on the bottom. We giggle as the long-necked feathered creatures dive in the water, honking as they surface. The warmth from the sun is on our backs, and we forget about time.

"Take me with you." Cous pushes me into the soft moss, kissing me, touching me, enticing me. I sink down in the moss, closing my eyes, enjoying the sensation.

"I will have you forever," I murmur in ecstasy. "Always together."

We rise and wash our bodies in the pond, looking at each other shyly. Then I turn and walk toward the red cliffs, my heart sad but exhilarated.

I leave the meadow with the fanged pup by my side. I follow the stream, listening to it gurgling as it flows from the cliffs, the sound getting louder. Another set of falls appears before me, larger than the ones at Father's camp. There is a ledge that juts out from the base of the cliff which the falls flow over. Behind the ledge is a small hole, an entrance into the rock face. I crawl along the ledge, my fingers touching the wet face of the wall. Water splashes up from the falls, tiny droplets landing on me. The rushing sound of the water is both exhilarating and frightening. I dare not fall off the ledge into the falls. At times the sun shines through the sheet of cascading water, casting shadows on the rock face behind the falls. I kneel, peering through the tiny opening, well hidden from most people.

"You have the gift of sight," Father would say to me. "Use it well."

I look inside. The walls are white with a band of yellow running across them. I place my bow and arrows beside the entrance before crawling into the cavern. The fanged pup sits at the edge of the falls, not daring to walk across the ledge. The air within the cavern is surprisingly dry. I sit quietly, letting my eyes adjust to the darkness.

A carving of a three-toed beast is on the far wall. This beast has scales on its back. It stands on two legs. Two toes point forward, and one toe points backward. Its tail is three times its length, its body twice my height. Wings without feathers protrude from its shoulders. It appears to have fire breathing from its mouth. Beside it is a carving of a being like me, with six fingers and six toes. I place my hands inside the carving. They fit perfectly inside.

Rocks are placed in a circle with ash in the centre. Bones sit on a ledge, surrounded by leather fragments. An object protrudes through the skull, an arrow with three feathers still on the end. Beside the bones are the remnants of a bow, its string long since rotted away. A small black stone, the length of my hand and the width of my finger, lies below the carvings. Its point is sharp. Another stone sits beside the first, its end blunt. I pick them up, pounding the one with the other to carve a picture of the fanged creature standing beside the carving of the six-toed being. Those who come later will see the images, not knowing they were carved in different eras.

I find wood stored inside. I place it within the circle of rocks. Like the six-toed being before me, I will spend my first night here. I must gather more wood, storing it inside for others who come after me. After I have a fire lit, I exit the cave, crawling back along the ledge toward the edge of the pool. I collect water in my flask to make a refreshing tea to remember Cous and Sis.

A red clay pot in the shape of the seven stars lies beside the rocks. It is in the same shape as the one Uncle makes. I pour water into the clay pot, then heat it over the coals. I sprinkle the dried leaves over it, watching as they float and spread apart like symbols in the water. One day I will read the leaves. I think of Uncle making symbols on the tablet. I dip a piece of the six-sided comb Cous gave me, dripping with the sweet nectar, into the steaming liquid. I take a sip, tasting its sweetness, thinking of Cous.

The moon circles the night sky, its silvery glow falling upon the earth. I fall asleep, dreaming wonderful dreams of Cous and I, our encounter in the meadow, the ecstasy I felt.

Howl! The fanged pup nudges me, its nose wet, its long tongue licking me, eager to get going. It has crawled along the ledge to come inside. Its fur is wet, and it shakes itself vigorously, water droplets splashing on me. I stretch, then rekindle the fire. I make a quick tea and then roll my belongings inside my mat while I wait for the water to boil. I eat a piece of the dried pink flesh of the finned creature along with a piece of bread.

Honk! Honk! A flock of the long-necked feathered creatures are flying back to camp. I watch them fly overhead, thinking of Sis in the sand, showing us how they fly in a vee. The strongest in the front, rotating through the lines to be both the follower and the leader. I lift the pot to my mouth, sipping the tea slowly as I think of her. I make sure the coals are cool before I leave; someone else may need them. Behind the waterfall is a hill. I scramble up it, following a path from long ago. Feathered creatures circle above me.

Screech! A red feathered creature swoops down at me, warning me not to come near her young. I hear a quieter screech, a troubled one. Crouching before me is one of its young, not yet able to fly. Its mother has kicked it out of the nest to make room for the other four. I kneel before it, whistling softly, then hold a wriggling creature above it. It opens its beak wide, and I drop the wriggling creature inside.

At the top of the hill is another meadow with a stream running through it. In the middle is a pool with a great tree growing beside it. I carry the red feathered creature in my hand, walking toward the small pool of clear, cold, water. The sun is settling over the cliffs, a brilliant red reflecting off the white clouds. I roll out my mat under the great tree. Above me is the red-breasted avian, building a nest of mud and twigs.

The red feathered creature hops on the ground, unable to fly. To keep the red feathered creature with me, I tie a string onto its right leg, and the other end around my wrist. The fanged pup lies beside me, sniffing at the red feathered creature. It lifts its tiny wings, screeching at the fanged pup. I laugh, feeling content, but missing Father's camp.

The night air is cool, and a slight breeze blows upon me. I look down where Father's camp is and see three fires burning around the tents. Father and Sis are sitting around one fire while Cous and Uncle sit around the second fire. Our brother and his wife are sleeping side by side, beside the third fire. A tear drips down my face as I see them staying warm around the fires. I look up at the sky, seeing thousands upon thousands of stars. I fall asleep, dreaming dreams that I do not remember.

I awaken to a tug on my wrist and a light pecking on my toes. The red feathered creature has woken and thinks my toes are its food. I untie the string from my wrist, picking the red feathered creature up. I believe it is female, so from now on I will refer to it as a "her."

Her beak opens wide as she squawks at me. I pick a wriggling creature from the ground, dropping it into her mouth. I give a piece of the dried finned creature to the fanged pup. This one I know is a male. He devours the tidbit hungrily, then looks up at me for more. Soon I will have to get more food for us. I will stay here for the length of the moon's cycle, bonding with the young creatures and gathering food to eat. Every night I watch the stars and look at the three fires burning warmly at Father's camp. I am torn between going back to Father's camp and searching for the end of the world.

There were seven of us, but now there are only six. The red feathered creature, the fanged pup, and I are alone. I wipe a tear from my eye. The red-breasted avian on the branch above me has finished its nest. Another one joins it, as red as the first. I cannot tell which one is male or female, like the black feathered creatures that caw, both male and female appear alike. I fall asleep with the glow of the moon above me, its face is large and round, like Sis's face. I miss her.

I awaken to the chirping of the feathered creatures. A large red feathered creature, similar to the other two but somewhat different, struts around, crowing loudly. This one has a large comb on top of its head and large tail feathers. Its legs are long and thin. It scratches the dirt, looking for small bugs and tiny wriggling creatures, picking them up with its beak when it finds them. A smaller feathered creature, like the first, but with a smaller comb and a shorter tail, clucks loudly, indicating it has laid an egg. I slide my hand under her warm belly, retrieving the egg. It is still warm. She clucks, then pecks at me. I crack the shell on a stone, then lift the egg to my lips. I suck the liquid into my mouth, the yolk is delicious, running down my throat, a warm, sweet taste.

The sun rises in the sky, its brilliant colours glowing on the clouds. The moon still has an orange glow as it dips below the water. Tonight it will be full. I search for berries and gather roots to eat. The fanged pup yelps at me, wanting meat. The red feathered creature screeches, also wanting food. A long-eared creature with enormous hind feet lopes past me, its tail a small fluffy button on its rump. Its colour is white, turning brown. The fanged pup bolts for it, his legs still clumsy, his gait like a pup. The long-eared creature dashes away, hiding behind a clump of dirt with a tiny bit of snow remaining beside it, blending in with its environment. The fanged pup sniffs around, searching for the long-eared creature.

Like me, no one has names yet. We are just creatures—fanged or unfanged, feathered or furry, scaley or without scales. Some live on land, some in the water, others in the air, and a few, like the long-necked feathered creatures, can live in all three environments.

A flock of the long-necked feathered creatures fly overhead. I hear the wind in their wings as they flap, landing in the pool of water, honking. They climb from the water, eating the fresh grass that grows on the sides of the bank. They hiss at the fanged pup as he nears them, their sharp beaks warning him to stay away. Their legs are long and thin, but unlike the feathered creature with the long tail and the comb on its head, they have webbing between their toes. I have never seen them eat the wriggling creatures from the ground, nor have I seen the feathered creature with the comb fly but a few feet above the lowest branch of a tree. The more I travel, the more I am learning about the different creatures.

What is the difference between a beast and a creature? I remember Cous asking me.

"The beast has solid hooves, and the creature has soft paws," Sis had replied as she held up one of the long-eared creatures, stroking its fur.

Soon the fanged pup catches three of the long-eared creatures. He brings them back to eat, dropping one of them at my feet. I pick the long-eared creature up, examining it. It has short front legs and large hind legs. Its back feet are long and flat, perfect for leaping. Its fur is soft and cuddly. I will make a pillow for Sis with it. It will comfort her when she sleeps on the cold ground. After I painstakingly remove the hide with a sharp stone, I separate the entrails from the flesh, and prepare the meat to roast over a bed of coals. I lay the hides in the sun to dry and cure. They will keep me warm when the nights get cold, a soft pillow for my head upon the stone.

I drop tidbits of meat into the red feathered creature's open mouth. She screeches, spitting the pieces out and giving me a murderous look. I remember that her mother would eat the rodent before feeding it to her young. Holding my nose and almost regurgitating everything in my stomach, I manage to chew the raw meat. Once it is softened and well chewed, I open my mouth, dropping the morsels into the red feathered creature's mouth, then watch her devour the pieces.

Her feathers have grown long, and I am no longer afraid that she will fly away from me. I throw her into the air, watching as she learns to fly. I wish I could fly to the highest treetop and soar above the tallest mountains with her, gliding through the sky. The red feathered creature learns to swoop down upon the rodents, then with a sharp whistle, I call her back to me. With a swoop, she lands on my arm, dropping the rodent at my feet. I no longer need to chew the meat for her.

Tonight I sit on top of the hill, looking all around. The glow of another fire shines a small distance from Father's camp. Staring closely, I see two young men sitting around the fire. One of them is motioning toward Father's camp. There are no weapons with them, and I have no idea where they came from, or where they are going. I lie down on the soft grass, putting my head on a smooth rock, hoping to dream of life beyond the cliffs. The moon shines above me, her bright face glowing down at me. I close my eyes and dream.

I awaken to a soft touch, a warm breath on my face. "I miss you," someone whispers in my ear, a soft body over mine. I open my eyes and look into Sis's eyes. Her round face is like the moon's, her breasts soft and full, pressing against my face. I put my arms around her, feeling her plump bum. Her aroma fills my nose like a sweet flower. The moon shines on us. She smothers me with kisses, tears of joy filling her eyes. She sits on me, her wide hips over my loins, her breasts firm, her nipples hard. She turns around, her bum facing me, round like the moon, her juices flowing. I touch her and she squeals with delight. The moon rises over us, and our bodies shine in the moonlight. We lie in each other's arms, twisting and turning until the moon dips over the horizon.

"I must go," she whispers, rising from me, trying not to show her tears. I watch as she descends the hill toward Father's camp. I am torn. Do I follow her, or do I continue?

"I will wait for you," she says as she turns toward me. "I am the red-breasted avian. I will fly back to you."

Chirp, chirp. The red-breasted avian dances on the edge of her nest, cocking her head at me. I smile, knowing I will return to Father's camp soon. I gather my belongings and roll them in my mat.

The red feathered creature sits on my shoulder while the fanged pup runs ahead, looking back at me if I don't walk fast enough. I follow the stream down the hillside, coming to another meadow. The sun is overhead, and the weather is unbearably hot and dry. The grasses here are a deep brown colour, and shorter than at Father's camp. My throat burns from the heat and the dryness. Removing my leather moccasins, I walk barefoot through the sparse grass, feeling the heat from the ground upon my arches.

Ouch! I step on something sharp. Sitting down, I see a large thorn stuck in my big toe. A trickle of blood oozes from it, a tiny pinprick, but so much pain. I lift my foot to my mouth and pick the thorn from my toe with my teeth, then stick it into my leather flask. The ground is covered with these plants with multiple thorns protruding from them. I must be careful where I step. The fanged pup is panting hard, his tongue drooling. We must stop and rest, cooling ourselves before we go on. We reach what appears to be a small dam. The stream flows over some sticks intertwined together and packed with mud. Tiny paw prints have embedded the mud between the sticks, filling the cracks to make a watertight seal.

Splash! A wide-tailed creature slaps the water with its tail. Its mate drops the branch it was carrying and scurries into the water, diving below. They are creating the dam, causing water to back up against it and form a pond. In the middle of the pond, they are building a home made from mud and branches. A wisp of steam rises from an opening at the top. I stay quiet, watching as they reappear, first their noses stick up, sniffing, then their tiny eyes, searching. When both creatures believe it is safe, five little pups with wide tails surface, gripping tiny tree branches, swimming through the water to help build the home.

I chuckle as I watch them work. I take the thorn that was in my foot and tie a small vine around its base. I poke the thorn through a juicy red berry, then drop it into the water. The water turns to a blood red colour around it. Immediately, a finned creature with scales pounces on it, swallowing it. I jerk the vine, embedding the thorn through its lip. With a quick flip of my wrist, I toss the finned creature onto the ground behind me. I must tell Cous that the finned creatures will eat the wriggling creatures and the berries.

Do all finned creatures eat meat and vegetation, or do some eat only vegetation, and others only meat? I wonder. I think of Sis when she caught her first finned creature and the excitement in her body as she stood next to me, her aroma enticing me.

The finned creature flops on the ground, trying to get back into the water. The red feathered creature looks at it, then she flies high into the sky, and with a sudden swoop, she dives into the water, pulling a finned creature out with her talons. She drops it beside mine, then flies onto my shoulder, nibbling on my ear.

I shrug. Why do some things come easily for some, and others must work hard for it? I wish I could be like the red feathered creature and the fanged pup. No need to wear clothing or work for food.

Before me is another hill. It is higher than the first, but unlike the first, this hill is barren; only short grass covers the knoll. Thousands of tiny flowers dot the landscape. Some have four petals, and others have three. I look for a flower that has seven petals, like the seven of us who were in Father's camp, but the most I see is six, like the six who are left. I will camp here before entering the cliffs.

Tonight there is no moon. The high altitude has a chill in the air. Soon it will be dark. I rub the two sticks that Cous gave me over dry moss, lighting a small fire. The wood is dense, and it burns hot. The trees here are small, some with oval leaves and some with tiny needles. When the coals become deep red, I roast the finned creatures over them, then share the meat with the fanged pup. The red feathered creature scoops another finned creature from the tiny body of water beside me. Like the trees and the shrubs, it is also smaller than the ones I caught below. It seems that the higher one gets, the shorter things grow. Even the fire burns low, just hovering over the coals, flickering, tiny blue tips extending from the orange flames. I must ask Father why this is so.

At the base of the hill is Father's camp. Sis and Cous are sitting beside their fire, joined by two young men. I cannot see the colour of these men, only that they are short in stature. At first I feel sad, but I am happy for them. Tomorrow I will look for a flower with eight petals on it, like the eight that are in Father's camp now.

I awaken to tiny feathered creatures fluttering around me. Even the feathered creatures up here are small. I get up and walk across the plateau. The fanged pup chases the long-eared creatures, catching one. I skin it, making a loincloth for myself. I roast the meat over the remaining coals, turning it a golden brown. I divide the meat in two, giving a portion to the fanged pup. The red feathered creature picks at the long-eared creature's entrails, the parts that I do not care to eat.

I continue my journey to the red cliffs, searching for the flower with eight petals. At the edge of the plateau is a trail leading the way down. Why is it that every time I climb a hill, I must descend back down, either the way I came up, or down the other side?

At the bottom of the hill, I come to a barren red land, a desert void of life. As I walk through this barren land, the fanged pup sniffs at some tracks. The ground is smooth and hard, yet these tracks are indented in the red clay. I kneel, scraping the dirt from the tracks. They are not carved like the ones in the cave, but real footprints. They are the same as the ones in the cave, with two toes pointed forward and one toe pointing back. A single line is between the tracks, possibly from the creature's tail. Beside the tracks are footprints like mine, six toes to each print. I put my foot inside. It fits perfectly, like the ones in the cave. These tracks are hard, baked into the red rock, just like the red pottery Uncle bakes in the kiln. I wonder how hot it would have been to preserve these tracks and how long ago it was. There are two sets of tracks, side by side, one with two claws in the front and one pointing back, and the other like mine.

Were they made at the same time or in different eras? Was one following the first, either a man or a woman, or was the great beast following a human? Was it a long-tailed creature that walks like I do? The length of the track is as long as my arm outstretched. I have never seen a creature that would make a track as large as these. My heart starts pounding as I look around to make sure no such creatures are hiding behind the cliffs.

The fanged pup walks beside me, his paws indenting the soft red clay that lies next to the hardened clay containing the two sets of tracks. The red feathered creature hops beside the fanged pup, leaving her own tracks, two toes in front and one pointing backward. I walk in the footprints like mine until they disappear. Only the large beast's tracks are left.

What happened to the six-toed being?

At this time of day, the sun is overhead, and the heat is almost unbearable. Only a few blades of grass are scattered about. Red sand blows everywhere, swirling around me, blinding me. The large tracks disappear at a stream, which is but a trickle. I stop and try to fill my flask with water. The water is red, the colour of blood, red from the mud. I drink thirstily, almost spitting out the muddy water. The fanged pup laps his long tongue into the stream, trying to fill his mouth with the living water. The red feathered creature has it the best. A small drop is enough to satisfy her. She tilts her head back, letting the water run down her throat.

I trudge forward, following the ghost of the sun through the dust. Tripping over something lying on the trail, I land on my face. Exhausted, I rise, dizzy from the heat and lack of fluid. I feel the urge to relieve myself, but I dare not, not wanting to expel any more water. I walk until the need is too great, then wavering on my feet, I relieve myself, the fluid leaving me in a circular pattern, putrid, dark and reddish yellow.

The fanged pup sniffs my urine, grimacing and panting from thirst. I feel terrible, bringing an innocent creature into this arid land with me to die. I think of Uncle and his last words to me: "Nothing can live in that heat. That is the end of the world."

If I could, I would cry, but I have no fluid in me for tears. I miss Sis, remembering the last hug she gave me, how she clung to me, her body full and warm, like the moon.

I sit on the object I tripped over. It is an aged skeleton, its bones almost a fine powder. Ivory tusks protrude from the sides of its mouth. Its tusks are longer than my body, its teeth bigger than my hands. Beside me is a rock, round and flat, like a disc. Lying across from the rock is another rock, shaped like a tree. It is taller than I am. There are rings on its base, circling its diameter, getting tighter as they near the centre, hundreds of rings. I remember Uncle telling us that the great tree at our camp has been there since eternity. But here is another tree, formed into a stone, with rings around its base, circling for eternity, like the gold band he put on Sis's finger. But this tree is dead, ancient, having become like a rock.

The fanged pup sniffs at a rock, digging around it. He looks at me, his eyes pleading. One eye is green, and his other eye is blue, like mine. He scratches furiously, uncovering the rock fully and exposing a small wall of smaller rocks laid in a circle. I roll the rock from the cairn, exposing a well. A dipper hangs from a tattered string, thousands of years old. I retrieve the dipper, careful not to break the string. The red feathered creature dances on the circular wall, screeching and looking at me, then down into the well. The fanged pup whines with excitement, licking me with his dry tongue. I drop a pebble into the well and hear a tiny splash, almost inaudible. My heart in my throat, I lower the dipper down the well, feeling the rope grow slack as it hits the water. I pull up the dipper, full of clean cool water, then hold it to the fanged pup's mouth, smiling as he laps it up.

The red feathered creature dips her beak into the tiny bit of water that splashes from the dipper, tilting her head back as she drinks. I lower the dipper again, then drink the cool water. Three times I do this, sharing it with the creatures beside me. I drink copiously, hiccupping from drinking so fast. Finally, stepping away, I relieve myself, a steady stream of clear fluid flowing from me. I sigh with joy. I will live.

"The earth and the body both filter the water," I remember Father saying.

"We are created from the red clay," Uncle once told me.

"Are the water and the red earth alive like we are?" I had asked.

Even though the air has been so hot during the day, it cools rapidly as the sun sets. Everything appears red as I prepare to sleep—the sun, the sky, and the hills. I look at my red skin, which is even redder from the sun's blistering heat. I lie under the stone tree like the people before me, who left their dipper in the well for those who would follow them.

As hot as it is during the day, it is just as cold during the night. I am thankful for the pillow that I made from the hide of the long-eared creature. I think of Sis and the night she laid with me. I will make her a pillow like this one, so she can rest her soft cheeks on it. The sky is dotted with stars; there is no moon in sight. I lie awake, hearing small rustling noises, little chirps and clicking noises. Something skitters across my legs. I lie as still as possible, lying close to the fanged pup for warmth and protection. The red feathered creature taps her claws twice on the stone tree, indicating that she will fly away. I do not blame her. This land is desolate, and nothing lives here. I watch her silhouette against the stars as she soars overhead. She turns to the fixed star, flying toward it. I dream of days gone by, of people digging a well into the hard rock to get water.

The sound of the red feathered creature scratching her talons on the stone tree awakens me. She is holding an olive branch in her beak, six olives hanging from it. She drops the branch into my hand. I pluck the olives from the branch, giving us each two. The fanged pup gulps his down, but I savour mine. The red feathered creature flips hers in the air, devouring them as they land in her beak. With the precious water, I make a weak tea from the leaves Cous gave me. Then I sit back against the stone tree, drinking the tea and thinking of Father's camp.

A knot moves on the tree, and a blade of grass moves with it. A sharp, rasping noise pierces the air. I tense, staring closely. Beady eyes stare at me as sharp teeth nibble on a blade of grass. A creature, smaller than my thumb, camouflaged to match the colour of the tree, is chewing on a piece of grass. A tiny branch, reddish brown, the colour of the rock, slithers across it, slithering in the shape of an ess.

A tiny feathered creature chirps, it is the same colour as the ground, hovering over a red flower. The feathered creature is smaller than my thumb. Its beak is long and thin, and its tiny wings flutter faster than I can see, yet it stays in one spot, its beak stuck inside the flower. Suddenly it rises, and darts away.

A scaly creature flicks its tongue into the air, catching tiny insects. I only hear their high-pitched whine. Even though I am staring closely, I can barely see them. Tiny flowers with thorns dot the landscape, both small thorns and large thorns. It is as if the plants do not want to be eaten, protecting themselves with thorns. This red barren land is full of life. I am amazed at what I see.

"Nothing can live in that heat," Uncle had said. "You will surely die if you enter it."

I spend the day here, exploring near the stone tree, finding relics from long ago. I rest under the shade of the tree during the intense heat of midday. The red feathered creature sits on the branch while the fanged pup lies at my feet. I pull a plant with thorns from the ground. Amazingly, it is in the shape of a phallus. I open the prickly plant and taste the delicious water stored inside. It is as cool and fresh as from under the falls. I will spend the next seven days here before moving on.

The red feathered creature flies ahead, leading the way. In the distance are enormous pyramids built from stone. They seem to reach the sky. I walk all day, and never seem to come closer to those great towers which reach the heavens. I drink water from tiny rivulets running down the hills. I pick berries and small nuts from various shrubs, some with thorns and some without. Beside me is a red mound of dirt. The mound is alive, crawling with thousands of eight-legged creatures with what appears to be two bodies. Their bodies are red, and their legs are black. They are as numerous as the stars in the night sky.

An army of these creatures build the mound higher, creating a small hill. Each one carries a piece of dirt in its mouth as it follows the other. I imagine an army of people from long ago, building the pyramids, copying the eight-legged creatures, walking single file, carrying stones for their tower. A multitude of tiny paths leads from the mound these creatures have built. The mound is their earth, the land they are created on. Do they know about the stars at night?

In the morning I will travel toward the stone pyramids. I fall asleep, exhausted, dreaming of eras long ago. The hide from the long-eared creature protects my head from the hard rock as I lie on it.

I awaken to the sound of wings as the red feathered creature circles above, scouting the way. The fanged pup growls as we near the pyramids, his lips curling, his stance ready to pounce. Two large beasts, carved in ivory, stand guard at the entrance of the pyramids. These beasts have large manes that reach to the ground. Their paws are enormous, their claws long and sharp, three times the length of my finger. They have wings attached to their shoulders, spread out, ready to fly. An eternal flame burns between them, coming from the ground. I will spend the night here, under the shelter of these winged creatures, then explore the pyramids when I awaken.

In the morning the sun glows on the center pyramid, a brilliant mirage of purple colours. A clear stone sits on top, reflecting the colours onto the pyramids on either side. In the morning, the sun's shadow from the centre pyramid will touch the one pyramid. When the sun is straight overhead, it is right over the pyramid in the centre. Then as the sun goes down, at its midway point, the shadow of the centre pyramid reaches the other pyramid. It is like the ancients divided the day into three parts.

The red feathered creature soars above the peaks of all three pyramids. How I envy her, to see what she can see. I cannot even climb the smooth walls of these pyramids; the ancients must have been giants to build such structures. The fanged pup sniffs at a circular stone covering an opening in the wall. With all my might I roll the stone away, then enter the cavern. Inside is a body, a head shorter than I.

A sweet smell fills the cavern. The fanged pup dares not come inside. It sits at the entrance, growling nervously. The body is lying on its back, wrapped in white linen. The sweet smell comes from the ointments infused in the cloth. I carefully unwrap the head, exposing a human face. Like me, it has long dark hair, but its skin is a deep brown. Its eyes are sightless, having been replaced by one green gem and one blue one. I kiss its dry forehead, then wrap it up again. I roll the stone back in front of the opening, wondering if I have released its spirit, either male or female; I cannot tell.

The red feathered creature appears to land on an invisible arm, screeching at what would be a person's face, as if talking to a spirit. She balances on the arm as the invisible body walks to the stone. As she drops to the ground in front of the stone, I realize that the body, which I cannot see, has walked through the stone and re-entered the cave. Shivers go through my body even though it is midday, and the sun is hot.

Since the night is cool, I walk through the desert at night, following the fixed star, letting the spirits of the tombs rest. I walk all night, listening to the sounds of the desert and hearing its life. In the morning, the red feathered creature lands on a tiny shrub beside a small body of water. Three smaller trees are growing beside it. A stream flows from the pond. I jump into the water, washing away my sweat and the dust of the desert. Feeling refreshed, I decide to rest here for three days, collecting fruits and roots for my journey toward the red cliffs.

Ahead of me is the great mountain that I can barely see from Father's camp. The mountain soars above the clouds in the sky, higher than the pyramids. I follow the stream that flows through our camp toward the great water. I come to the base of the mountain. Water trickles down the hill, pooling at the bottom. Higher up, the water falls down the edge of the cliff. Its bronze walls shine in the sun, wet from the falling water. The fanged pup and I jump into the pool. Gulping a mouthful of water as we enter it, we take a refreshing drink. The water is crystal clear, cold, and refreshing. This must be where the hard, pale-green ice starts. I rest by the pool and prepare to climb the mountain. I will see the end of the earth from its peak.

The sun is high in the sky. The air hotter than I have ever felt before. A school of finned creatures float at the base of the waterfall, their shimmering sides glowing as they leap, catching bugs above the surface. I dip my small line with the thorn into the water and soon catch a finned creature.

Gathering a handful of dry twigs, I rub the two sticks together, lighting a fire to roast the finned creature. With a sharp stone, I cut off the finned creature's head and tail to feed to the fanged pup and the red feathered creature. The eyes I eat raw, savouring them.

Uncle had told me to do this. "So that your eyes will always be keen."

The fanged pup is now used to me feeding him whenever I eat. He waits patiently for me to drop him a morsel of food. He has become the child and I the provider. The red feathered creature soars through the heavens, swooping down to pick up finned creatures from the water and rodents from the meadows. At times she will eat berries from the shrubs. I must learn how to keep an ember of a fire going, so when I am travelling, I will always have a fire ready to start. It takes too much time to rub two sticks together to create a fire. I wish the fanged pup could light a fire with his breath, like the etchings of the fire-breathing monsters on the cavern's walls.

The hill gets steeper as I climb. The ground turns to a reddish-brown colour, and the grass is yellow. I enter a meadow where the wildflowers are all the colours of the rainbow and every shade in between. A beast is chewing the yellow grass on the side of the hill. It has two short, curved horns pointing to the back of its head. A smaller beast is beside it. Both beasts have small beards hanging from their chins. Behind the pair is a small herd, also grazing on the dried grass. I count the beasts to be about the same number as the fingers on my hands. Some have little ones beside them, suckling on their mothers' teats. One has three suckling on her, bunting her, taking turns, since the mother only has two teats. These beasts are very nimble, easily climbing and jumping from crag to crag, almost seeming to climb the cliffs straight up. Their fur is long and white, and their hooves are split and pointed. With their horns they playfully butt each other. The young one's leap on each other.

I decide to spend the night among these beasts. As I gather wood for a fire, I find an old horn lying in the dry brush. The inside of the horn is hollow, with a tiny opening at the narrow end. Its shell is hard and crusted. It looks the same as the horns on the beasts' heads. I hold the horn to my mouth and blow through the narrow end. A deep, eerie sound resonates from it, bouncing off the red cliffs, and echoing back to me. The fanged pup lifts his head, howling in return, making the same sound as the horn. I will carry the horn with me, alerting others whenever I sense danger.

The evening air is damp and humid. A warm breeze blows from the cliffs. I lie among the flowers, sleeping in the open. The smells are wonderful, and the hues of the night sky are amazing. Soon the stars will come out. The moon is full and round once again as it emerges over the mountaintop.

After I have eaten a mixture of berries and roots, I sit by the fire, watching the moon rise. I rub the horn clean with a soft stick until it is a shiny amber colour. I polish it with moss, making it smooth. I lift the horn to the moon and blow into it. The fanged pup sits on his haunches, his head lifted, and he howls at the moon as I do. The sound from the horn changes depending on how I change the position of my mouth, and how hard I blow. Sometimes it is eerie, and other times it is calm. Using a piece of hide, I fashion a belt. This belt will always hold the horn by my side, ready to be pulled out if I need to blow into it to alert the fanged pup of danger. I wear the horn on my right side and my arrows on my left. I carry the bow across my back.

I sleep among the horned beasts with beards. The fanged pup sleeps by my side, warming me. The horned beasts and the fanged pup get along well with each other. During the day the fanged pup practices herding these horned beasts into a circle. But they are agile and lively, giving the fanged pup a hard time, not allowing him to round them up easily.

The night sky is full of stars. It seems that I can almost reach up and touch them. When I climb the mountain, I hope to walk across a star. I have climbed all day, climbing higher than ever before. Here the trees are no taller than I stand, and snow is still amongst them. Although the air is cool, I will not light a fire. I want to see the moon as it travels through the sky, watching its eerie glow.

The other fanged creatures are silent, but the great feathered creature with small, tufted ears hoots all night long, catching small rodents to eat.

Who! Who! They hoot, calling to one another. These feathered creatures have round faces and tiny tufts of feathers on their heads, which look like small horns. I wonder if their horns will harden and grow like the horned beasts with the split hoof. They stand as tall as my arm is long.

They sit in the tree branches, as still as the branch itself, I must look closely to see them.

I lie awake, watching the stars revolve around the one star. Father said it is the true star, for it is in the centre of all the stars. He showed me how to use this star for direction, since it never changes. It is on the tail end of the handle of the seven stars that make the little dipper. The two stars on the front of the large dipper point to this star.

A tear flows to my eyes as I think of Cous and Sis. "We are the two stars that point to you," I remember them whispering to me. "You are the true star. The star that shows the way." I pull out my satchel of dried leaves and make tea, remembering them as I drink it.

In the morning I awaken after the sun has risen over the great mountain. A mist is rising from the ground. Once again the fanged pup nudges me to get moving. The red feathered creature flies above me, screeching, ready to show me the way. I gather my belongings and roll them into a tight bundle. There are still a few pieces of dried meat from the finned creatures and some of the red berries left.

I eat these, remembering Uncle's words: "Never eat the red berries, for they will cause certain death."

I share the berries and the dried meat with the fanged pup. He sits on his haunches, waiting for me to give him a bite. After we have eaten, we take a long drink from the stream. The red feathered creature flies up, landing on a small shrub, screeching for us to follow her. I climb the trail up the great mountain; a plateau stretches out before me. The ground is white with snow. The trees have disappeared, and only a few sparse rocks and crusty snow cover the ground. Although the ground is still covered with snow, the air is warm from the sun's heat. The path is becoming slippery and dangerous. Any slip will cause me to fall a long way down. I look back. The horned beasts are eating and playing in the meadow below me. Two of the horned beasts with split hooves follow me up the side of the mountain. Although the path looks dangerous, I am excited to climb the mountain and will travel on.

Once again I remember Uncle's words: "You will climb to the top of the world and stare into the vast emptiness beyond the red cliffs."

But I know that when I reach the top, I will be able to jump across to the moon, and my mother will be waiting for me there.

As I climb, the stream disappears, and only deep snow is around me. The air becomes thin and crisp, and I struggle to breathe. The fanged pup pants hard as we both struggle upward. The wind is howling. The crustiness of the drifting snow bites into my exposed skin. The fanged pup's fur protects him. It becomes difficult to see if I am climbing up or going down the mountain. I almost despair, wanting to lie down in the snow and rest. The horned beasts lie in the snow below me, watching me continue. I am not sure if they will follow me. I can no longer see the sun because of the blinding snow. An eerie whiteness covers me, the sun barely shining through.

I trudge on. At long last I reach the peak of the mountain, coming to the very top. Instead of the moon before me, there are three large rocks laid in a circle. I climb between the rocks, crouching down, the rocks protecting me from the howling wind. The fanged pup crawls beside me. Even the red feathered creature struts inside the den. I carve out a space to sleep in the deep snow, piling the snow up high to make a mound of snow around me with a small opening in front for a door.

The fanged pup digs his paws into the snow, helping to make the den. It is as if he knows how to make a den, like he has done it before. The heat from our bodies and our breath creates a small layer of ice along the walls, and the roof of the den. It is as if I am in a tomb or inside a womb. I am comfortable and warm, tucked inside our cozy den. I desire to make a tea, and dream of Sis and Cous lying next to me.

The wind howls outside. It is pitch black in the den. Even though I have keen eyes, I have only the sensation of sound and touch inside the enclosed tomb. There is no sense of time because everything is dark. I think of Father's camp by the great water. I am excited that when the wind quits, I will emerge from my tomb and climb to the peak of the hill, viewing the edge of the world. I wonder what I will see. Will it be a dark abyss like Uncle said, or will I step on a star, seeing a glorious white light all around?

For three days and three nights I stay in my tomb, listening to the wind howling. The fanged pup curls into a small ball and does not move. I think of how memory is created, and birth. I remember what I have been taught and what I have seen, but how did the fanged pup know how to dig a den, never being taught by his forebears?

At last, the wind is silent, and all is quiet. The morning sun is just starting to shine through a small crack in the tomb. I share the last of the meat from the finned creature with the fanged pup, and the red feathered creature. After I eat, I remove the pile of snow that blew in front of the entrance to our rock shelter. I remember the birth of the one-horned beast and think of how I will come out of my tomb, which has become a womb. A new sight to behold after the darkness of the last three days and nights. I press my hands between the cracks, prying the snow apart.

The fanged pup goes wild, digging through the hardened snow. The red feathered creature chips at the ice with her beak. Once we have spread the crack wide enough for us to emerge, we crawl through the opening. It is like being expelled from the womb, entering the heavens, the sun blinding us. The centre of the three rocks which we have sheltered under is the tallest, so I climb upon it, excited to see where I have come from and to see the other side of the mountain.

I am not sure what the fanged pup is expecting to see as he leaps up beside me, or the red feathered creature as she flies to the top of the tree above us, but I know, that I will see the ends of the earth, covered in a brilliant white light, and I will be able to walk across the mountain peak onto a star. I will be the guiding star, the first star for others to follow.

I stand upon the rock, peering around me. As my eyes adjust to the brightness, I look down upon the way I have come. Below me a pair of the horned beasts are resting at the base of the last hill, chewing their cuds. Below them is the meadow where the woolly beasts are. The little ones are jumping among the flowers, skipping gaily through the meadow, suckling on their mothers' teats while they drink from the stream.

The beginning of the stream emerges from under the snowpack before it winds through the different waterfalls and meadows as it travels toward the red cliffs. At the bottom of the red cliffs, it becomes a waterfall, pooling at the base of the meadow, where it flows past Father's camp and into the great water beyond. I see the cavern beside the waterfall where I carved the image of the fanged creature on its walls. I can barely make out the seven tents at Father's camp. Against the backdrop of the green grass, the white skins of the tents shine in the midday sun.

I turn around, looking down the mountainside opposite the way I came, toward the end of the earth. At first all I see is more snow and ice, but as I peer farther, I see another stream flowing through a meadow. A meadow like the one I came through, both streams flowing from the same source in opposite directions, both travelling through different meadows and hills to the great water below, joined together by the great water alongside the base of the mountain, two different streams of water becoming one.

A herd of the horned beasts graze in the meadow below me, another herd grazes in the meadow I came through. One group has long white hair covering their bodies and short horns pointing up. The other group has short, curly wool and horns that circle around before pointing up. Both groups have split hooves.

A waterfall drops off a ledge, falling into a pool of water below it, just like the waterfall at Father's camp. With my keen eyes, I see finned creatures with scales swimming in the crystal-clear water. The red feathered creature swoops down, her wings tucked beneath her. It dives into the water, catching a finned creature with scales. It flies back to us, dropping the finned creature at our feet. We eat ravenously, scales and all.

Another group of trees grows by the stream, a small cove like ours, with a great tree growing in the centre. The tree of knowledge. It is amazing; from the mountaintop, I can see both streams flowing from the same peak, one stream flowing down one side of the mountain and the other stream flowing down the other side, joined by the great water. At the bottom is another village like Father's, with a great tree in the centre.

Beside the great tree are seven dwellings, built from mud and sticks with dome tops. Mud is placed between the branches to make it watertight. At the top a small amount of steam or smoke is coming through an opening. I have seen this type of dwelling before. I have watched the family of the wide-tailed creatures build one of these huts, the five little pups carrying small twigs to help make their home.

Once again I am reminded that we are all the same creature, birthed from the same red clay: feathered, finned, furred, and some naked of fur or feathers, like me.

In front of one of the mud dwellings is a fire with a round pot hanging from a rod over it, boiling with roots and vegetables. Beside the fire is a large rock with a loaf on it, not thin and flat like the ones that Sis bakes, but round and full, like the moon. Stirring the pot is a being like me, except with bright yellow hair and white skin. I can not see the person's eyes, and I wonder what colour they are. Is one eye green and one eye blue, like mine? A child sits in the person's arms. The person turns toward me. It is a lad with a young child cradled in his arms, a girl, still searching for the breast.

I have not walked upon a star, but I do see another village below me. I am surprised, disappointed, and excited. I have climbed the great mountain past the red cliffs and the red barren land to see the brilliant white light at the end of the world. Instead, all around me I see another view of our world, another group of people who live as I do, like me but different.

I will follow this stream down the opposite side of the great mountain. I will walk toward the mud dwellings and meet these people, who are like me. I will see a world that I was told never existed. I will learn other stories that are told in other lands. I can return to our camp by going down the way I came, or I can descend on the opposite side. Once I reach the great water at the end of the stream, I can travel along its shore back toward Father's village. It seems that all of life is a circle, from beginning to end.

I descend the mountain, opposite the way I came, sliding down the snow until I reach the meadow. I envy the fanged creatures with their fur and the feathered creatures with their feathers, keeping them warm. Why was I born naked and alone?

I reach the first meadow below the snow-covered peaks. The brilliant red colours reflecting on the clouds are the same as the colours reflecting on the clouds over Father's village. The same sun shines on both. I roll my mat beside the stream, then gather berries from the meadow and catch finned creatures in the pond. The fanged pup leaps happily around, sniffing out the long-eared creatures, chasing them when he sees them. The red feathered creature flies to the treetops, swooping down into the meadow to catch rodents scurrying through the grass. Five tiny beaks peak over the rim of a mud nest. The red-breasted avian lands on the edge, depositing wriggling creatures in her chicks gaping mouths.

I think of Cous as we lay together in the meadow, the red-breasted avian chirping above us, the long-necked feathered creatures flying overhead. The ecstasy I felt, the tremors in our bodies.

I take out the two sticks Sis gave me and rub them together to light a fire for making tea. As the water heats, I stare into the fire, the curling flames mesmerizing me. I sprinkle the leaves Cous gave me into the bubbling water, watching them spread around and trying to read the leaves. I think of Cous and Sis, missing them. Do they miss me?

Beside me the horned beasts with split hooves happily eat the new grass, chewing on small trees while they skip and jump. I fall asleep to them nibbling on the grass beside me, at times nibbling on my toes.

Cock-a-doodle-doo! A red feathered creature with a comb crows, awakening me as the sun rises. Another one clucks. I slip my hand under her body, retrieving an egg. The egg is warm, freshly laid. I crack the egg on a sharp rock, sucking the liquid into my mouth, the yolk warm and delicious.

I will spend the day here, resting and contemplating. The sun rises and sets here as in Father's camp. The moon is white as it disappears over the horizon. Tonight it will be full. The moon and the sun appear to be opposites, one ruling the day and the other ruling the night.

"The earth is flat." Uncle had told me. But now I believe that the sun, moon, and the earth are round, circling each other. How else does the sun go down on one side of the earth and then come up on the other side? And how else would the moon rotate around the earth, opposite the sun? Flat objects only spin in the same direction. It would be like a flat stone skipping across the water, never returning to shore.

I am excited to explore this new meadow I have entered. I eat the berries and some flakes of meat from the finned creatures. I make myself a tea, sweetened with the golden liquid. I wish Sis and Cous were here with me in this new land, a land like Father's camp.

Between the dense brush on the hillside, a vine climbs along the ground. This vine has hard, oblong fruit growing on it. I find one that has fallen off and is shrivelled and dry. Its top has been cut off, allowing rainwater to collect inside its empty shell. I lift the gourd to my mouth, drinking the water. It is still fresh, just like it came from the spring. I dip it into the flowing water, filling it up once more. Then with a soft piece of wood, I plug the hole, keeping the water inside. The water will provide a refreshing drink when the weather gets hot. I gather more gourds, remove the tops, and scoop out their tender flesh. I place the outer shells in the hot sun to harden them. This way I can bury several gourds in the sand, and the water will stay cool for days. Whenever I am thirsty, I can easily retrieve a gourd, drinking the lifesaving water within it.

Many of the flowers I see in this meadow are the same as the ones in Father's camp, although some of the flowers have slightly different colours and shapes. I find a patch of berries with large thorns growing on the stem of the plants, protecting their berries. I surmise that if a plant has thorns, the berries will be delectable and tasteful. Why else would the plant try to save its berries from being eaten?

I remember the time when Sis got deathly ill from eating the red berries. We were all scared that she was going to die. Her skin became cold and clammy. Her usually bright red lips were instead a blue colour, and her breathing became raspy and shallow. Uncle was worried sick, fearing that she would die. He cradled her head in his arms for days. Then on the third day, she opened her eyes. Once she got better, Uncle told all of us that we were never to eat the red berries again. It was after this that he formed the yellow band, embedding the shiny rock in it, and put it on her finger.

I pick berries that grow close to the ground. They are the sweetest I have tasted, almost as sweet as the golden liquid from the six-sided hives. I eat these berries, savouring them, wanting to share them with Sis and place them in her lips. I can almost taste her lips on mine, remembering the day she took me to the edge of the meadow.

"Taste me." She had winked, her face mischievous.

As I travel across the meadow and see a berry that I have not yet tasted, I will eat one at a time, waiting to see if I get ill from it before eating another. There are bearded beasts in this meadow too, and the woolly beasts with split hooves. One type has black wool and a white face while the other has white wool and a black face. Both pairs have split hooves, unlike the one-horned beast back in Father's camp, which has a solid round hoof. Some of the bearded beasts are white, and some are black with white spots. Horns curl from their heads. One type of woolly beast has two sets of horns on its head, one set pointing forward and one set pointing backward. Their wool is white with brown spots, the same colour as their face.

"Freckles" I call them.

In the distance toward the wooden camp are a range of hills covered with a vast forest. The hills are beyond a valley. Everything on the other side of the valley is a shade of blue. It is amazing to see all the colours of blue in the distance. The sky, the hills, and the great water are all different shades of blue: turquoise, sky-blue, deep blue, and blue-green. I think it would be boring to live in a world full of blue. In Father's camp we have blues, browns, reds, yellows, and greens, all the shades of the rainbow. I will call those hills beyond the valley the Blue Hills. Will the people I meet be blue skinned like we are red skinned, created from the red cliffs?

I think of the red cliffs beyond Father's village, with muddy red water running through them, becoming clear as it reaches the village. Trees with green leaves and brown trunks, fields full of different hues of grains, flowers of all colours and sizes.

I rest here, setting a hook in the flowing water and catch a finned creature with bright rainbow colours running along its sides. Stringing the finned creature over a pole, I let it dry in the hot sun. As the sun beats down on me and I wait for the finned creature to dry, I lie in the shade of the tree, looking at the sky as white clouds form above. A breeze blows across the meadow. The billowing white clouds turn grey, then change to black, rolling through the sky. A chill comes through the air. The clouds change shape, becoming large creatures, the shape of the monsters that made tracks in the red clay long ago. Long necks, tails that sweep from side to side, winged creatures with scales covering their backs, feet with large claws; black and large, how scary these clouds become.

Boom! The thunder rolls, the winds blow, and sheets of rain pelt down in the distance. I look for a fallen tree to hide under for protection. Running as fast as I can, I crawl under three trees that blew over from the wind, the noise deafening as they fell. Gathering branches, I place them across the fallen logs, creating a shelter from the storm. As soon as I finish building the shelter, there is an enormous flash of light from the clouds above. A bolt of brilliant white light hits the ground beside me. The hair on my head stands on end, my skin tingling as an enormous amount of electric current is pulsating through the air.

Boom! I jump, the loudest sound I have ever heard ringing in my ears. Lightning flashes from the clouds to the ground, from cloud to cloud, the bolts criss-crossing each other. Thunder rolls and echoes, shaking the ground, booming. The sensation is the strangest I have felt yet. Darkness is followed by intense light, sudden quiet, then deafening thunder. The ground shakes. The wind roars through the leaves, rain pelts down, and branches fly through the sky.

Crash! A large tree crashes upon my shelter. The air turns cold, the sky opens, and sheets of water pour down from the sky. Uncle's flat earth has turned on its side. The great waters run down the earth. Soon there will be another flood, worse than the one Uncle says happened before. The stream is roaring. Finned creatures leap in the water, crashing onto the shore. Feathered creatures huddle under the brush, their wings spread out, hiding their young. The rains pour down, and everything is soaking wet, yet the fanged pup and I stay dry inside our shelter. The red feathered creature huddles at my feet.

The clouds swirl, shape changers, monsters lurking in the darkness of the meadow. The flash of lightning exposes them as its bright light hurtles through the air. The whole earth is charged with electricity, intense white light exposing the blackness. The lightning bolts are like flames shooting from the scaled creatures open mouths, flying, lighting the earth on fire, the rain trying to quench the flames. A stand of brush ignites, and flames soar upward, crackling and hissing as the rain pours down. The fire spreads, the wind blows, and a sudden gust brings cold rain pouring onto the fire, smothering it.

I am no longer afraid of these storms. I love watching the lightning strikes and hearing the echoing sound of the booming thunder. I imagine the winged creatures with scales fighting in the heavens. The winged creatures that left their footprints on the earth many moons ago, fire breathing from their nostrils. Soon the storm clouds are gone. The sun appears in the sky, chasing the clouds away, and the sky turns blue once more.

I gather wet leaves and pick up some of the coals from the fire that was ignited by the lightning bolt. After arranging the coals in a circle, I place wood over them, and blow onto the coals. When I blow on them, they turn a warm orange colour, igniting the wood. Soon the fire is burning, crackling, and hissing from the wet wood. The flames make shapes like the clouds did. An image of a fanged creature appears, howling at the moon, changing to a winged creature with scales, breathing fire through its nose.

I gather rocks to circle the fire. The heat from the coals causes steam to come from the rocks, cracking some into pieces. How can steam break rocks? How can water come from rocks? I pass my hand through the steam, feeling its heat, my hand moving easily through it, easier than water. Steam is lighter than water and hotter, yet both seem to have the ability to carve the rock or break it in two.

Pop! A rock has just split in half from the heated steam. The outside has been smoothed by the flowing water, but the inside is coarse, rough to the touch. In the centre is a smooth, dull yellow metal, untouched by the water. I place the split rock on the hot coals, and the yellow ore starts bubbling inside the cavity of the rock, becoming a molten metal, pouring from the rock. I tip the rock over, letting the molten metal spill from it. I shape it into a crude ring. When I find a sparkling stone, I will heat the stone and embed it in the yellow band. I will give it to Cous to remember me.

I sit by the fire, soaking in the warmth reflecting off the rocks. The coals turn from orange to black and then back to orange as the heat moves across them. I purse my lips, blowing into the embers. The coals turn a bright orange once again, and the fire burns hot. When the fire cools, I add more sticks to the burning coals, watching the flames rise, lighting up the air around me. The circle of rocks absorbs the heat from the fire, reflecting it to me, keeping me warm. Steam rises from the wet ground beside me.

The fanged pup sits by my side, licking his lips, whimpering at me. I take three of the finned creatures that I kept in moist leaves within my satchel and place them on the rocks. The smell of the finned creatures reaches my nostrils as they sizzle on the rocks, tantalizing me. Soon the meat is crisp and tender, a pink colour inside. As I eat the crisp, tender flesh, now a golden colour, I think of Sis.

The sun becomes large, settling over the water at the end of the earth. It turns into hues of orange, the colour of the heated coals. Soon the sun will go down, and everything will turn black once more, like a coal removed from the fire. I surmise that the sun must be a huge lump of coal in the sky, warming up the rocks on the earth below during the day. Each morning I must put fresh sticks on the black coals, blowing on them until the flames curl upward, surrounding the coals once more. I imagine that a powerful being is adding wood to the morning sun, causing it to warm the earth for the day. Then in the evening the being rests and lets the sun die down to an ember, causing the earth to become dark and cool once more.

I lie awake, looking at the stars shining in the sky. The fixed star is shining above me. I curl under the three fallen trees, rolling into a ball to sleep. The air is warm, and the night creatures start to make their nightly noises, humming to the sounds in the meadow. I look at the seven stars and ponder what I have seen so far. How far away are the stars? They are higher than the highest mountains, higher than the feathered creatures can fly. The moon rises over the blue hills, a large orange disk in the darkened sky, shining its light down on me.

Tomorrow I will walk to the blue hills and try to see how creatures can live in a blue environment. I fall asleep and dream of Sis and Cous, their bodies snuggling next to mine.

Before sunrise, the red feathered creature scratches the dirt by my head, anxious to get going. I walk all day, coming to a place where the earth divides. Ahead of me is the deep valley that I must cross. Beyond the valley, the blue hills shine in all their glory, a deep blue, deeper than the blue sky at noon. I gather vines, braiding them together to fasten a rope.

"Three is better than one," Father had told me. "A three-cord rope is seldom broken."

I fasten one end of the cord around the base of the largest of the three trees. The other end I throw to the bottom of the gully. Then I let myself down along the rope, gripping it with my hands. The fanged pup looks at me curiously, then crawls down the gully, using all four paws to hold himself back from going too fast on his way down. Smoke fills the air, coming from the fires ignited from the lightning bolts. It is hard to see the other side of the river because of the thick smoke. The sun is right above me, but with all the smoke obscuring it, it appears to be an orange disc in the sky, flat like the rock that covered the tomb. I look into the sun without even squinting.

As I climb down, I brace myself against the larger rocks as I descend the slope. The few trees and rocks allow me to rest against them as I make my way down. It is dark before I reach the bottom of the gully. Once again I find three stones that are side by side, allowing the fanged pup and I to crawl between them and rest for the night.

The wind howls all night while a strange glow shines in the sky, and dark ash blows all around me. The fanged creatures howl in the darkness, the noise echoing back at me. I must be near the end of the world where the fires are eternal. The sun becomes dim, and its ash flies all around. I listen to the howls of the wind and the howls of the fanged creatures. Above their howls, a deep roar, and a crackling noise comes from the other side of the gully. The night is eerie. The noise, the ash, and the glow create a sign of the end. I dare not sleep, for I am sure that I will fall into the deep abyss at the world's end. I lie between the three rocks for protection, staring at the moon as it moves through the sky. The moon appears blood red, then the greyness of the smoke from the world's end covers it.

I hear another noise above the wind and the howling of the fanged creatures. It is the sound of the feathered creatures flying overhead, fleeing the flames. I listen to their sounds as they fly. Some honk while others chirp. The feathered creatures are leading the way, followed by all manner of beasts. Two by two they come, both male and female. Split hooves, solid hooves, paws with three, four, or five toes. Horned and un-horned; long, pointy ears; short, stubby ears; or long, floppy ears; some with tails and some without.

All manner of beasts run past me, coming from the burning meadow, crossing the river, thundering up the steep hill to the land above, safe from the fire. A deep red glow shines in the sky while a heavy, acrid smoke billows through the air. The colour of red against the black is vivid. The intense noise of the thunder is worse than any summer storm. A steady roar comes from the river. Beasts run under the glowing night sky, red like the hottest coals. The red feathered creature and the fanged pup stay by my side. A heavy rain starts. Water is flowing everywhere, soaking everything in its path.

All night the beasts run past me, following the feathered creatures who lead the way. For three days and three nights the rains continue, it seems like forever, but soon the intense noise dies down. The beasts quit running past me, and the feathered creatures land once more in the trees. The red in the sky disappears as the sun rises. The day is once again becoming light. I am joyful to see the sunshine. I was afraid that the sun had fallen into the earth, causing the acrid smoke.

All is quiet, and I can see everything around me. The river flows over its banks, engorged by the rains. Large, finned creatures swim upstream, dancing over the rocks. So far I have not seen any of the finned creatures swimming downstream, so I have no idea where they are all coming from, or where they are going.

I set a hook in the water, catching more finned creatures. The finned creatures in the stream fight vigorously once I hook them, sometimes breaking the line and disappearing back into the water. A large black creature with no tail is sitting by the water's edge. As soon as a finned creature swims by, it swats it with its long claws onto the shore. After it has swatted twelve of the finned creatures onto the bank, it wanders over, sits on its haunches, then picks up the flopping finned creatures to eat them. It holds them like I do, and like me, it has no tail. This creature can also stand on its hind legs for a short while. But unlike me it has thick black fur and a white streak on its forehead.

As I walk along the river, I search for a shallow spot where I can cross. The pounding of the beasts' hooves has created a trail along the river's edge. I follow the trail, crossing the shallow water to the other side. Once across, I climb the gully. The feathered creatures have found the easiest way for the beasts to follow, safely crossing the divide.

A cloud of steam rises from the blackened earth. Amazingly, there is a patch of green, untouched by the fire. In the middle of the trees is a body of water. I see thirteen wooden houses within the forest, two rows with six houses each. The farthest house from the water is burnt to the ground. Only twelve houses still stand. The dwelling in the centre is the largest. Beside it is a stone table. At the head of this table is a shiny object, its tip buried in the stone. The glimmering object stands up in the form of a cross. The handle is an oval pattern, the length of my palm. Below the handle, the glimmering shaft has a double edge, sharper and harder than anything I have ever felt before. The blade is the colour of seven different metals hammered together to form a sharp edge. I run my finger along the edge, drawing blood.

The handle and the hilt are made from three gold-coloured metals—rose, white, and yellow—interwoven to make one. Twelve rocks that glitter like stars are inlaid in the handle, like the hard rock that Sis found, and Uncle embedded in the soft yellow metal, a bond to last forever.

I call this instrument a cross, a flaming sword. The colours reflecting off the sword are the colours of the sun, the colour of the eternal flames from a fire. The handle of the flaming sword is the same size as my fist. I reach for the sword, and because of my strength, I easily withdraw it from the stone. The sword is well balanced, fitting perfectly in my hand, I practice swinging it.

"You must never cut your hair," Father once told me. "Or you will lose your strength."

"It is the gods who created the sword," Uncle would say, "the gods who separated us from the beasts."

I look at the sword and wonder why I can do things that the beasts and the creatures cannot do. Only the great creature that has hands like mine can grasp the sword, yet it cannot swing it like I can. Even though it has no tail, and a face like ours, it can only do simple things, following a simple pattern in life. Does the great creature worry like we do? Can it reason and logic like we can? I used to tease Sis that we came from them, but then gained knowledge once we lost our tails.

On each side of the stone table are six stone seats. A thirteenth seat at the far end is broken, like the thirteenth dwelling burned to the ground. I wonder about the significance of this. I will stay here for forty days, search for the lad I saw tending the fire, and learn his ways.

The red feathered creature with the comb crows three times, awakening me from my sleep. The morning air is cool, crisp, and clean. I breathe in deeply, feeling refreshed. The fanged pup slurps as he drinks from the stream. I kneel over the stream, cup my hands together, then dip them into the cool water. I lift my hands to my mouth, the water dripping off them, then drink the living water. I listen to the tinkling sound of the water flowing over the rocks as I drink.

In the distance are the blue hills. The morning haze makes them appear a darker shade of blue than when they were last night. The dark blue of the hill's contrasts with the lighter blue of the sky. Beyond I see the blue-green water of the edge of the world. A place I will never return from if I reach the edge, falling forever down the falls at the end of the world.

The red glow in the morning sky changes to a clear blue as the sun rises over the water. I wonder why at this time of day everything in the distance appears to be a shade of blue, but in the early morning and in the late evening, the rising or setting sun turns the sky into all hues of red. Wanting to get an early start to continue my journey, I quickly make tea from the leaves Cous gave me.

I collect a few red berries along the way to eat with the dried finned creatures. Leaving the woolly beasts behind, I resume my journey toward the blue hills. A pair of the horned beasts follow me. One is a large male with horns pointing up and out. Beside him is a smaller female with short horns pointing straight up. The male has a coat of long black hair like mine while the female has a coat of short white hair. Nibbling on the purple flowers with their lips curled upward, they walk ahead of me. I am grateful for this since they also eat the thorns from these flowers, saving my feet from stepping on them.

I follow the flow of the stream through the meadow, walking a trail travelled centuries ago. Was it the same group of people who made the trail on the other side of the mountain? I come to an area where the stream widens. A doe walks over to the stream, bending her head to take a drink, taking huge gulps from the flowing water. The ram walks behind her, sniffing her backside as she drinks the cool water. She gives the ram a swift kick under his chest before scrambling up the bank, running back to the meadow. Startled, the ram jumps backward, then reaches forward to get a quick drink of water. Whirling, he lunges after the doe. Suddenly, the doe stops, puts her head down, and lets the ram mount her from behind. Planting her feet firmly on the ground, she pushes back against the ram. Grunting, he mounts her, his tongue curled upward and his body rocking back and forth, his phallus inside her. As he snorts, a strong smell emanates from him. Finally, he dismounts and steps back. The doe runs away, snorting.

I smile, thinking of Cous kneeling by the stream, drinking the water.

I am excited to see what the horned beast's kids will look like when they are born, frolicking around in the meadow, nibbling on the flowers. Will they be born with horns or without?

When I reach a rocky ledge, I stop. I hear the sound of a waterfall ahead, water tinkling upon water. At the base of the waterfall is a small pool in which a school of finned creatures are swimming, silvery flashes with rainbow colours darting through the water. With their fins stretched out, they leap through the air, their forked tail fins facing up and down, their backs arched as they leap from wave to wave. Their tiny bottom fins are like small legs that have not developed yet. A flock of feathered creatures with small white bodies and blue wings flit among the leaping finned creatures, catching insects on the water, wings flapping, forked tail feathers side by side. Finned creatures and feathered creatures alike, one swimming in the water and one flying through the air, one with scales and one with feathers. One with fins and one with wings, one with clawed feet and one with fins under their bellies. One with forked tail fins up and down and one with forked tail feathers side by side. Both picking the insects from the water with their mouths, one with a beak and one with a pointed mouth.

I poke a thorn through a thin vine seven times my length. Grabbing a small insect, I poke it through the thorn, then with a flick of my wrist, I throw it over the water. Flash! A silvery flash leaps for the insect, catching the thorn in its open mouth. I feel the excitement of the tug on the line, then pull in the silvery catch. Reaching into its mouth, I release the thorn. The finned creature's many sharp teeth, which point backward, gash my finger, causing red blood to flow. As I stick my finger into my mouth to stem the flow of blood, I taste its fishiness combined with the saltiness of my blood.

I toss the flopping finned creatures onto the rocks as I catch them. I catch three more to eat, they will sustain the fanged pup and me. I toss a finned creature to the fanged pup; he eats it whole. I bite into the delicate eyes of the finned creatures, tasting their saltiness and tenderness, then roast the pink meat over the fire. I dry the other two over the coals to eat after the sun goes down.

Finding a bush of blueberries growing in the soft wet ground, I gather them to eat with the pink meat of the rainbow-coloured finned creature.

The soft moss is greenish-blue, moist, and soft to the touch. I must be near the blue hills, judging from the bluish tinge on the finned creatures' sides, the blue-winged feathered creatures, and the blueberries growing among the greenish-blue moss, a sure sign that I am close. I am excited to try the tea made from the leaves of the blue trees. I will eat so many berries that my hands and tongue will turn blue.

I walk past the small pool beneath the falls and follow the stream. The stream comes to a ravine, spreading out across small rocks. I love the sound of the flowing water trickling down the hillside, the roaring getting louder as the stream flows faster. Feathered creatures sing in the trees at the edge of the stream, swooping down to catch insects flying above the water. The finned creatures jump upstream, catching insects as they soar through the air, silvery flashes darting across the ripples. The gully that I must descend has many rocks strewn across it. The farther down I go, the more treacherous it becomes. While crawling across the rocks, I must be careful. One smooth rock will slide down, picking up another rock, and carrying it with it, gathering more rocks as they fall.

I stop so as not to disturb more rocks, letting the rocks settle. Then I inch my way down. The whole hillside becomes a rocky shale, with some large boulders scattered about and a few small trees growing among the boulders. I can see that there have been many rockslides over the years. Rocks of all colours and shapes are scattered across the hillside. Water trickles over them, rounding them, smoothing their rough corners. When I step across a small boulder, I stumble, causing it to tumble. The rock glides over three more rocks, causing them to fall with it. Each of these rocks gathers more rocks, causing larger rocks to fall with them. Leaping behind a large boulder, I watch as the combined weight of the smaller rocks pulls the larger rocks along with them. The rocks pick up speed with a slow roar, continuing to pick up larger rocks on the way down. Dust flies through the air, choking me. The roaring gets louder as more rocks fall. It seems like the whole hillside will slide into the water below. I grab onto a small tree root growing from under the boulder and hang on, praying. The boulder starts to tremble, the roots wiggle, and the ground shakes from the moving rocks.

A pink granite rock hurtles past me, smashing into a large black boulder behind me. I crouch as the fanged pup hunches down beside me, both of us staying low to the ground. It seems like forever, but soon the rumbling stops. As I wait for the dust to clear, I raise my head. Three massive trees at the bottom of the hill have stopped the rocks, not allowing them to go any farther. Only a few stones made it past the trees.

The trees tell me that no matter how small a thing is in the beginning, or how large it becomes later, it can only cause so much destruction until it is stopped by a greater object. I will keep this memory in my mind, remembering the three large trees, branches spread out like crosses, soaking in the sun.

At the bottom of the trees, the stream rushes through the hardened rock, carving a deep gully through it, exposing all colours of the rock. Crawling to the safety of the trees, I climb onto a low branch that spreads out over the flowing water. With my heart pounding, I look down to the bottom of the carved rock, the water churning white at the bottom of the spasm. Resting on the cross of the branch, I watch the water flow continuously. It has no beginning and no end. The water is fluid, yet it carves a beautiful canyon through the rock, exposing all the colours of the rock, seams of white, grey, black, red, and brown. Each layer has a different colour and hardness to it. Some layers are coal black, glistening in the water, and some are shiny white, tiny sparkles like diamonds scattered throughout.

A large, bearded beast with ringed horns curving backward stands on a boulder on the other side. Its long white hair flows to the ground, its pointed ivory horns curving outward. Crossing over the tree branch, I drop to the other side. The fanged pup leaps across the stream with ease. The white-haired beast lifts its head, looking at me. It has a mouthful of green grass, which it chews slowly. I believe it is a male. Bending over, it licks the white powder that is on the boulder. Then it turns to me, shakes its head, and moves off the boulder. It nibbles on the small trees growing around it, stripping the leaves from the branches.

I pull a piece of dried flesh out of my leather satchel. I sprinkle some of the white grains from the rock on it. I am amazed at the taste; it is seven times better with the white substance sprinkled on it. Also, it seems to help in digestion, the dried meat feels much better in my stomach. This white substance has the same taste as my sweat. Who taught the bearded beast to lick the white substance while eating? Collecting some of the long white fibres from its hide, I place them in another small satchel to store with me. I hope I can knit them together, making a small blanket to keep me warm during the chilly nights.

I come to another waterfall, smaller than the first. Kneeling, I drink from the stream and taste the crystal-clear water. I call it the living water, sweet and pure. The horned beasts that followed me bleat, indicating they are near. I start climbing down the rocky ledge. The horned beasts jump from rock to rock. I crawl down the slope on all fours, like the long-tailed creature that walks like us. The difference between us and the creature that looks like us is that it has a tail. Its skin is like the horned beasts, coloured and furry. The horned beasts only have a short tail while the woolly beasts have long tails, hanging to the ground.

I have no tail, and my skin is bare. I need the skins of the beasts to keep me warm when the wind is cold and icy.

A few large boulders sit alongside the stream with small trees growing between them. The sun is high in the sky. At this time of the day the sun is a bright white colour while the sky is a light shade of blue. In the mornings and evenings, the sun changes to a red colour, and it can be looked at with the naked eye. I crawl upon the first boulder to rest, feeling the sun's warmth reflecting off the rock. The fanged pup lets out a low growl, staring at the boulder in front of me. What looks like a short, curly tail with smooth skin is swaying back and forth. I have never seen this type of creature before. At one end of the tail-like creature is a bulbous head with two intense eyes staring at me. Darting from the creature's mouth is a forked tongue, flicking in and out.

The only time I have vaguely seen an image like this was after Sis fell through the ice under the falls. Her teeth and her tongue were chattering as she crawled up onto the rock. She blamed me for the fall, and her intense anger showed in her eyes and in her tongue. When I get back to Father's village, I will tell her that the reason we have no tail is because it fell off in the icy water and became its own living being, a slithering creature. After the newly formed creature swam from the icy water, it crawled on the rock to warm up, and having no legs, it slithered into the dust.

After warming up on the rock, I continue walking toward the blue hills. The terrain becomes rolling hills covered with small trees. The leaves on these trees are green like in our camp at the great water. The hills in the distance are still a bluish colour, but the closer I get to them they are turning into a more blue-green colour. The red feathered creature flies ahead of me as I walk to the blue hills. If I could communicate with her, I would ask her what colour she sees.

Are the hills blue? What colour is the sky? Does the fanged pup see the same colours as I do?

As I get closer to the hills, I realize that the colour of the leaves and grass are still green. The sky above is blue. The blue hills seem to be a mirage, always in the distance. The trees are getting larger, with vines hanging to the ground. I must be careful of the slithering creatures camouflaged as vines, ready to pounce. The fanged creature growls when the slithering creatures are near, warning me.

I can barely see the sky through the large leaves and the towering trees. The vegetation is thick, and under the canopy of leaves and vines, it is dark and humid. I wonder how the plants can grow under the towering trees with no sun. The stifling air is hot and heavy as I walk through the vegetation. Everything is wet. It seems that these large trees give off a light mist, creating their own rain. The stream has become a river, and the water is reddish brown, like the mud I must walk through at times. I look for the blue mud, but only see red mud mixed with black. At times a small amount of light comes through the trees, but the sun remains hidden. All kinds of shadows are lurking around me. Feathered creatures fly from tree to tree. With curved beaks and large talons, they easily grip onto the tree branches as they land. Their feathers are the colours of the rainbow.

The slithering creatures are like vines, some black, some green, and some brown. They are large, small, or in between. Fruits of all colours hang from the trees, larger than the berries that were in the meadow. I pick a fruit that I have seen a feathered creature eating. If the feathered creature can eat it, I should be able to eat it too. There are also finned creatures in the river, which I catch, feeding the fanged creature and me. The finned creatures dart through the water, having many colours too. Sometimes the red feathered creature catches a slithering creature by its head and crushes it, shaking it violently. Often a rain shower will pour down on me, dripping wet through the trees.

I have no sense of time because the sun is mostly hidden in the dense canopy of the vegetation. I come to where the river widens into a large body of water. The dim light becomes darker, so I decide to camp for the night. All kinds of bugs fly around me, and insects with multiple legs crawl upon the ground. I gather large leaves from the trees to make a shelter. I crawl inside to eat the remaining fruit and tidbits of dried finned creatures. The tidbits of dried meat are no longer dry but soggy and wet, and they taste bitter. I must find a different way to keep food here. The air is hot and humid, yet there is so much food all the time that there seems to be no reason to store food.

I make a small cup of tea, thinking of Cous. Are the long-necked feathered creatures still flying over the meadow? Does Cous look up at them and think of me?

Tonight it is totally black. I listen to the night sounds, waiting to fall asleep. I know I will dream tonight, and in the morning, I will try to remember my dreams. The fanged pup also dreams, I hear his feet moving and the sounds he makes as he dreams. Most likely he is dreaming of the slithering creatures in the vines or the long-eared creatures bounding across the rocks. Does Sis dream of me?

Caw! Caw! I awaken to the loud sound of one of the multi-coloured feathered creatures. Light filters through the leaves as the sun rises. The multi-coloured feathered creatures are cheerful, singing brightly. The slithering creatures swing from branch to branch, watching me. No sound comes from their fanged mouths, their forked tongues darting in and out. One is wrapped around a long-eared creature. The only parts that I can see are its long ears and large hind feet. I shudder as I watch the slithering creature's fanged mouth stretch over the long-eared creature's face, swallowing it whole.

I gather leaves from the trees to make tea. The blue tea will have to wait until I reach the blue hills where everything is a shade of blue. I will stay in this forest until the moon is full again, then I will continue my journey to the blue hills.

During the next full moon, I continue onwards, coming to another lake. Smoke drifts up from a small fire across the lake. A group of people are there. Their huts are made from the fabric of the trees, whitened from the sun. The people's skin is pure black, and they have the whitest teeth. Their hair is short and curly, and their eyes are dark brown, surrounded by whiteness. The insides of their palms and the bottoms of their feet are pale. Even when standing tall, they are a head shorter than I am.

I walk around the lake to greet them, then stop when I see an enormous beast coming toward me from across the river. What appears to be a slithering creature comes out from above its mouth. The enormous beast's appendage sucks up water from the muddy river, curves around, then blows it into its open mouth. The beast has a short curly tail at its hind end, but coming from the middle of its face is a larger tail with two openings at the end. The beast's ears are wider than my arms stretched out, and it stands three times my height. Suddenly, it looks at the fanged pup and me with its tiny eyes. Its ears stick straight out, and the appendage on its face points straight ahead. It glares at me, unearthly noises coming from its appendage. Horn-like tusks hang down from the back of its mouth, curving inwards, unlike the bearded beasts' horns, which curve up from their heads. Its feet are large and round with five short toes on each. There is no split in the middle. They are round like the one-horned beasts' hooves, except it has five small toes with flesh, not solid hooves. The beast stands still, snorting loudly. Then it squats. Another long appendage between its legs lets out a stream of liquid, steaming as it hits the ground. The beast is a male. Behind him is a smaller beast with two young suckling on her udder. Like me, these beasts have no fur or hair covering them, only thick grey skin. Thin hair covers the hides of the young, soon to disappear.

I was told that we were the only people left, and our tribe was pure, but tomorrow I will meet another group of people who live in dwellings made from the fabric of the trees. They wear dark green leaves for covering, hanging from their waists. I remember the lad I saw from the mountaintop, the yellow-haired, light skinned-lad, sitting by his fire, cradling a young child, a fresh mound of dirt next to his wooden dwelling.

Who will mother his child?

The red feathered creature swoops into the water from time to time, lifting the finned creatures up in her talons. At times she has a slithering creature dangling from her talons. She flies to a high, rocky crag, screeching. I travel all day along the body of water, seeing many things I have never seen before. When the sun goes down, it's a brilliant red colour.

I gather sticks and leaves, intertwining them to build a shelter for the night. The fanged pup sleeps at the entrance, guarding it. The seven stars shine in the night sky. I fall asleep listening to the sound of water washing upon the shore.

In the morning the red feathered creature pecks on the wood, awakening me. She is ready to go. I gather my things and start walking. The bow is still by my side and the horn slung over my shoulder. I have not needed to use them yet. Fortunately, the large-eared beast seems to be friendly. It reaches out with its long appendage to sniff me as I walk by.

Across the lake a group of the dark-skinned people have built a raft from reeds and leaves. With this contraption they float on the water. They also have baskets made from the reeds, which they use to dip into the water. Their muscles bulge as they lift a basket of finned creatures onto the raft. As the basket comes up, the water drains from it. They tip the finned creatures into another basket in the middle of the raft, one that holds water.

I continue walking along the edge of the lake. At the next bend is a spot where the lake turns once more into a river, where the water flows continuously. Somehow I must cross the rapids. I find a few fallen trees along the path that are small enough to carry to the river's edge. I lash some vines around them, making a raft. The fanged pup fears getting onto this contraption, but with much coaxing, he finally leaps aboard. I climb aboard the raft, then push it away from the shore with a stick. The raft carries us as we drift downriver. With the stick I can push myself across the river, but soon I am no longer able to reach the bottom.

I drift downriver with no control of the raft. I have no idea how deep the water will become. Floating down the river beside me is a creature with enormous front teeth, and a wide flat tail which it uses to propel itself through the water. I realize that I will have to come up with a design like this to propel my new mode of transportation toward shore. A small piece of driftwood floats past me. I use my stick to pull it toward me. With some leftover vine, I secure it to the end of the stick. I use it as a paddle to propel my raft.

Slowly, the fanged pup and I reach the other side of the river, but I am quite far downstream from the lake and the group of the dark-skinned people. The paddling has been hard and strenuous. I pull the raft onto the shore, placing one end on a log. My food is soggy, making it undesirable to eat. I manage to eat some anyway, then I crawl beneath the raft to sleep, dreaming of floating on the water.

In the morning I awaken to the chattering of voices, guttural sounds that I cannot decipher. I crawl out from under the raft, holding onto the fanged pup, so he does not chase anyone. I do not want to scare anyone away. Three dark-skinned people are standing by the raft. Their skin is as black as the rock in the canyon. The tall one in the centre has a bow drawn, ready to shoot. I draw my bow, and suddenly there is a squeal beside me as a beast falls with an arrow through its heart. The three hunters walk past me, putting a stick through the curly-tailed beast's mouth. The other end comes out of the dead beast's rear end. Two of them pick the stick at either end, then the leader nods at me to follow them.

The fanged pup licks up the blood from the ground as I follow the three dark-skinned hunters. Twelve of the curly tailed beasts are still left, rooting in the ground, eating the roots of the reeds by the river and frolicking in the black mud. This beast is like a smaller version of the enormous, large-eared beast with the long appendage for its nose. Its ears are long and pointed, its tail short and curly, and its snout is long with two large holes at the end. It has short legs, but instead of round feet like the larger beast, it has split hooves like the bearded beasts and the woolly beasts with horns. Ivory tusks hang from its jowls like the enormous beast with the large ears.

We reach the camp, and the two men holding the beast with the short curly tail place both ends of the spear onto two forked sticks, the length of the beast apart. An older woman comes out of the largest hut and lights a fire under the beast, singeing its hairs. She uses embers wrapped in wet leaves to ignite her fire. When the fire reduces to hot coals, two young lads take turns rotating the curly-tailed beast over the hot coals.

I count sixty-eight people in total, twelve sons with their wives and forty-four children. I have no idea where the men's wives came from. There must be another camp nearby, maybe in the blue hills, which I hope to reach soon. Like me they have no sense of writing, but they speak with gestures and fluid sounds that come from their mouths. They look at my bow and arrows and the horn I have made, murmuring to one another. They also use a gourd like mine for water.

One of the girls leads me to a hut, gesturing for me to follow. She appears to have been born during the same moon as I was. She shows me how to intertwine leaves and vines to build a strong hut, one that will withstand the heavy rain and wind. The green fig leaf covering her loins blends in with her dark skin. With a wink, she grabs my hand, then leads me into the centre of the hut. Smiling, she squats in front of me. The insides of her legs are as dark as the night. She gestures as she runs her hands along my hips, indicating that she will make me a garment like hers. She fashions a covering made from fig leaves around my loins. Smiling coyly, her fingers touching me, she ties the vine around my hips. Her full lips brush against my folds, her tongue tasting my nub. The touch is sensational. I close my eyes; a feeling of ecstasy flows through me. My body tingles, moistness oozes from me. I smell a musky aroma emitting from her as her fingers touch me, caress me. Her tongue tastes me, darting in and out of my petals, swirling around my sensitive nub. Total exhilaration flows through me. I throw my head back, my loins pressing into her face. My folds are wet, my juices flowing.

She smiles, giggling, her white teeth sparkling. Her nimble fingers rub my wetness over her erect nipples, nipples as black as the night. I sink down, her full breasts in my face, nuzzling them, my mouth enclosing over her engorged nipple. My tongue swirls around it, tasting her delicious fruit, dark, wet, and juicy. I suckle on her, her warm milk running down my throat. Then I look into her eyes, soft and warm.

On her shoulder is a small feathered creature with short, stubby ears and a small hooked beak. "You have eyes like the feathered creature," I say as I touch the feathered creature, feeling its soft, downy feathers. "And its face is round like yours but white, surrounded by black feathers."

She picks the feathered creature up in the palm of her hand. The feathered creature looks at me, its face rigid, its black eyes boring into mine. I brush my hand against the girl's cheek. Her cheeks are soft like the feathered creatures, her eyes a deep brown, almost black in colour, also like the eyes of the feathered creature. I grin at her, feeling ecstatic. She hugs me, her body soft and desirable.

I show the men how to make a bow from the seven woods, a bow almost strong enough to take down the large beast with ivory tusks. Its ears are as long as I stand, its snout like an enlarged phallus hanging to the ground.

The dark-skinned girl teaches me her words. She tells me that her people were created from the black mud and that she was created from her brother's rib. She tells me that every living being was created from the black mud, even the beast with the short curly tail that we are about to eat. "That is why they love to wallow in the soft mud; it reminds them of the day they were created." She chuckles as we watch a herd of the beasts with long snouts, blunt noses, and short curly tails root through the mud, eating the fresh shoots that grow at the edges of the swamp.

She takes me to a place deep in the forest, to a garden filled with trees, fruits, and all colours of flowers. The lake in the middle is teeming with brightly coloured finned creatures. All colours and sizes of beasts and feathered creatures live here. In front of the garden is an image of a powerful being, three times my height. Beside it is another image with large paws and claws. This second being has a huge head with a full mane of black hair. Its back is lean and muscular with short black hair. Its tail is long, curled around its body. Its huge eyes stare ahead. Both beings were created from the black stone. They are so ancient that green moss is growing on their feet. In front of these images is a pit of bubbling black mud with a flame continuously burning in the centre of it. She tells me that the image is the creator of all living beings.

"The image of the black-maned creature is our protector, always watching over us. The flame is eternal. All living things were created from this black mud," she says in a hushed tone. "In the beginning all beings were equal, each one having the same thoughts and language."

Her slender black arms point to a shadow that reflects off the image of the creator. "That is the shadow from the sun. This shadow always points to a certain spot as the earth rotates around the sun. The shadow is dependent on the time of day and the time of its season in the rotation of the earth."

I stare in awe at all the sights while the fanged creature looks on as if everything is as it should be. The red feathered creature flies to the top of the image, landing on its outstretched arm.

"There is the centre of the earth. The shadow continuously circles around the image." She points to four rivers flowing from the black mud. "The four rivers of the earth flow outward from here toward the four corners of the earth."

I am amazed at her knowledge. I ask her about snow and the mountaintops filled with ice, the eternal streams of water running from the ice. She has never seen snow or felt its coldness. She only knows the bubbling black mud and the rivers flowing from it.

"Everything starts from here," she tells me. "All beasts and creatures were created here, and after death, all beings and all living things will return here, even the grasses and the trees. All things will join once again, having the same thoughts and once more be connected to one another."

"Are we beasts or creatures?" I ask.

"We are neither." She smiles at me, her eyes twinkling. "We have neither fur, nor feathers."

We leave the garden of a multitude of colours and all species of beings, the eternal flame at the entrance, guarding it, and we go back to the camp of the dark-skinned people. I will stay with these people for one more full moon, learning their ways.

I show them how to make paper from the reeds by the river, the same way the black insects with stingers make paper for their nests. After letting the paper turn white while drying in the sun, I show them how to mark the paper with a stick of charcoal. I draw a picture of the seven tents that are at Father's camp. I also show them how they can use the thorns and the liquid from the plants to mark their skin. Each son puts a symbol on his right hand, except for the youngest, who puts the mark on his left hand, the hand he uses.

When the time comes for me to leave and for us to say our goodbyes, I tell them that I will come again. I leave them the bearded and woolly beasts that have come with me from the meadow. Only the fanged pup and the red feathered creature will travel with me to the blue hills. I have stayed here for seventy days, learning their ways. We drink tea together and say goodbye to one another. They give me an enormous bag filled with dried fruits to take with me. They also give me many kinds of dried leaves for all colours of tea.

The fanged pup and I walk for three full days, following the stream before we reach the edge of the forest. Finding a small grove of trees, I set up a shelter for the night, setting up camp. As I watch the sunset over the hills, I wonder about the image of their creator and how the shadows always point with precision to the rocks placed around it at different times. The image that is in the centre of all things.

In the morning as I watch the sun rise, I make a black tea from the special leaves that the dark-skinned girl gave me, hoping to reach the blue hills before nightfall. All day I travel up the hill toward the blue hills. The stream I am following turns into a river, cutting a deep gorge into the ground as it continues to flow ahead. The trees have become sparse, and there are once again open spaces. In the distance I see the wooden camp.

The blue hills must be over the next ridge. The river has become large and difficult to cross. I cross many streams flowing into the river. It is almost dark when I reach the top of the next ridge. I spread my mat out in the open and watch the stars as they appear in the darkening sky. Hopefully, I will see a few shooting stars moving through the sky before they disappear into the blackness of the universe.

There are a multitude of stars in the sky, so many I can't even count them. Many stars are shooting through the sky faster than I can shoot an arrow from my bow. The flash of a shooting star is swift before it drops out of sight, arcing through the night sky. All stars revolve around the fixed star, like the shadows revolving around the image of the creator.

I awaken to the fanged pup howling, in the distance there is another howl, answering back. I raise my head, squinting into the morning sun, hoping to see the blue hills. All I see in the distance is another plateau of blue hills. I look back to the way I came and the hills I have just walked through. The hills are dark blue in the morning sun. The large trees and the forest of many brilliant colours of flowers and grasses shine blue in the distance. The centre of the earth with the eternal flames and rolling black mud were in the blue hills. I have walked through the blue hills, the home of the dark-skinned people.

It is now that I see that colour is an illusion. The sky changes from black to orange to blue, and back to red again, from when the sun comes up to when it goes down. Water in the distance appears blue, but when I get close to it, I see that it's a clear liquid.

The child within me is almost due. For eight full moons my belly has been growing and my breasts getting fuller. I will search for the lad with the young child in his arms. I look at the long-necked feathered creatures flying overhead. It has been eight full moons since I left Father's camp, since the time when the long-necked feathered creatures flew over Cous and I as we lay in the meadow together. How I screamed in ecstasy as his seed entered me.

I think about the girl who fashioned a skirt of fig leaves around my loins. The colour of her skin as she squatted in front of me, the smile in her eyes as she winked at me, the touch of her hands on me.

I wonder if I will see her again.

THE OPEN WATER

The fanged creature and I set sail across the great water on the raft which I have built. The water is calm with a red glow shining across its tiny ripples, reflecting from the morning sun. The air is warm and moist. It feels good on my skin. I wear the fig leaf covering that the dark-skinned girl fashioned for me. The smell of salt is in the air. I shinny up the mast, balancing on the cross beam. The mast sways slightly in the breeze.

I look down into the water below. Schools of multi-coloured finned creatures swim along the sandy bottom. The water is clear and inviting. The sand glimmers as the sunlight reaches it. I remove my fig leaf and drop it onto the deck below. Leaping into the air, I somersault down, straightening out just before I hit the water. I enter it with barely a splash. My breath leaves me, tiny bubbles floating up. My ears hurt as I enter its depth.

A tiny finned creature with a large gaping mouth swims to my face, nibbling on me. Its little fins moving back and forth, its gills moving in and out. I turn upward and swim toward the surface. The pressure on my ears eases as I rise from the depths. As my head bursts above the water, I gulp an enormous breath of fresh air before sinking back down. I rise once more, inhaling and exhaling rapidly. A wave splashes over me, inadvertently causing me to swallow a huge gulp of water. As fast as the water goes into my mouth, I spew it out with a huge rasping noise. I have never tasted water so salty; it burns my throat. How can anything live in this brackish water? I think of the living water at Father's camp, water so pure and refreshing as it gurgles from the ground.

I climb aboard the raft, grab a gourd of clean water, and gulp it down, swirling it in my mouth to get rid of the taste of the bitterness that remains.

I realize it will not be possible to drink from this body of water. I will have to ration my drinking water. Knowing this, I place the gourd in an upright position beneath the sails in hope of collecting the rain. Although the water is salty and unfit to drink, it is soft on my skin and soothing on my aching muscles. I reach my hand into it and bring it to my lips. The taste is like the sweat that drips off my brow.

Why is this great expanse of water so like my sweat? The water from the streams and rivers that flow into this great expanse of water is pure and safe to drink, yet this water is brackish and unfit to drink. How can water change its consistency?

The fanged creature nudges me, indicating he is hungry. I dig into the reed basket that the dark-skinned girl gave me, retrieving a piece of the dried finned creature and a slice of bread. Once my hunger and thirst are dissipated, I dive into the water once more, feeling its buoyancy while floating in it. I swim as the fanged creature does, paddling with my arms, my head above the water. The fanged creature swims faster than I, since he uses all four of his legs, while I only use my arms. I move my legs up and down, learning how to kick with my feet too. When I use both my arms and legs, I am able to swim faster than the fanged creature. Tiny finned creatures swim past me, silvery flashes darting by.

Boom! The sky darkens. I look upwards. Enormous black clouds are gathering and billowing above me. I swim back to the raft, grabbing onto the vine that I have hung over the side, and clambering onto the deck. Rain pelts down, stinging my bare skin. The wind howls down on me, and waves crest over each other, creating white-caps, washing over the raft, and tossing it like a leaf in the wind. It takes all my strength to take the sail down and strap it across the mast.

I lash the skins for collecting rainwater to drink. Once the sail is fastened to the crossbeam, I crawl under it for protection from the pelting rain. The wind rocks the raft back and forth in the waves, tossing it up like a leaf before throwing it back down. The mast hits the crest of a wave as we turn sideways, swinging up and hitting the waves on the other side. I fear that the raft is going to turn over and sink. My stomach churns, I feel ill, and my whole body turns green. It is the most sickening feeling I have ever felt. I lean over the edge, struggling not to throw up the finned creature and the loaf of bread I have just eaten. I retch, my stomach heaving as much as the raft is rocking in the waves, the taste of bile filling my throat.

I lose all sense of time as I fashion a device to remove the water that is pouring over the raft, collecting in the hold, and tossing bucket after bucket over the side. The rain and the wind seem to last for eternity, blocking out the sun. I lose all sense of direction. Land is nowhere in sight. I fear this is my last night on earth. Uncle was right. The end of the earth is at the great water, and soon I will drop into the abyss, falling for eternity. Exhausted, I close my eyes, awaiting the sensation of spiralling downward continuously. Suddenly, the wind subsides, and the water is calm once more. As quickly as the wind came up, it disappeared.

A large white feathered creature with a wingspan the length of my arms outstretched, circles me. A branch hangs from its beak. The raft rocks, and a large black shape swims up to the surface, nudging the raft with its enormous nose, turning it toward the setting sun. The beast from the sea leaps high above the water, blowing a geyser of water from a hole on top of its head. The water rises three times the length of my mast, spraying a mist above me. With a great splash the beast lands back in the water, rocking my raft once more until I almost tip.

This enormous beast of the sea has smooth black skin and a large head with tiny eyes. Where its arms or wings would be instead are small fins that it uses to guide itself along. Its tail is powerful, and with a sudden thrust it can propel itself right out of the water, blowing water up from a hole in its head before landing with an enormous splash. The beast is seven times the length of my raft. Its mouth is as long as my body, and its teeth are numerous and tiny. Seeing its gaping throat, I fear that it can swallow me whole, raft and all. This beast swims with its mouth open, collecting all kinds of tiny finned creatures, and a green substance that floats in the water.

I watch it for a period of time. It seems to breathe as I do. For a short while it will swim under the water before resurfacing, then exhale its breath through the small hole at the top of its head, and with a loud snort it blows the water from its head. I believe it must take in a huge gulp of air before it dives once more into the water, or how else does it breathe?

The smaller finned creatures that I have caught before have slits on the sides of their mouth, inhaling water, then exhaling the water through these slits. It is like they are breathing underwater. These finned creatures also have scales, like armour on their bodies, protecting them. It appears that this enormous beast has a smooth skin like mine. It is like the scaled creatures as far as swimming and diving in the water go, yet it is different, more like me. A tiny calf, just like its mother, suckles on her.

A feathered creature flies toward my raft. Its feathers are as white as snow, and its beak is large, curved, and black. It lands on the cross of the centre beam, looking down at me with its glittering eyes. The raft is steady as the wind has calmed. I reattach the sail to the mast. When I am done, the feathered creature flies away and looks down at me as if I should follow it. I tilt the sail toward it, cruising at a good clip. The enormous black beast that spews vapour from the top of its head dives back into the depths.

I follow the white feathered creature across the water. In the distance I see a grove of trees. The red sun is at the height of the tallest tree. Once more the dry earth is before me. The white feathered creature flies to the tallest tree, landing at the top of it. It turns its head to me, indicating I should stay. I lower the sail and slow myself down with the oars as I back paddle.

I come to a beautiful bay protected from the waves by a layer of multicoloured rocks. The rocks are in a semicircle around the bay. A white layer of the most beautiful sand lies on the beach. Large trees with broad green leaves rise on the hills behind it. In the centre of the bay is a river, its blue-green water flowing into the bay. A large mountain rises in the distance, trees growing halfway up it. The top half of the mountain is barren and rocky. White clouds drift across its peak. The trees are full of leaves and fruit. The grass is tall and lush. All kinds of berries grow amid the bushes.

The white feathered creature turns its head to one side and looks at me as if to say, "See? I have brought you here safely."

I will follow this feathered creature every time I am out in the great water. I will trust that it will always keep me safe and close to shore. This land I have reached is like another garden. It reminds me of the land where the dark-skinned people live. Swinging through the treetops is a small creature whose face is like mine. This creature has a long tail which it can use to hang from the tree branches. Its hands and feet are almost like mine, with four fingers and one opposing digit for grasping things. I have yet to see another creature or being that has six digits like I do.

I float toward the mouth of the river. The fanged pup stands at the helm, anxiously waiting to get on solid ground once more. A rock ledge juts out from the bay. On one side of the rock, the water is murky like the great water. On the other side where the river flows, the water is clear. I follow the river until the water is crystal clear and safe to drink. Sandy ripples run along the bottom, flowing toward the salt water. The ripples are the same below the water as on top. Multiple finned creatures of all shapes and sizes swim amid the rocks, searching for food.

Deciding stay here for a while to prepare for the rest of my journey, I steer the raft into a small cove. A large tree grows near the shore, reaching up toward the sun. This tree will provide shade when the sun gets hot. I tie the raft to the tree, lashing the vine three times around its base. The fanged pup jumps off the raft and runs into the bushes in search of the long-eared creature with the button tail.

The ground sways as I walk on it, like when I first sailed on the raft. As I walk on land, it is as if I am still floating on the water. My stomach feels queasy, even though I am on dry land. The creatures that look like me chatter incessantly. They throw large fruit down at me from the treetops. The fruit has a hard outer shell with coarse brown hair covering it. I gather the fruit that the creature's throw down from the tree, storing it aboard the raft. I drop the thorn with the wriggling creature, deep into the water and catch a finned creature swimming along the river bottom. Its silver body thrashes as I pull it up.

The fanged pup and I return to the raft to spend the night, a much-needed rest from our travels during the storm. At night as I lie awake, looking at the stars, I ponder what I have seen so far. Why does this great body of water taste like my sweat, but the streams and rivers that flow into it do not? Why do I get sick at the beginning of going onto the raft, but after a few days of being on the water, I get used to it? Then when I return to land and walk once again on solid ground, I get queasy, and have trouble walking? It is like I'm walking on the raft while floating on the water. The solid ground heaves like the raft upon the water. Is it an illusion, or is it real?

I awaken to the sound of the creatures that live in the trees chattering. They are creatures like me but with long tails. Did I come from them?

Around me a group of people are bustling about, some collecting fruit from the trees, some catching the finned creatures from the river. Children are diving from the rocks into the water. The larger children dive on the deep side of the rocks into the salty water, and the smaller children dive on the other side, into a pool of clear water beside the river.

These people have skin the colour of ivory, and their eyes are a soft green. Their skin is smooth and void of hair, both male and female. The hair on their heads is flaming red. The women have two braids flowing past their hips. The men keep their hair in a single braid, flowing down to their backsides. The women are as tall as the men, but the men and women are two heads shorter than I. The women are beautiful to look at. They gaze at me with their large round eyes. Their lips are red and full. Some of the women have a child in their arms, suckling on their breasts, drinking their mother's milk.

The men appear to be strong and solid. They carry short spears for protection. They also have hollow rods into which they place small feathered objects, pointed at one end. They dip the sharp ends into a pouch containing serum, then with a quick puff, they shoot the dart into the creature with a tail that walks like us. The creature spasms, then falls to the ground, its body twitching.

The women skin the creature, using a stone, honed razor sharp. They spread its insides on a rock, scraping the offal from the soft material of the stomach and intestines. They save the soft material for later use. The women put the meat into a cauldron of boiling water while the men gather roots from the ground, mixing them with the meat. They sprinkle a small amount of a dried black substance into the mixture, which creates an intense heat in one's mouth. A young girl sprinkles a tiny amount of a white substance into the cauldron. "It will enhance the taste," she says, smiling at me.

She gestures for me to share the meal with them. The thought of eating the creature with the same face as ours makes me queasy, but I am hungry and willing to try it. The food is delicious with a hint of heat in it. The meat is dark yet tender. The fanged pup sniffs the meat but will not eat it. He bounds into the bush in search of other rodents. The children giggle as they touch my bare skin, while pulling on the fig leaf I wear. I am amazed at these people. How did they get here? The air is always warm and humid, and food is plentiful. The people smile often and laugh quickly. I spend the day with them, picking up a few words. The sunsets are beautiful, always a brilliant red as the sun goes down, sometimes a deep purple.

The fanged pup and I sleep on the raft, awakening as the sun rises. I walk along the smooth rock toward the salty water. A mist rises from the rock as the rising sun warms it. I feel the sun's warmth on my bare feet. At the edge of the rock, I dip my feet into the water, feeling its coolness. My legs appear bent where they go through the water, yet they are straight when I pull them out. I splay my toes apart, wondering if my legs are bent, or if it's an illusion. I dip my arm in, and it also appears bent. Startled, I yank my arm out, but it is as straight as it was before. I realize it is the reflection of light passing through the water that causes things to appear differently.

The fresh water on the other side of the rock is almost the same temperature as my body, while the water on this side is considerably cooler, yet they join at the end of the rock ledge. The water in the distance appears blue, yet the water at my feet is murky white, like my sweat. I remember the bearded beasts licking the white substance from the rock, and how, when I tasted it, it also tasted like my sweat. Is it the saltiness of the water that makes it murky, like the tears in my eyes? My eyes do not burn when I am under the water, even though the water is salty. Whenever I sweat, I can taste the salt on my skin. It is like my tears and the salty water are the same. I think of Sis as she clung to me, the tears in her eyes, the taste of her tongue on my tongue.

I dive into the water, finding that I float easily, buoyantly. I move my arms and legs, treading water. With my keen eyes, I can see down into the depths of the water, the ripples in the sand along the bottom of the water matching the ripples of the water on the surface. Buried at intervals in the sand are rocks of various shapes and sizes. Did they fall from above, or were they pushed up from the bottom?

Finned creatures of many colours and sizes swim at different levels. Most of them have scales on them, but some creatures have no scales, and numerous appendages on their bodies. I see a creature that has eight legs spreading out in a circle from its head. It appears to have no body. Its legs have a row of circular discs along the insides. A dark cloud surrounds it as I come near, obscuring it from my eyes. It is as if it releases a substance to hide in, and its discs are used for grasping onto things. Other creatures are long and thin, like the slithering creatures that crawl in the dust. Some have heads and tails; others appear to be the same on both ends.

Small oval shells sit on the sandy bottom, looking like smooth stones. These shells are two halves hinged together, opening and closing slightly as if they are breathing. They have no legs or fins, but they move slowly with the motion of the water. A small piece of flesh peers from between the two shells that are partly open.

A slithering creature with a pointed mouth swims near me. It is three times my length. I watch as it swallows a finned creature, then sinks to the bottom, a bulge in its belly.

I try swimming to the sandy bottom, but although I am strong, I am unable to swim lower than twelve times the length of my body. The pressure under the water crushes my chest. It feels like my chest will collapse from the weight. My ears can barely stand the pain. But how can water have pressure? It seems the deeper I go, the greater the pressure, yet I can move through the water with little resistance. Having no air left in me, I swim upward, gasping for air as I surface, breathing deeply. I swim toward the rocky ledge, anxious to get back on shore. I crawl onto the ledge, exhausted and panting. I lie on the rock, my body absorbing the heat from the sun.

In the distance the enormous black beasts are swimming toward shore. They swim and frolic in the water like the horned beasts frolic and jump on land, bunting each other with their noses, leaping up, and playing with each other. It is amazing to watch them jump out of the water and discharge a large breath of air from the top of their heads. They swim in the water like it's natural for them. I would like to dive in the water like the finned creature, and soar through the heavens like the feathered creatures. I lie on the rocks, listening to the waves splashing against the shore. My eyes close, and soon I am fast asleep, unaware of anything or anyone around me.

I awaken to the sound of a splash. A girl from the village dives into the water beside me. Two other girls dive off the ledge, following her. I sit up, watching them swim to the depths. The eight-legged creature swims away as they come near it. The multi-coloured finned creatures gather around them, their mouths opening and closing. The girls swim like the finned creatures, kicking their feet in one fluid motion like the finned creature moves its fins. Soon they reach the bottom and sweep their hands along the ripples in the sand.

Bubbles rise through the water from their mouths. They scoop up the hinged shells from the sand. As soon as each girl has three shells, they rise to the top, blowing small bubbles as they ascend. At intervals they stop and hold themselves in place, slowly moving their arms and legs before rising again. As I watch the fluid motion of their bodies swimming through the water, a warmth flows through me, a feeling I cannot explain.

The girls rise to the surface; I watch the reflection of the light ripple across their bodies. The reflection changes as they roll over, their arms and legs outstretched. It is the most beautiful sight I have ever seen. Their long red hair accents their ivory skin, their hair always floating upward, sometimes obscuring their faces, other times covering their bodies, twisting around them as they turn. Their ivory bodies and glowing red hair are set against the backdrop of the multi-coloured creatures swimming among them. I picture it in my mind, creating an image that will stay with me forever.

The girl in the centre is the taller one. She rises from the water and swims toward the sandy shore. As soon as her feet touch the bottom, she stands, walking through the water toward me, waves lapping at her body as she emerges from the water. The other two girls follow, one on each side of her, their hair dripping wet and clinging to their backs. The morning sun shines on the girls, glowing red in the sky, accenting their bodies.

I watch them walk toward me as they hold onto the shells they have picked. The movement of their legs, their narrow waists, their breasts thrusting out in the cool air. Water glistens on their smooth skin. Small goose bumps appear on their arms and legs, covering the rising swell of their breasts. Their bodies are in rhythm as they walk in unison to the rock I am lying upon.

As they sit in front of me, I see their curves, the smooth folds between their legs, their firm breasts, peaked with dark red nipples, hardened from the cool breeze. The small indent of a button in the centre of their bellies. Their eyes smile at me, dimples appear in their cheeks. Their pupils are wide with excitement. Their red hair hangs over their shoulders, covering their right breasts. Their skin is soft and glowing, and faint scent emits from their bodies.

The girl in the centre passes one of her shells to me. She smiles, motioning for me to spread the shell apart with my fingers. "Open it," she says, grinning.

"It's delicious!" the other girls exclaim.

I take the shell from her, accidentally dropping it into my lap. The shell is smooth and slippery, the smell of the ocean emanating from it. As she retrieves the shell, her hand brushes against my loins, her eyes smiling as she pulls back.

"Open it like this." She grips the edges of the shell, prying it open.

Inside the hard shell is a layer of soft meat. Within the layer of meat is a round stone, luminescent in colour. She separates the stone from the meat and places it in her mouth. She sucks the tendrils of flesh from it. After removing the stone from her luscious red lips, she holds it in the sunlight, colours radiating from it.

"Here." She passes the stone to me, pressing it into the palm of my hand. "Feel its hardness."

I hold the stone between my fingers, then hold it up to the sun. The stone glimmers, its colours changing in the light. The stone is hard and translucent, accenting the colours of the sun. She leans forward, uncrossing her legs as she takes the stone back, then holds it between her forefinger and thumb. She lifts it to my lips, motioning for me to suck on it. I taste the stone, being careful not to bite it, or swallow it. She places it in a small pouch so she will not lose it. Then she picks the soft meat from inside the shell and places it in my mouth.

The taste is sensational, moist, exquisite, with a texture I have never encountered before. She places a piece in her mouth, chewing seductively. I watch her lips move as she chews the delicate meat and her pale throat as she swallows, the blue veins pulsating in her neck. With her legs uncrossed, I see the part of her that glistens, moist, emitting a pleasant smell, the tip of her pearl exposed.

The two girls on either side of her lean forward, kneeling. They each lift one leg as they pry open their shells, removing the pearls and tasting the delicate meat, sharing it with me. Their breasts are soft, the colour of ivory, their nipples the colour of red berries, hard with small dots surrounding them. The two girls are identical. They rise, stretch their arms toward the sun, then bend over backward until their hands touch the ground, their palms flat on the rock. Somersaulting backward, they leap into the water, swimming to the bottom like the finned creatures.

"They show off," the tall girl says, smiling at me. "Our mothers were twins."

I look at the girls and their likeness as they swim through the water. "Let's follow them." She rises, pulling me up with her. Her hands are soft, yet I feel her strength as she grips me. She stands before me, her nipples brushing against my chest. Spontaneously we touch our lips together, our hands clenching each other's. The touch is sensual, as if an electric current flows through us. We look into each other's eyes. Her eyes shine, glimmering like the sea. She places her hands on my shoulder, facing me, a radiant glow emitting from her body.

"Come, let's swim," she says, breaking the spell. She leaps into the water, the cold water splashing me. I leap in behind her, the coldness shocking me as I enter the water. We dive toward the bottom. Like the sea creatures, we turn, somersaulting underwater, blowing bubbles at each other. We swim toward the two girls, rising to breathe like the great beast of the sea, spewing our breath from our mouths. The four of us cavort and play in the water like we are part of it. The finned creatures nibble at our bodies, tickling us.

The girls show me how to dive to the bottom to gather the shells that contain pearls. I watch how they breathe deeply, expanding their chests. Slowly they let little breaths out, one breath at a time. I mimic them. They show me how to move my arms and legs, helping me to swim deep into the water while exhaling, releasing little bubbles from my mouth. Once the pressure gets too great, they stop and rest until their bodies become accustomed to the pressure.

I follow them, swimming as they do, holding my breath, letting little breaths out one at a time, watching the bubbles rise. The eight-legged creature swims past us, as do the slithering creatures that live in the water. I swim behind the tall girl, watching the way she moves her arms and legs, her legs opening and closing smoothly as she swims deeper. The other two swim beside me, moving their arms and legs in unison. Their breasts are buoyant, their bums' firm and taut.

My eyes see every movement of the girls as they swim like the finned creatures. The glimmering light shines through the water, accenting their bodies. One of the girls reaches for a rainbow-coloured finned creature swimming by, holding onto it gently. She passes it to me, stroking its belly until it relaxes. I watch the finned creature as it breathes in and out of its gills. I feel its smooth underside, which contrasts with the roughness of its outer scales. The other twin holds up a string of a jelly-like substance with black dots inside it. She places it in my hands. It is soft and slimy.

"Roe," she mouths to me.

With my breath almost gone, I rise to the surface. The three girls follow me, making sure I am okay. I hold onto the string of roe, long and slimy, letting it twist around my fingers. I take a deep breath as I surface. One of the girls takes the string from me, then swims to shore, and places it inside a pouch of wet seaweed.

"Later we will eat it." She rubs her belly.

The tall girl grabs my hand and pulls me downward, the girls following us. We reach the bottom. I sweep my arms from side to side. Sand rises as I run my hands through it. I touch something hard; a shell is buried in the sand. I pick it up and show it to them. They smile at me, then they find more shells, gathering them with their hands.

The tall girl motions upward. We start rising to the surface, careful not to move too fast. Suddenly, I experience excruciating pain throughout my body. The girls swim to me. Grabbing my arms and legs, they hold me level until the pain subsides. The tall girl locks her lips on mine, blowing her breath into me. I feel I have a new life with her breath entering me, her lips clasped to mine. She lets me rise, stopping me before the pain starts again; she lets my body adjust to the density of the water. I rise to the surface, gasping for air.

"We must rise slowly," the girls explain. They place the shells between their teeth. With both hands they swim to shore, pulling me with them. My feet touch the bottom first. I stand and lift the girls by their waists, carrying them to shore. When we reach the rock ledge, I lift them onto it one at a time. Their inner thigh muscles flex as they scramble onto the rock. I glimpse their smooth folds as they pull themselves up. The tall girl comes behind me, her hands clasping me. She pushes me onto the rock. I turn, reach for her arms, and pull her up. She kisses me once more as her body rubs against mine. A jolt flows through me as our lips touch.

"The tide will be in soon," she says with a grin, her eyes ecstatic. "Let's stay and watch the waters rise."

The four of us turn, facing the water. Sitting on the ledge, we dangle our feet over the rocks, the waves lapping against our ankles. The enormous black beast of the sea blows vapour into the air as it exhales before diving once more into the deep. A baby calf follows her, suckling on her teat.

"Do other finned creatures suckle on their mothers?" I ask.

"Only the ones without scales," the tall girl replies.

Soon the water is up to our shins, making them appear bent. We laugh and giggle as we lift our legs and then put them back in the water, spreading our toes and splashing each other.

"How high will the water rise?" I ask.

"The water will come to our waists," the girls say in unison.

"But what causes the water to rise, and why is it only the salt water that rises, and not the freshwater on the land?"

"We don't know," the three answer together.

The water splashes against our thighs, tickling our loins. We spread our legs slightly, letting the waves splash against us. The girls' smooth folds are slightly parted, exposing their pink inner petals. They giggle as the water laps against them. Feeling shy and timid, I cover my loins with my hands. The twins look at me coyly, their eyes twinkling. The tall girl smiles. She places her hand on my thigh.

"Lets swim." The twins jump into the water one last time. The tall girl jumps in behind them, pulling me with her. We tread water before climbing back on the rock. I lift them by their wet dripping bums, tossing them onto the rock ledge. Their knees buckle slightly as they land on their feet, their smooth bums flexing as they straighten. Once we are all on the rock, we walk over to where we left the string of roe. The twins walk in front, leading the way. One of the girls bends over, picking up the string of roe wrapped in the wet seaweed. She has a tiny red mark under the crease of her right bum cheek which becomes visible when she bends over.

Otherwise, I see no visible difference between the two. Even their small pert breasts are identical, rosy, pink nipples perched on their ivory globes.

"I will cook the roe for us tonight," one of the twins' whispers to me. A dimple appears on her left cheek as she grins.

The tall girl squeezes my hand. I put my arm around her slim waist as we walk along the sandy beach, feeling the wet sand squish between our toes.

"We must go back to our village," she says huskily. "Come taste the finned creature's roe before the sun goes down." She presses her body against mine, kissing me.

"Yes, come!" the twins say in unison, smiling at me. They hug me, kissing me on my cheeks.

I watch the girls walk away. The tall girl is in the centre, the twins on either side. The three hold hands as they walk with a spring in their step. They turn to look at me, smiling. My body stirs, and a warm feeling flows through me. The day has been sensual, vivid, and erotic. Tonight I will dream. The sounds of waves splash against the raft. I roll over, not wanting to wake. My dreams were vivid in the night; I want to stay in them.

The fanged pup licks my face, whining. I take him to the edge of the ramp going to shore. He bounds down the ramp into the shrubs. Seconds later, his body relieved, he bounds back up the ramp, excitedly licking me.

I feed him a piece of the dried finned creature. Then I also eat a piece, along with a loaf of bread. The bread is stale; fresh fruit and bread would be lovely this morning.

I watch the sun rise over the water. The morning sun is red, almost the same colour as the girls' hair. I wonder if I will see them today. The water rose again during the night. It rises twice daily at evenly spaced intervals, but this morning it is higher, separating me from shore.

The full moon is going down on the horizon, departing for the day. It seems that the phases of the moon, and the rise in the water coincide with each other. When the moon is full, the water rises higher. I walk to the edge of the raft and stare at the water, contemplating the relationship between the water and the moon.

A school of multi-colored finned creatures swim below me. The eight-legged creature with suction cups hangs onto a rocky outcropping under the water. Another eight-legged creature skitters across the deck. This one's body is black and furry. It does not swim, but it can scurry on top of the water. It can even walk upside down on the underside of the mast. The long-tailed creatures with faces like ours chatter as they swing from tree to tree, using their tails.

"Ocean, ocean," a multicolored feathered creature with a large bulbous beak repeats. *How can the feathered creature speak*? I wonder. *Yet it only repeats one phrase.* "Ocean, ocean. Where are you?" the feathered creature says again.

I think of the tall girl, remembering her face. She is the most beautiful girl I have ever seen. My body stirs when I think of her. The voices of children chattering fills the air. In the distance I see the tall girl walking toward me. The multi-coloured feathered creature flies to her, landing on her shoulder and pecking on her cheek. Twelve children are following her, seven boys and five girls. Giggling and laughing, they follow the tall girl. The twins follow the children, making sure they do not stray. A warm feeling comes over me as I watch them walk.

I return to my sleeping mat, and grabbing my loincloth, I cover myself, then dive off the raft. The fanged pup follows me. I reach the shore just as the girls and children arrive at the rock ledge. My loincloth is wet, hanging loosely on me. Laughing, the children reach for it to feel what it is made of. I explain that it was made for me in another village, and it is what the people of that village wear. I tell them that in my village we wore skins made from the beasts of the field. They have never seen or heard of another village. No one here wears any clothes. Everyone is naked like the beasts.

"The air is always warm here," the tall girl explains. "There is no need for clothes."

I gather driftwood, then rub two sticks together to make a small fire. The children gather around me. They have never seen a fire started like this before. The oldest boy gathers two flints. He strikes them together, creating sparks. In less time than it takes for me to light my fire, he has his lit beside mine. The rest of the children giggle, clapping the boy on his back. I smile at the boy, then slap his right hand with mine, congratulating him.

I pour water into my red clay pot and make a tea from the leaves of the sacred tree of the dark-skinned people, then I share it with the girls and the children. I explain to them that I was created from the clay of the red cliffs. All life was moulded from this clay, the breath of life breathed into each being. That's why my skin colour is red. I tell them about our small tribe and how my father said that I was never to cut my hair or touch a corpse.

"We must not cut our hair either," the oldest boy replies, running his finger along his braid. "My uncle made a blowgun for me from the special tree," he adds.

He proudly shows it to me along with the dart his uncle helped him make. The dart is small with tiny feathers on the end. I show him the bow I created from the seven different coloured woods and tell him about the seven stringed instrument my sister created, and the beautiful sound it makes as you strum the tight strings.

I tell them of the storms I have seen, intense lightning and thunder. I also tell them about the blue-green ice on top of the world, the tall trees I have seen, and the dark-skinned people's camp with the eternal flame. The children listen intently. The tall girl gives me a loving look, her eyes glowing. I remember the feel of her lips on mine when she blew her breath into me, the breath of life.

"But we are created from the water and given the breath of life from the great spirit in it. At one time we were a small dark dot, floating in a piece of jelly, growing slowly into who we are now," the smallest girl says, looking up at me. I smile at her. She is young and has not yet seen things. I remember when I was young, playing in our camp, learning things. I would listen to what Uncle told me, believing what he said.

She picks up my red clay pot, holding it to her mouth, and blowing into it. Then she puts it down on a grassy ledge beside a small puddle. "When we get back to the stream, your pot will still be there. It will still be a red clay pot, not eating or drinking water from the puddle. It will have the ability to hold water but not to contain life or a spirit." She gives me a sly look.

When we are done drinking our tea, the girls gather all the children together. The tall girl takes my hand, leading us to a small swampy area with a stream flowing through it. We come to a series of three puddles among the grass. In the first puddle is a string of opaque fleshy material with black dots spaced apart in it. It is almost the same jelly-like material that I saw floating in the bottom of the great salt water. With her deft hands, the tall girl explains to the children that once we were just an egg floating on the water, surrounded by a sac of jelly.

In the second puddle, numerous black creatures with large heads and tiny tail-like fins, no bigger than my smallest fingernail, are swimming. She calls these tadpoles. The oldest boy cups his hands together and scoops the tadpoles up, showing them to the rest of the children.

The third puddle shows how these tadpoles lose their tails while growing legs and arms. Their heads appear normal now, large eyes blinking at us. With webbed feet they swim to shore, then crawl out of the water and onto the land. Their long tongue flicks at small insects, sucking them into their mouths. They have soft underbellies. Some have lumpy backs while others have smooth backs. I cannot explain their sitting behaviour. They sit hunched over in a crouched position. Then they hop with their back feet from place to place, croaking loudly. She calls the ones with the smooth backs, frogs. The ones with the rough backs are called toads.

The little boys delight in picking up the toads and tossing them to the girls. The boys laugh while the girls squeal and try to run away. Some of the girls pick up the frogs to hold them, watching their tongues flicking out and catching bugs, rapidly swallowing them.

"Its belly is soft," a girl says, lifting the toad to her lips, and kissing its nose.

The tall girl explains that is how we all came to life. All things start as a blob surrounded by jelly, floating on the water, then separating into other species. Some with fins and some without, some with legs and some without, all shapes and sizes of creatures.

On the rock sunning itself is a hooded slithering creature, flicking its forked tongue at us. Singing softly, the tall girl picks it up, holding it in her hands. With its slitted eyes, it stares at us, its head turning from side to side, its forked tongue flickering in and out as the rings on its tail rattle. Two of the smallest girls go into a trance, hypnotized by the slithering creature's movements. They freeze, unable to move. I pick them up and hold them tight. The other girls step back while the boys look on with awe.

The tall girl strokes the slithering creature's throat while humming a beautiful tune. The slithering creature turns its head this way and that. She places her hand around its head, putting a small amount of pressure on it, and forcing the slithering creature to open its mouth, exposing its two large fangs, ivory in colour. From a sac behind the front teeth, a small amount of white liquid is secreted. She holds a large leaf under its head, collecting the serum. She folds the leaf in four, handing it to the oldest boy to keep. Later this child will be taught to become a snake charmer, collecting the serum to be used for the darts that kill, releasing the poison into the blood.

The oldest girl will also use some of the serum to save anyone who has been bitten by the slithering creatures. She will become the tribes snake healer. The serum is both the healer, and the slayer.

The tall girl then places the slithering creature on the rock. It slithers to a dead tree with a branch shaped like a cross. Circling around the pole, the creature rests its head on the cross. She says that in the days of old, the slithering creature was the healer, and whoever knelt before it wrapped around the cross would be healed. She explains that not all beings were meant to have arms or legs. Some beings crawl in the dust but also have the ability to swim in water. Some beings are dangerous to us, and we must learn the way of all creatures as well as the difference between good and evil.

I watch her arms and legs move. The sway of her body as she gestures, her smiling face with large, intense eyes. The tiny dimples on her cheeks. The children look at her adoringly, intent on every word she speaks. She looks at me, raising her arms and smiling. Her green eyes are large and twinkling as she gives me a playful wink.

The twins find a large slithering creature, longer than both of their bodies together. Unlike the hooded one, this one is harmless. They let it curl around their bodies. The children are in awe as they watch. The girls tell the children to be careful because some slithering creatures will circle their prey, squeezing tight around their bodies until their breath is squeezed out of them.

On our way back to the meadow, the children find a round fruit, its inside is eaten and its outside is a semi-soft shell that has hardened in the sun.

"Let's play ball!" The oldest boy runs for it, kicking it to the oldest girl.

"Teams!" he shouts. "Boys against girls!"

"You're on the girls' team!" the boys shout at me.

We pick opposite ends of the field, the girls separating from the boys. The smallest girl gathers branches, making posts for our end. The smallest boy gathers sticks for his end.

"Your goal is shorter than ours!" he yells.

He runs to the centre of the field and drops the ball between the oldest girl and boy. They tousle each other, battling for the ball, each one's teammates cheering them on.

The girl drops down, puts her shoulders between the boy's legs, and lifts him up. The smallest girl dashes under them, kicking the ball in the air. The rest of the girls converge on the ball, not letting the boys reach it as they pass it between themselves. The smallest girl runs to the goal, standing beside it, she deftly kicks the ball between the youngest boy's legs, scoring the first goal.

The girls cheer, but the boys yell, "No fair!"

"The winning team is the first to eat the delicious fruit!" the girls yell, leaping up and down.

Sweat drips off us as we play. The girls kick the ball to me, letting me score a goal. They leap on me, cheering me on as my long hair swings in their faces.

"You must braid it." A girl pulls me aside to do just that. Then she hugs me as she runs back to the field, her little feet pattering on the soft ground.

The boys run down the field, kicking the ball between two girls who are standing as posts. "Tied!" The boys leap, cartwheeling down the field.

I chuckle as I watch them play. The tall girl and I lie down together, side by side, hands held tight. Our backs are to the sun, we feel its heat on us. The twins lie on either side of us. We listen to the children running and laughing together. Soon the children are quiet. The team with the extra boy in it has lost the game. The twins climb the tree and pick the fruit, giving one to each child. I think about the things I have seen and wonder about my red clay pot sitting by the water. Will it have life in it?

When it's time to walk back to the village, the twins lead the way, followed by the children. The tall girl and I walk in the rear, making sure the children are safe. We come to a small pool of crystal-clear water. All the kids dive in, jumping and splashing. Some crouch down imitating the frog, and others slither through the water like the slithering creatures.

A small waterfall is pouring into the pond. I bring out my gourd and fill it from the waterfall. The children come in turns to drink the crystal-clear water from my gourd, placing their lips over the opening and lifting it as they drink. After each one drinks, I rub a piece of moss over the opening to clean it, explaining the importance of cleanliness.

On one side of the pond is a grove of tall slender trees, their long leaves branching out at the top. A hard round fruit with hair on it has fallen to the ground. The twins wrap a piece of vine around the tree. Holding onto the vine, with their feet gripping it, they are easily able to climb the tree. I watch their toes curl around the trunk as they lean against the vine, pulling themselves up. Their bum and thigh muscles are tight and flexing, their every curve exposed. When they reach the top, they grab a branch, then each girl grabs some fruit, throwing it down. After they throw down eight each, one for each of us, they climb down the same way that they climbed up. The children want to learn how to climb too, so each girl takes one child at a time, tying the vine around the tree and boosting the child up.

I help the tall girl drill a hole into each round shell, then hand one to each of the children and the rest of the fruit to the four of us. Inside the shell is a white milky liquid. It soothes our throats as we drink it, sucking the liquid into our mouths. After the fruit is empty, the boys use rocks to split the hard shell in half. The girls laugh as they pick up the broken shells, holding them to their chests. They prance up and down as milk dribbles from the shells. Inside the fruit is a solid white substance that tastes delicious and sweet. These round nuts provide us with much-needed fluids and solids. I show the children how to fill the unbroken shells with water and plug the hole with a stick. We fill them with water from the falls, saving the water for later. Once we have eaten the flesh and drank the milk from the fruit, we rest in the meadow.

The youngest girl points to a red-breasted avian picking a wriggling creature from the wet ground. With her swift hands, the tall girl also plucks one from the wet earth. Showing it to the children, she explains that some beings were created both male and female. We cannot tell the difference between the wriggling creature's head or its tail. On starvation days they will eat them, but now there is enough food for everyone.

"This is the same red-breasted avian that nests in my village," I tell the children.

One of the girls picks up a blue egg from the nest and shows it to the rest of us. She asks how the red-breasted avian came from the blue egg. "The blue feathered avian must have laid an egg in the red-breasted one's nest," she says. She wants to stay there until the egg hatches to see the colour of the chicks. Rubbing my skin, she smiles, telling me that it is the same as her skin, only rougher since I am a male.

When we reach a rocky ledge above the waterfall, we follow the trail up the hillside. First, I lift the twins onto the ledge. Once they are up, I pass each of the children to the twins, who, in turn, reach down to grab their arms, pulling them up. I grab the tall girl by her slender waist, lifting her over me, then playfully spank her as she scrambles up. Laughing, she kicks her feet back at me. Then she turns, bending down to lift me. I let her pull me up, then give her a quick kiss as I jump onto the ledge beside her.

The twins lead the way, followed by the children. I stay in the rear, lifting the children and the two girls up as they need it. Soon we hear a slight roaring sound. A dim glow shines in the distance; steam rises high into the air. I remember the fires I saw at the white man's camp when it seemed the whole earth was burning. When we reach the top of the hill, the youngest children are breathing hard from the long climb. At the top is a grassy knoll with a ledge running along it, making a perfect bench to sit on. The tall girl and I sit in the centre with the twins on either side of us. Six children sit on the left side, and the other six on the right, from the tallest to the shortest.

I tell them about the round table at the yellow-haired person's camp and how the thirteenth seat was broken in half. I tell them about their leader and his twelve knights and the one knight who betrayed him. The youngest girl tells me that this ledge is better because we have sixteen seats, eight on each side, like the eight legs of the furry creature that can scurry upside down. She picks up an eight-legged furry creature in her hand, passing it around. The tall girl tells the children about the eight-legged creature in the depths of the water. Like the slithering creature, some eight-legged creatures are harmless, while some have a poisonous bite.

As I look across the water, I see a small mountain forming. The rock is molten, with fluid bubbling up from the water. As the molten rock spews from the top of the formation, it flows into the water, causing it to bubble and boil. The sudden cooling causes the molten rock to become hard. Different gases within the earth rise with the molten rock, causing different shapes and types of rock to form. Some rocks are white, and some are red, black, or brown. Some rock is a mixture of many colours. I tell the children about the blue hills and how they were not blue, but green and filled with all kinds of colours. I point to the blue water in the distance.

"But the water in the gourd is clear," a child says. "How can water in the distance be blue?"

"But what is colour?" another girl asks.

"Colour is a reflection of light," the tall girl replies. "Without light, there is no colour."

I tell the children to close their eyes, then ask them what colour they see. The youngest boy giggles. His eyes are open as he points to the great white feathered creature that led me to this land. A large scat falls through the sky. It lands on an area of the rock that has already cooled, right into the centre of seventy little fruit trees that are growing in a circle. The tall girl reminds the children that at this time last year, seventy of the long-necked feathered creatures flew over that area, eating the small grasses that appeared. Each one ate the berries from another land before pooping the seed out.

"So, did the feathered creatures create the trees?" the youngest boy asks.

"Yes, this will be a new land with new creatures on it, isolated from the rest by the water," she replies.

He then points to a creature climbing from the water onto the rock ledge. This creature is smaller than he is. It has gills but breathes like we do. It has a long body with short legs, and its tongue is long and thin. Along the centre of its back, from the top of its head to the tip of its tail, are ridges like armour. Its feet are webbed, with claws like the feathered creatures. The tall girl says that this is the sea dragon. At one time it had wings without feathers. It would fly through the sky, blowing fire out of its mouth, and terrifying villagers. The children giggle, saying that one day they would like to fly and blow fire at one another. Laughing, they jump up and flap their arms, blowing at each other.

I grab the youngest girl by her waist, pulling her toward me. She has gotten too close to the edge of the cliff. I remind the children that we are not yet feathered creatures and cannot fly. I lift her long red hair above her head, telling her that underwater her hair will float upward, but on land her hair, and her body will fall to the ground.

"But how do I float in the water and fall to the water from the cliffs?" she asks. Then she laughs, thanking me for saving her, and gives me a quick hug followed by a kiss on the cheek. I slap her lightly on her backside, then set her on the ground.

The tall girl smiles at me. We look at the other side of the hill. She points to their village. The oldest boy shows me where he lives. The dwelling is built on stilts, made from the stalks of thin trees, elevated above the ground. It has a small ladder made from vines to climb up. It has short walls and a roof. On hot summer nights, the breeze flows through, keeping everyone cool. I see the fanged pup in the village with his newfound friend. Other children have gathered around it, petting it.

The tall girl tells me that in three days there will be a dance, and they must prepare for it. She invites me to the dance but tells me that she cannot see me tomorrow. She shows me the dwelling where she lives with her grandfather.

"My parents died from the sickness when I was young," she whispers, giving me a sad look.

"The oldest girl with us today will be given to one of the men for marriage. She will become his third wife. The child to be married is younger than the man's youngest daughter. I and the twins are not married yet. I am to become the priestess of the tribe. Our grandfather saved us from being married as children, but soon he will pass on like the ones before him. When he is gone, one of the older men will bribe the leader to make us his wives. We collect the pearls to bribe the leader, so we will not be given in marriage. I gave my pearl to you to keep it safe." She kisses me, her lips soft and tender.

"I will keep it forever." I promise her. I kiss her, then pull the pearl from my pouch, rubbing it between my fingers. Her eyes glisten with tears.

With the two of us in the lead and the twins in the rear, we make our way back to the waterfall. Whenever we reach a rocky ledge, I turn to help the children down, sometimes turning them around and around before setting them on the ground. They squeal with delight as I do this. I lift the twins up and over me, turning them around over my head. Then I set them on their hands, their feet in the air, and watch them roll over onto their feet. Grabbing the tall girl, I hold her tight to me, then kiss her as I lower her to the ground, savouring her salty taste and her scent. We reach the waterfall and climb down one last time, lowering the children one by one.

"How can these girls be married at such a young age?" I ask the tall girl. "They are just children."

She shrugs, "It is the custom."

We come to my red clay pot; it is still lying beside the water. A piece of dirt with a small bug on it is floating on top of the water inside the pot.

"See?" the youngest girl laughs. "Even though your skin is red, you couldn't have been created from the red clay. Otherwise, you would be like the red pot, with the ability to hold life, but not to have life inside you."

I chuckle, then pick her up and swing her around. I give each child a hug, then kiss them on the cheeks. I also kiss the twins and give them a hug. I hold the tall girl tight, lifting her up to me, and kissing her lips. Then I set her down, and we all turn toward the sunset, glowing red in the sky. I remind the children that earlier in the day the sun was yellow, and the sky was blue. But now the sun and the sky are multiple shades of red and orange. I watch the three girls and the children walk toward the sunset, their backs to me, shaded from the sun. The tall girl turns and waves, blowing me a kiss.

As I watch the silhouette of her shape against the sun, something stirs within me, a feeling I can't explain. I raise my hand and wave at her. Tonight I will listen to the waves as they rock the raft, and dream of her.

**

The young lad leads the way back to camp, followed by the rest. I walk behind the children, lost in thought. The twins walk beside me, smiling at me, teasing me. Today has been exciting. My whole body tingles with excitement. I have never felt this way before. I look at the young lad walking in front and his strong stride. He is quiet. When he glances back, our eyes meet.

The girls hold my hands, walking in unison with me. We have been together ever since we were born, sharing our secrets. Our fathers were twins, a sacred thing in our camp. Our mothers were also twins. Ever since the girls were conceived, they did everything together. The youngest was hanging onto the hand of the firstborn when she entered the world.

Although I never mistook who was who, most of the villagers could not tell them apart. Many of the men in camp wanted both girls together as brides, offering many pearls to our grandfather for their hand in marriage.

The three of us learned at an early age to dive for pearls. In our camp, pearls were worth more than food. We would collect the pearls, giving them to our grandfather. He would give the pearls to the clan elders in exchange for protecting us. Our grandmother taught us the ways, protecting us, making sure we learned everything.

I was born during the full moon of the night when the ground shook. A thundering roar was heard all night. The sky was as bright as day, and hot ash rained down from above. Our grandmother climbed the hill in the early morning hours to pray for our safety. She was the first to see the new land being formed. Molten lava flowed from the sea, spewing up from the ocean floor. Volcanic ash rose high in the sky, creating blackness all around. She felt the heat from the molten rock and the cool breeze from the splashing water as it cooled in the darkness.

Every year after this, at the time of my birth, we would go to the hills for three days and three nights, the length of the full moon.

It was in the second year of my birth that my cousins were born during the same season as I was. After they were born, our grandmother would take all three of us to the hills. On the night of our bleeding, she told us to go to the hills alone. This was a special time for us. Every year after that, we would travel to the hills alone, watching the newly created land growing in the water.

Our clan calls our grandmother the creator. She is the oldest alive. She was the first to see the new land being formed. Her long white hair flows to the ground. The clan believes all beings come from her. I am to become a priestess of the clan. The twins and I will take twelve children from the clan for seven years, teaching them, showing them the ways, like our grandmother taught us. They will, in turn, discipline seventy others. This way our clan will survive.

Turning back as we walk, I see the red man watching us. His arms are outstretched, the small fig leaf covering his loins. The backdrop of the raft's mast is behind him. It is in the shape of a cross, glowing red in the setting sun. A warm flush flows through me. My nipples ache, and moistness emits from me. The girls see me looking back, and they smile knowingly. The children walk ahead. I watch them, thinking of their future. The young lad in front, leading the way, is an adept student, always asking questions. The eldest girl of the twelve is beside him. The twins and I walk hand in hand as we enter the camp, past the leering eyes of the men, who hang out by the fermented grapes. I think of the red man and his smiling eyes, one blue and one green, shining at me, the feel of his hands as he caressed me.

We walk past the dwelling of the man who will marry the young girl tomorrow night. His youngest daughter is helping to prepare for the feast. She was one of the twelve last season. Her belly is swollen, her breasts full, and her nipples are engorged. Soon she will give birth to a child. Last season she was given in marriage to her uncle, her father's brother. The children walk side by side into the camp, the three of us behind them. We enter our grandfather's hut, all of us crowding inside, jostling for position. The young lad stands behind me, his hands on my waist. Someone jostles against him, pushing him against me, his phallus touches me.

Our grandfather gives each child a blessing before they go to their homes. "Protect the children, as I have protected you," he tells the three of us. "I have climbed the hill today. I have seen a raft with a cross on it. I have seen a man with long black hair and red skin. This man was one of us from a long time ago. Learn his ways, as he will learn your ways."

I return to my cot, and the girls each go to their own cots. We give each other a quick hug before retiring for the night. I wrap grandmother's warm robe around me, thinking of the red man's body lying next to mine, dreaming of life to come. I touch my breasts, feeling their fullness. My flower is wet, wanting to be touched. Falling asleep, I dream of the young lad leading the children. It is a strange dream. I writhe during the night, tangling in my blanket.

The feathered creature with the comb crows at sunrise, waking me. The girls are already up, offering me a sweet drink, giving me the special fruit for breakfast.

"Today will be busy," I say as I sit across from them. We must prepare for the dance. After the dance is over, we will climb the hill, staying for three nights and three days, during the length of the full moon.

I bake flat cakes over the hot rocks, heated from the darkened wood. Once they are cooked to perfection, I spread berries across the centre. The young lad comes, carrying three eggs with him. He cracks the eggs over the heated rocks, turning them over once before putting them in the centre of the cakes.

"What will you eat?" I ask as I look at him, his body lean.

"Nothing," he replies, smiling.

"Here, take mine." I pass him my hotcake.

"You eat." He passes it back to me. "I will make another." He mixes flour with water, adding an egg to it, then kneading it as he rolls it into a ball. His strong fingers flatten it, making a circle. He throws berries on it, then bakes it on the flat rock.

"The new earth," he says with a grin, breaking the hotcake in four and passing us each a piece, keeping one for himself. "The four pillars of the earth!"

We eat the flat bread, its texture is soft, yet sticks together, a golden brown.

"Delicious!" The girls bite into it, savouring it.

I stare into the lad's eyes as I eat mine. *What does he mean by the four pillars of the earth?*

Even though the morning is busy, I still have time to think of the previous two days, and a smile comes to my face at times. The girls and I are smiling and laughing as we prepare, teasing one another. Seeing this, the children giggle and smile at us, some shyly and some brazenly. The young lad helps us, getting things for us and helping us prepare the food. The young girl to be married smiles, but I can see a faraway look in her eyes. I watch her, wondering what she is thinking.

She has not bled yet, but she will be married tonight to an older man. She will not spend the night with her new husband until she has spent her first seven days becoming clean after her first bleeding. She will live with the older man's first wife, being prepared to serve her husband. Sometimes the young girls are beaten in jealousy, and sometimes they are treated indifferently. The girls are so young.

The young lad grabs the fruit from the vine, then tosses it into the vat. He helps me crawl over the sides of the vat, his hands lingering on me. I turn to him and smile, helping him climb inside. We step on the fruit, side by side, our feet touching each other's, squishing all the juice out, making a sweet drink for the feast.

"I will get the sweet nectar," he says, grinning. He wipes the skins of the fruits off me, his hands touching me lightly.

"Hurry," the girls tell him, lifting him over the sides of the vat.

He runs to the hive and gathers the combs laden with the sweet nectar. The fuzzy yellow insects circle him as he runs back to us, throwing the six-sided comb into the vat.

"Would you like some?" he asks as he sweeps the fuzzy yellow insects off, then holds a piece up to me, dripping with the sweet nectar. I stop and look at him. My heart flutters as I see his glowing eyes. I accept a piece of the comb and taste its sweetness.

"Thank you!" I murmur. I hold a piece to my lips, biting into it, then lifting it to his lips. He smiles at me, licking my fingers as he eats the comb.

"I will get more." He dashes back to the hive, careful not to get stung. He sings to the insects as he takes the sweet nectar from them. I have watched him work with the hives. Sometimes when he gets stung, he comes to me to rub the special ointment on him. In a matter of hours, the swelling goes down, and the red marks disappear.

I smile inwardly as I remember when he got stung on his chest. "My breasts are larger than yours," he had said with a giggle when I rubbed the healing lotion on him. Then he grinned as he dipped his finger into the lotion and rubbed it into my nipples.

The fuzzy yellow insects are amazing creatures. As soon as the hive gets too big, they raise a new queen. When the queen is mature, she exits the hive, followed by the males. Only one will mate with the queen before she returns to the hive, laying eggs inside the six-sided cells. The females will nurture the eggs, collecting the nectar and the pollen from the flowers, bringing it back to the hive.

"You are the queen!" The young lad grins at me as he holds a fuzzy yellow insect up, cradling it in his palm. "More beautiful and taller than the rest."

He blows on the larger bee, urging her to go back into the hive.

"When the cold weather comes, the females will kick the males out." He shows me the difference between the males and the females.

"Only the females have stingers." He holds one in his fingers, nudging it gently so as not to get stung.

"And this is its tongue." He points to the appendage coming from the fuzzy yellow insect's mouth. "It sucks the nectar from the flower."

Soon we are sticky with the sweet nectar, laughing as we tread on the grapes. Our bodies are wet, and skins from the fruit cling to us. We scrape the skins off each other, sometimes with our lips, eating it. The young lad swats the insects that fly around us, making sure we don't get stung.

"Some bite and some sting." He slaps my bum, pretending to swat an insect. The girls giggle, pushing him between themselves, sometimes pushing him into me. Whenever he brushes against me, he lifts a comb to my mouth, letting me taste the sweet nectar inside. After all the fruit from the vine is trodden and the juice is flowing through the spigot, we climb out of the vat and run to the water to wash. The girls leap through the air, swan diving into the water. I leap behind them, followed by the young lad. We swim to the shallow end, washing the sticky nectar from our bodies.

A fuzzy yellow insect lands on me, its long tongue sucking the nectar off me. It tickles as it crawls across my breasts. I yearn for someone to wash me, to lick the nectar off me, and to feel the sensation of their tongue on me. I glance at the young lad washing himself, his eyes glowing as he returns my smile. His thumbs are strong and slender, his four fingers sticky with the sweet nectar. I sink down in the water, scrubbing myself clean, wanting instead to rub my hands over his body.

"Let us wash you." The girls smile at the lad, then pick up a piece of clean moss. They scrub him clean until his skin glows.

"We better go back," I say, feeling strangely jealous.

"Some of the men are taking the pulp and remaining juice," the girl to be married says as she stands on the bank, watching us. I look up and see the men taking the spilled fruits and juices, running to where they ferment it. One of the men is the one whom the young girl will marry tonight. I look at the girl and worry for her. What will her life be like?

"I will watch over her," the young lad assures me, his fingers pressing into my bum as he pushes me up onto the ledge.

"Thank you," I whisper to him.

I lift him beside me, feeling his strong hands grip mine. He touches my sensitive area before walking over to the young girl, leading her away. I watch them walk away together, my face pensive.

"Come, let's give grandmother some of the freshly squeezed juice." The girls grab my hands, and we skip along the path to the vat, bringing a gourd along with us. We fill it with the sweetened juice, bringing it with us to our grandmother's house.

"She has not been well," our grandfather says as he greets us at the door. We walk inside the dim room and see our grandmother lying on her cot. She lifts her head when she sees us. I kneel on one side of her while the girls kneel on the other side.

"We brought you the sweet juice," I say as I lift the gourd to her lips, letting her sip the amber liquid.

"Tonight will be my last feast," she says after she takes a sip. "I will return to the stars soon."

She squeezes my hand, my tears dripping on her as she struggles to raise herself up. The girls hug her, rubbing their hands over her forehead, crying softly. She has been like a mother to them. Even though she is old, her eyes and her mind are still sharp, missing nothing.

"We came as a seed upon the water to this land, and we will leave it as a ray of light, soaring to the stars." Her arms encircle us. "Tonight during the dance, I will go to the hills where I first saw the new land being formed."

Tears glitter in my eyes as we leave our grandfather's hut. He hugs us, his shoulders stooped and his eyes sad.

"Take this with you." He passes us each a pouch, filled with pearls. "I have kept them for you."

We walk past the men standing by the fermented fruit. "I am never to cut my hair or drink from the fermented juice," I remember the red man telling me.

The village is bustling as everyone prepares for the feast. Ladies wash the fruit, and men prepare the circle. Children play, pretending to be finned creatures swimming in the water. The red man walks up the path toward us, a glint in his eyes, and his long black hair flowing behind him. Tonight I will dance for him. As soon as the children see him, they run toward him, hugging him. He throws them high into the air, then grabs their arms and twirls them around.

"Throw me up again!" they cry, giggling as he catches them.

A few of the clan give him a strange look. They have never seen anyone different from themselves.

"Our clan is the world," I hear someone mumble. "It is only us."

Gourds of sweetened juice are passed around. Dancers gather in the middle of the circle. Women circle around the outside, shaking rattles made from the tails of the slithering creatures that sit coiled on the rocks. The young girls tap their sticks together, and the boys tap their feet and clap hands. Men hand out the sweetened and the fermented juice. Neither the red man nor the young lad drinks the fermented juice, only the pure drink from the fruit of the vine, sweetened with the nectar from the hive.

As the women shake their rattles, it is like the rhythm of the waves crashing upon the shore. The young girls tap their sticks together to the sound of finned creatures leaping over the waves. They slither through the circle like schools of finned creatures swimming through the water. The boys clap their hands to the sound of waves lapping upon each other, bobbing up and down as they dance through the girls like waves. The older girls join in the dance while the men stamp a rhythm with their feet. The young lads enter, swimming like dolphins trying to catch the finned creatures. The girls scurry around the boys, everyone moving like finned creatures in the water. I move toward the red man, swaying my hips and moving my arms as I slither toward him. I place my arms around him, sliding them up his body, feeling his muscles, my nipples pushing against his chest as I slide against him. I remove his fig leaf.

"We are all naked like the finned creatures in the water, our smooth, slippery skin rubbing against each other," I whisper in his ear as I rub my body against his.

Looking into his eyes, I see his soul and feel the caress of his hands on me, his six fingers touching me. I savour the feeling, pouring the sweetened drink into his lips and licking the sweet nectar from his tongue. I feel his phallus touching me. I step back, dancing with my arms raised, swaying back and forth, and side to side. I feel his eyes on me, feeling the warmth in them as they move up and down my body. I watch his eyes pause as I twist my hips back and forth, my breasts jiggling up and down. His eyes rest on mine, and we gaze at each other, then he reaches for me. I stand on my toes, flexing my arches and leaning forward on one foot, my other leg stretched back. I circle, pivoting on my toes and reaching for his hands.

The girls tap their sticks faster, twirling around, to the sound of waves splashing. The men stamp their feet harder to the sound of waves crashing upon the shore. The boys clap their hands faster as they move in a circle, swimming like finned creatures. The women shake their rattles to the sound of raindrops falling on the water. The red man spins with me, pivoting on his toes. I watch his form, his rippled muscles, his rough hands holding mine. I see his wide shoulders and his muscles tense as he turns. I see every form of his body, yearning with desire.

The girls come swimming up to us like the slithering creatures. Grabbing our arms, they spin us around them, lifting us up and spinning us over their heads as they hold us up with their hands. The children dance around us to the sounds of waves splashing, the steady slapping of waves upon waves. My love grabs the girls one at a time and throws them into the air. He catches them on the way down, spinning them around, their red hair flying outward. He grabs the girl to be wed and lifts her high in the air. Then he swings her around, tossing her to me. I catch her, then throw her back to the girls. They catch her, passing her back and forth between themselves. She laughs with delight, giggling like the tinkling sound of the waves. The other children scramble over to be thrown into the air as well, everyone laughing and giggling.

The newlywed girl smiles, her belly swollen with child. I lift her carefully, passing her to my love. He holds her in his arms, rocking her back and forth, causing her swollen breasts to sway. She giggles and holds her stomach, feeling the child move within her.

The man who is about to wed the young girl, drinks the fermented juice, along with his brother, their eyes red as they stare at us. I look at the two men and worry for the girls, the one to be wed and the one ready to give birth. We turn the girls away from them, swinging them around, dancing with them. The women join in, as do the men who do not drink the fermented juice. Everyone surrounds the girls like a school of the finned creatures protecting their young. Hands touch my waist, and the young lad faces me, dancing with me, his lips brushing against mine. He turns away, dancing toward the young girl.

The full moon rises in the sky. The girls dance toward me, putting their arms through mine. Tonight we will go to the hill. I grab my love, pulling him along. At the edge of the circle, I cling to him, feeling his body against mine. I lift my lips to his, kissing him. I feel his flesh against my flesh. I fall to my knees, quivering. I tell him I will journey to the hills, but I will be back before the moon disappears. I squeeze him tight, telling him to look after the children. Turning with our arms linked, the girls and I walk the moonlit path toward the hills.

Moonlight shines all around, illuminating the way. Our legs tremble as we climb the steep parts. The girls pull me up, and I, in turn, pull them up the rocky ledges. As we climb, the sound of waves crashing on the shore drowns out the sounds of the dance. Clouds drift across the sky, covering the moon, then allowing it to reappear again as they pass. When we reach the stone seats, we see our grandmother sitting in the centre seat, her long white hair touching the ground. The seven stars shine in the night sky, brighter when the clouds cover the moon and dimmer when the moon shines bright, uncovered by the clouds. Placing my hands on our grandmother's head, the girls on each side of me, touching her shoulders, we bless her, knowing that tonight she will reach the seven stars.

She points to a ship sailing toward the new land. Standing at the helm is a man with pale white skin. His hair is the colour of the sun, long and flowing across his shoulders. Beside him is a woman, her skin almost as black as the night, her hair short and curly, and her belly starting to swell with child. Standing behind the man and woman are two men, shining white in the moonlight, their hair the colour of the sun, braided in three strands, hanging down the centre of their backs. All four wear a small white tunic, made from the softest cloth. I look at my love's raft, rocking in the waves. The cross in the centre glows white in the moonlight. Our grandmother grabs my hand, pointing for me to follow the path toward the raft.

"Go," she urges me.

Grabbing the girls' hands, she points down another path, to where the taller vessel sails toward the new land, coming to a grove of trees, freshly growing in the new earth.

"Go," she tells them.

I walk down the trail, excited and full of anticipation, almost feeling the red man's hands on me, guiding me. The night air is cool and moist. I see the hooded slithering creature glide past me, its tail rattling. I tread carefully down the trail. My breasts are firm, my nipples sensitive and erect. Thoughts of my love as he lifted me over the ledges drift through my mind, his hands touching me. The feel of his phallus as he brushed against me, the feel of his tongue on my pearl as I kneeled over him. I arrive early, before the moon fades. It is glowing bright in the sky.

A cord is tied from the base of a tree to the helm of his raft. It's made from the long vine that grows at the bottom of the hills, woven together with three strands intertwined together. I think of the girls and me. Even though we are separate, we are entwined around each other. That is what gives us our strength. I climb along the braided vines with my arms and legs encircling the cord, sliding along it toward the raft. Climbing aboard, I see my love sleeping in the centre. He lies beside the mast, lying on a mat of fig leaves. At the helm, swinging from a bed made from reeds, the young girl to be married is sleeping soundly in the hammock.

Another hammock is across from hers. The young lad is sleeping in it, his face glorious in the moonlight. My body stirs, filled with sudden desire as I remember the feel of his lips as he kissed me. The moonlight glows on the red man, his fig leaf lying beside him. I creep toward him, careful not to awaken the others. I sway with the rocking of the raft, my toes lifting up, balancing, then stopping briefly when I hear a creak on the deck. Moving forward, I feel the cool breeze across my body as I crouch down and touch my love's feet. I lift them up, kissing his six toes, nibbling on them, rubbing my fingers between them. I look into his eyes, one blue, and the other green.

On my knees, I smell his scent. I straddle his loins, my nipples engorged with desire, my pearl throbbing as I listen to the waves lapping against the raft. The moon shines on his phallus, hard and rigid. I raise myself over him, my hands clasping his rigidness as I guide him to my swollen folds, wet with anticipation. I lower myself on him, feeling the tear, the sharp pain, followed by utter bliss. The raft rocks from side to side. My wetness glides on his phallus, glistening in the moonlight. My hands grip his shoulders. My knees press down, my legs gripping him as I look across the moonlit water. I see the shiny blackness of the great beast rising above the water, arching through the air. I thrust hard on the red man.

The great beast blows, its breath spewing from its head, vapour raining down on us. My love rises; his head thrust back. His hard phallus trembles and jerks. I convulse on him, milking him, feeling his spasms, my petals tightening around him. Feeling a deep rush through my body, I want to scream with pleasure. Instead, I whimper quietly so as not to wake the two who are sleeping.

I sink down onto my love. A cool breeze blows as the great beast dives back into the water. I feel the cool breeze against my bare bottom, cooling my wetness. Looking up, I see a star hurtling through the sky. I close my eyes, resting in his arms.

I awaken to a soft touch, tender hands on my waist. I look across the vast expanse of water as the cool breeze blows against my wetness, tickling me. Four fingers touch me, slender thumbs spread my flower. A phallus enters me. As it quivers upon release, another star shoots across the sky, soaring through the heavens.

I weep in ecstasy.

THE THUNDERING

Hungry, I stop for a bite to eat. The meadow I have come to is sparse. I do not see any fruit growing on the trees around here. The air is dry with only a few clouds in the sky. In the distance are a range of towering mountains, covered by ice and snow. The trees are small in stature. Boulders of all shapes and sizes are scattered throughout the meadow. Small creatures stand guard over tiny holes in the ground, standing upright on two legs, like a man, facing eastward, toward the rising sun. These creatures have tunnels buried in the ground. Their dens are at the ends of the tunnels. The white-headed feathered creature flies overhead, swooping down to catch an inattentive rodent, scooping it up with its talons. Soon there is nothing left of the rodent.

    A thundering roar of dozens of hooves comes from the distance. I feel the vibration coming from the ground as the noise intensifies. Galloping past me are thirty of the hoofed beasts. Their heads are high, their long tails flying straight back, and their manes lifting in the air. At times one lifts both back legs up, giving the one behind it a swift kick in the chest. There are twenty-seven females and three males. The three stallions are herding the mares, guiding them. All the beasts are white with black spots on their hind ends.

    Behind the herd is a young girl riding a stallion. She has two ropes strung around its nose, and she tugs the rope in the direction she wants it to turn. She keeps the whole herd galloping in a straight line, her long hair flying straight back, like the stallion's tail. She appears to be the same age as me. With a jerk of the reins, her stallion rears up, standing on its hind legs, its forelegs moving in the air. The girl stays on its back as she lets the reins loose. The stallion comes down, snorting. The herd stops, neighing as they all prance. The mares and the three stallions eat the grass as they rest. Some roll on their backs, their long legs kicking in the air.

The girl is wearing loose trousers, bound to her waist by a sash. Her top is loose, her slender arms coming out of the sides. Her face is dark from the wind and sun. Her hair is black like mine. Her eyes are a light grey, having a perpetual squint, as if she is always looking into the sun. Her stature is short and slim. On her feet she is wearing leather coverings, sewn together. Her stallion snorts and shakes its head, prancing up and down. Swinging off the beast with an agile grace, she lets the reins drop to the ground. Then she walks over to me and bows, with a grin on her face.

"Drink." She passes her leather flask to me.

"Thank you." I bow, taking a sip of the cold water.

I pass it back to her; she tilts her head and pours the precious water into her mouth. I watch the movement of the muscles in her throat as she drinks, a tiny trickle of water running down her chin. Wiping it with her hand, she puts the flask back around her slender waist. She pulls some dried meat from another sack and breaks off a piece.

"Eat!" She passes it to me.

I wait for her to bite into hers before I bite into mine. Having some dried blueberries left, I share half of them with her. We eat slowly, savouring each bite. I gather wood and dried moss, then spread it inside a circle of rocks. Lighting a fire with my flint, I warm a cup of tea and share it with her. It is the tea I got from the blue hills.

As the steeds' graze, we sit by the fire, watching the feathered creatures swoop down on the rodents. The fuzzy yellow insects are flying around the flowers, gathering nectar from one flower, then flying to the next, and depositing the nectar inside its open petals. Their pollen-laden legs wiggle in a dance, alerting others to the sweet nectar of the flowers. The girl plucks a flower with a fuzzy yellow insect on it. She shows me how the insect crawls over the male parts of the flower, collecting the pollen from it, then flies from flower to flower, depositing the flower's seed upon the female parts of other flowers.

"It is the fuzzy yellow insect that spreads the male seeds of the flower to the female parts," she explains as she touches the different parts of the flower. "Flowers are both male and female, but they need the seed from the one to be deposited onto the other. It cannot pollinate itself even though it is male and female. It needs the help of the insects to pollinate it."

I pluck a flower with a fuzzy yellow insect crawling on it. "Ouch!" I feel a sharp prick as it stings my finger.

"It has a stinger for protecting her hive," she says as she lifts my finger to her lips. "They will only sting once, since they lose their stinger and die. Be careful, we do not want them to die."

As my finger swells, she leads me to a stream of cold water, and holds my hand in it until the pain subsides. With her deft fingers, she removes the stinger using her fingernails. She smiles at me, revealing a gap between her front teeth. I grin back at her, loving the dimples in her cheeks.

"Let's follow the fuzzy yellow creature back to her hive," she says, her eyes shining.

We follow the insects, dodging the workers as they fly from the flower to the hive. She removes a piece of the comb from the hive.

"Taste." She places a piece of the comb, dripping with the sweet golden liquid, into my mouth. Carefully, so as not to get stung again, I remove a six-sided portion of the comb, then give it to her.

"What's sweeter than honey?" she asks, grinning.

"Nothing is sweeter than honey," I reply as I give her another piece. "Taste and see that it is the best."

Soon we are both sticky from the sweet nectar. Laughing, we go to the stream to wash off, licking our fingers until the stickiness is gone.

I show her my bow. I explain how to pull the string back, and hold it to her cheek, keeping her form straight, and her arms tight.

"You must stand straight," I place one hand on her shoulder and my other hand on the curve of her back. "Bring one leg forward and move the other back." I put one hand under her thigh, moving it forward. "Stand tall, lift the bow, sight down the arrow, and look straight at your target." I put my other hand under her elbow. "Breathe in, hold, release," I whisper, stepping back.

Twang! The arrow releases, flying straight into the centre of the tree. She turns to me, smiling.

"Where did you get the wood for the bow?" She rubs her fingers along the length of the bow, admiring the seven different colours of wood, moulded together. "We do not have such wood here."

"My father designed the bow from the seven colours of the rainbow," I reply.

Prancing, her stallion comes to us, sniffing at me.

"I will teach you to ride." She grins as she throws me the stallion's ropes, grabbing my waist, and lifting me onto it. She jumps up behind me. "Yee haw!" she cries as she digs her heels into its flank.

I grab its mane, gripping tight. Her body presses against mine as the stallion rears up, then leaps forward, galloping fast and smooth. I hang on, feeling the wind in my face as we soar ahead. She wraps her arms around me, holding me tight, so I don't fall. I grip my knees against the stallion's sides, the movements of its strong muscles coursing through my body. She holds on tight, her body moulds into mine. We gallop among the herd, the mares kicking their hooves in the air as they run with us.

I listen to the thunder of hooves behind us. The beasts' tails are flying straight out, and their manes blowing in the wind. My long black hair flies in the girl's face as we gallop. She reaches over and tugs the rope, turning the steed in the direction she pulls. Her hand is on my shoulder, pushing gently; she leans me with the steed. When we come to a stream she pulls on the reins. We stop at the water's edge, all four of the stallion's feet digging into the ground. I slide up its mane, stopping behind its ears.

The girl jumps off the stallion. She reaches for me and swings me down to the ground. Even though she is slender, I feel the muscles in her arms. As the steeds' drink, we walk upstream, dipping our faces into the water, drinking like the hoofed beasts until our thirst is sated. The mares run to us, water dripping from their mouths. The stallions prance, wanting to run.

"Ride." She grabs me and throws me onto her stallion, then slaps its rump.

I feel its power through my legs as we gallop across the meadow. With my hands on its mane, and my legs gripping tight, it feels like I am flying in the wind. The thunder of hooves follow me as I soar ahead, floating on the stallion's back. As we turn, I feel the rush as my knee scrapes the ground. I gallop full speed toward the girl. Reaching down, I grab her waist and pull her up in front of me. As I lift her over the stallion's mane, her hair blows in my face. We gallop past the other steeds, jumping over the stream. Laughing with delight, I feel the power of the stallion's muscles coursing through me.

I feel every move of the girl's body as I hang onto her. Pulling on the rein, I turn us back to the stream, yanking it as we reach the water's edge. The stallion rears up, causing us to slide off its back. Giggling, sweating, and smelling like a steed, we dive into the water. After ducking under the water to remove our clothes, we rinse them while washing our bodies in the stream, then climb onto the rock ledge above us. The rock is white with numerous black specks in it, the colour of the steeds. I watch her as she walks, water dripping from her body. Her waist is slender, her legs straight and true. She walks with a spring in her step.

"Pass me your clothes," she says as she holds out her arm to me. "I will hang them to dry." She reaches over, lifting one leg as she drapes our clothes over the branches of a tree. Her body is slender, wiry, and athletic. Her skin is light brown, her eyes are grey, her hair is wavy, long, and black, hanging down past her waist. Her breasts are small and her nipples pert. Her arms are long and thin.

"Our clothes will soon dry," she says as she turns to me, her body lush, and her eyes glowing.

Beneath the tree is a bed of soft moss. We lie on it, facing the sun, its rays shining on our nakedness. I tell her about my father's village and how he built my bow. I also tell her about the hoofed beasts with horns coming out of their foreheads and the wings they have on their shoulders.

"They were pure white in colour," my father used to tell me.

"They would soar through the clouds," my mother would say.

I tell her about the red cliffs and how my father's uncle believed he was created from the red clay of those cliffs. I tell her how my mother travelled across the cliffs, passing through remnants of villages, seeing things from long ago. I tell her about the blue hills that she travelled through and how they were full of colour. I show her how the bow was made from seven different woods, compounded together. I tell her about the seven-stringed instrument that my father's sister made as a child.

She tells me of her tribe, how they follow the steeds, learning to ride as soon as they can walk. She tells me of the rugged barren land we are in and how it once was always ice. She tells me how they were taught to follow the horned beasts, driving them over cliffs for food. She shows me her short spear and the leather whip she uses to chase the long-haired beast with the split hooves. She tells me about the rodents that tunnel into the ground, letting water into the dry earth with their tunnels, bowing to the east as they wait for rain. She shows me how to crack the whip and tells me never to touch the beast with it.

"Beasts are temperamental, but they can be friends for life if treated right," she says as she rubs the steed's mane.

A cloud covers the sun, sending a chill through the air. Goosebumps spread across our bodies. "We must dress," she says. "It will cool off soon."

She stands up, reaching her hand out to me. I grasp her hand, letting her pull me up. Her dimples appear as she smiles. Her eyes glint in the sunlight; I see a myriad of grey as she squints. She pulls her top over her head. It fits loosely on her, allowing her movement as she rides. Placing one leg through her pants, she balances as she wiggles her hips, then she stands on the other leg, pulling her pants up, and tying them with a sash around her waist. She watches me as I dress, her eyes roving over my body. Finally, we pull our leather coverings over our feet. Her clothes are different from mine, the hems are elaborately embroidered. I remember the warmth of our village, where there was no need for clothes. She whistles, a shrill echo reverberating in the meadow. Her stallion gallops to us, stopping in front of her.

"Jump on." She lifts my leg, pushing me onto the beast. Grabbing my waist, she swings up behind me, her legs clinging to me.

I carry my bow strung across my shoulder. Her hands grip my waist as we gallop to her village, followed by the rest of the herd. Her village is a series of round tents, dotted around each other, each with six sides like the honeycomb. Hoofed beasts and fanged creatures wander through the camp. The fanged creatures pull little children on carts and older children ride the steeds. These fanged creatures are like the ones in the wild, but more docile, barking gleefully at us. Boys and girls wear the same pant-like outfit. Their shirts slung loosely over their shoulders and tied around their waists with a coloured sash. The women's faces are smooth while the men have scraggly beards. Men and women have the same grey slanted eyes. At the edge of the camp is a herd of the long-haired beasts. The ratio of cows to bulls is seven to one.

A child is milking one of the long-haired beasts, collecting the milk in a bucket for the evening meal. Its calf is bawling nearby. Women are brushing the long hairs from the beasts, collecting the fibres for making warm outfits to wear. The men are stretching a hide out, drying it in the sun, curing it to make another dwelling.

We dismount from the stallion, and she introduces me to the rest of the village. She lives in a yurt with her mother and father. Her younger brother also lives with them. Her father invites me to stay until a dwelling can be built for me. This is the last year that she will stay in her father's yurt since this winter she will be of age. In the spring she will choose a young lad, and both will live in his parent's yurt until they can build their own.

The men look at me curiously, eyeing the bow I carry. The women and girls smile shyly at me, their gapped teeth brilliantly white. One of the older girls dips a ladle into a jar surrounded by ice. She gives me a refreshing drink of cold milk. I will stay with these people for the cold season. Soon the snow will fly and travelling will be unsafe. The girl and I become fast friends. She teaches me her ways, and I teach her how to use the bow. Over time I become excellent on the stallion, while she can easily shoot the long-necked feathered creature from the sky.

I learn about the fuzzy yellow insects and the flowers. The queen lays all the eggs. The males only job is to mate with the queen. Only one male will get the chance. The females do all the work—collecting pollen, feeding larvae, and making the sticky nectar. Their combs are all six sided. I learn about flowers, which ones to use for aches, and which ones to use for indigestion. She shows me the male parts of the flower. How to take the seed from the pistil of one flower, then deposit the seed onto the stamen of another flower, causing more flowers to come to life.

The snows come and everyone gathers wood to keep the fires burning. I gather wood with the men, stockpiling it near the yurts. I teach the lads how to shoot the plump feathered creatures with the bow. I also help them improve the bows they use while they teach me how to tan hides for blankets and coverings for yurts. We keep a hole in the ice at the river. We keep a bucket beside it to use for carrying water to the village. The hoofed beasts and the long-haired beasts are adept at chewing the long grass under the snow and eating snow for their liquids. The rodents have long since buried inside their tunnels. They will return when the days get longer.

When the fanged creatures howl at night, we keep watch over the hoofed beasts and the long-haired beasts. Sometimes a great furry beast with no tail will wander into the camp, scaring the children. The men will jump up, throwing their lances at it. The meat will be cooked over a fire and the hide will be tanned for a new rug for sleeping on. Most furry beasts with no tail are black in colour, but some are shades of brown. These people revere the white one, with blue eyes.

I tell them about my mother and how she travelled from her village with a fanged creature beside her. I show them how to write things down, using a thorn dipped in certain coloured flower juices, and how to make marks on the white inner bark of special trees, marking symbols to remember a place or an event.

One night during the new moon, the wind blows, sending snow swirling all around. We cannot see in front of us; the whiteness of the snow is too thick. For three days and three nights the wind blows, piling up snow and covering the openings of our dwellings. I think of the rodents, safe in their tunnels.

One of the young men goes out to get some food for his family. We wait all night and day for him to return. His young wife cries as she cares for their little boy and girl, her baby girl still suckling on her breast. On the third day the men search for him. They bring back a cold body, frozen in time.

It is decided that I will stay with the young family whose father just passed away. I help the young mother, milking one of the long-haired beasts for her, heating the milk, and giving a cup of it to her little boy and girl. I also boil dried grains and make a mash for them, sprinkling a few dried berries on it, and spooning it into their mouths with some cream. After we eat, I tell them stories about my travels. Once the coals become embers, we crawl into our robes, draping them around ourselves and sleeping on a rug on the floor. I sleep across from them, a small robe covering me. In the center of the yurt is a bed of coals, creating heat to keep us warm.

The young mother nurses her youngest child. Her breasts full, she lets her child suckle her milk until her breasts become flat. I heat a pot of water over the coals. Then I place it in front of her, washing her body with a white bar of ash mixed with fat. Using a soft cloth, I rub her body dry until her skin glows. Then I dip my finger into a jar of salve and rub a small amount on her nipples, feeling a slight erection as I massage them. After dumping the dirty water outside the yurt, I fill the pot with fresh water. I wash the child, listening to her cooing with contentment. After she is clean, I place her in her mother's arms.

"Thank you," the young mother murmurs, covering herself with her robe.

Her children sleep beside her, a robe covering their nakedness. I lie awake, watching them sleep, thinking of the girl in the tent I just left and how I first saw her naked body in the stream. I watch the woman dream, wondering what her dreams are about. Her body moves as she dreams, and her night robes slide off. I cover her, then lie next to her, comforting her.

During the next new moon, the sky is clear, and the air is cold. Millions of stars shine in the night sky. I hear a rustle at the door, followed by the girl entering our yurt. The young mother and her children are sleeping soundly. Grabbing my hand, she pulls me outside. "I miss you," she whispers. "Come, let's go outside and look at the stars. Tonight there's no moon, so it's the best time for stargazing. The night is dark, and we will see stars shooting through the sky." I grab my robe and follow her.

"There is the perfect spot." She points. "Let's lay our robes on top of the knoll. We will be able to see all around us." She stops when we reach the knoll. Kneeling, she brushes the snow together to make a smooth bed. I throw the robe upon the snow, then spread it out with my arms, smoothing its folds. We lie together, staring into the night sky, feeling the coolness of the air, our naked bodies warm under the robes. The heat from our bodies warms us as we lie against each other.

I tell her about my mother's grandmother, how she became a shooting star. I also tell her about the warmth in her village, which never sees cold or snow. She reaches for my hand and squeezes it, telling me that we should go back in time to see my grandmother's village. I squeeze her hand and smile, feeling a warmth inside me. I point to the fixed star, explaining how my father used it as a guide when he sailed upon the great water and how the star led him to my mother's village.

She reaches over and kisses me. We lie side by side in the deep snow, looking at the multitude of stars shining against the blackness of the night sky. "Listen to the fanged creatures howling at the stars," she whispers.

A star soars through the sky, and we gasp in awe, watching until it disappears. "That star is the spirit of the young man who froze," she says. "His spirit is flying through the sky, looking out for us from above. We are only here for a season. Even the stars have a lifetime. When they die, they come back to earth." She squeezes my hand.

Soon it is time to go back. Wrapping our robes around our bodies, we hold hands as we walk through the snow. As I drop her off at her yurt, I kiss her lips.

"I will come see you tomorrow," she promises me, hugging me.

I make my way back to the yurt. Once inside, I see the young mother nursing her child, a sad look is on her face. I stir the coals in the fire, creating warmth inside the yurt. I tell her about the star I saw and how I believe it was her love travelling through the sky, looking for a place for them in the afterlife.

She stares at me, a scared look in her eyes. "Come, lie with me," she whimpers, tears rolling down her cheeks.

I bring my sleeping robe beside hers and put my arms around her. She cries softly as I massage her belly. I feel her stomach tremble as my fingers caress the stretch marks that reach across it. A fanged creature howls outside, long, eerie; the sound echoing inside the tent. I feel a small movement along her stretch mark, a slight kick, answering the call of the fanged creature. Another fanged creature answers, and I feel another tiny kick. I feel the wetness of her enlarged nipples brush against my chest as she turns to face me, wet from the child suckling her. The fanged creature howls again, and a light flashes through the sky. Once again, the child kicks inside her womb.

Soon she drifts off to sleep in my arms, her body nestling against me. I feel her twitching as she dreams, her steady breathing matching mine. I am aroused as I lie beside her, our bare skin against each other. I think of the girl, her promise to see me tomorrow, and our parting kiss. I dream of her with me as I lie beside the young mother.

In the morning I milk the long-haired beast. There is only enough milk to feed the children. The youngest child will have to be weaned from her mother, as her mother's body prepares for another child. The dried meat and grains for mash are almost gone. The light in the doorway dims as the girl enters our yurt. She gives me a quick hug, then picks up the youngest child, rocking her as the mother rests. I tell her that the young mother is with child again. Squeezing my hand, she tells me she will help the mother too, but she also winks at me and tells me not to fall in love with the young mother. I smile back, hugging her.

"Teach me to hunt," she implores me. She whistles at the steeds, and her stallion comes running toward us. After feeding him some grain, I throw her onto the stallion's back. I whistle at the red stallion, red like the colour of my skin. His one eye is blue, and the other is green, like mine. I jump on him, bareback. We use our legs to turn the steeds, signalling the way to go with slight pressure on their sides.

Skittish from not having been ridden since the snow fell, my stallion bucks. I grip its mane with one hand, my other arm outstretched for balance, then dig my heels into its flank. It leaps forward, galloping toward the forest. She follows me on her stallion, clutching the bow I made for her while hanging on tight. We pass the herd of the long-haired beasts, digging through the deep snow for grass. We gallop past the rest of the mares. When we reach the edge of the trees, we slow down, hoping to catch sight of the multi-horned beasts, their horns like tree branches on their heads.

Swoosh! An arrow whizzes past me.

Swoosh! Another arrow flies past. It whistles as it flies by my ear. I duck as she gallops past me, her bow ready for another shot. On the ground, bleeding, is the multi-horned beast, nine points on each side. Behind it is another multi-horned beast with seven points, both shot through the heart, killed instantly with one arrow each. She turns to me and grins as her stallion prances. I am in awe; I never even saw the beasts.

Grinning, I salute her, telling her that she is a better shot than I am. The village will be happy with her. She smiles, her eyes glistening. After quieting the steeds, we dismount. It takes both of us to lift the two beasts onto the stallions. They are skittish from the blood and want to gallop away. As soon as they are calm, we jump on their backs and return to the village. We will have enough meat for a couple of full moons.

The men watch us as we enter the village, some with jealousy and others with admiration. The women and girls look at us shyly, grinning as we enter with the beasts. Snorting, the stallions will not go any farther. We dismount, then pull the beasts off our steeds. The women help us cut the meat and bring it to the hanging rack. After seven days, the meat will be distributed among the villagers.

The girl invites me to eat in her yurt that evening. I accept and eat a delicious meal with her, and her parents. Her younger brother eats with us also, and the young mother. The days have been hard on her. The girl's parents thank me for bringing her on the hunt.

"A girl going on a hunt is unheard of," her mother says, her face proud.

"She is an excellent hunter," I reply, beaming at them. I will call her my love from now on.

"The village will need more meat. The young mother was with child before her husband passed," I say to her family.

"I want to stay with her too," my love tells her parents. "She will need help looking after her two children."

"Yes, please stay with us," the young mother begs the girl, her eyes pleading. I smile, a warm feeling inside me. After some discussion, it is decided that the girl will also stay in the young mother's yurt, helping with her children. After we eat, I share my tea with everyone.

"I will bring my sleeping robe," my love says after she finishes her tea. Then she rises and gets her sleeping robe, bringing it to the young widow's yurt.

She will sleep beside the young widow and children. I will sleep on the other side of the yurt, keeping watch over the fire. Today has been busy. After we settle down in the yurt, we feed the children. The young girl cries as we feed her some mash. She wants her mother's milk. The young mother squeezes her nipple, forcing some milk into the palm of her hand and feeding it to her daughter. She must rest, saving her body for the young child growing inside her, the child with the spirit of the fanged creature.

My love reaches for the hem of the young mother's dress and pulls it over her head. Her naked body is starting to show the rise in her belly.

"Lie down," my love whispers.

She gently pushes the young mother onto her robe, then she places her hands under the young mother's head and turns her onto her back. With her smooth hands, she massages her belly, smoothing out her stretch marks. She does this to soothe the child inside. Motioning for me to come over, she places my hands on the young mother's belly, letting me feel the child move inside her womb. After covering the young mother with her robe, my love holds the baby girl in her arms until she falls asleep. We hug each other goodnight, then I take the little boy and cover him with his robe. I lie awake, listening to the soft snores of the young mother, and the lonely howls of the fanged creatures in the hills. I think of the child growing inside the young mother's womb, remembering her stretch marks. She is only a few seasons older than my love and me.

In the morning I take the boy, letting him help me gather wood for the night. I let him sit on the red stallion, holding him so he does not fall. I also let him help me milk the long-haired beast, teaching him how to pull the teat and squeeze the milk into a bowl. Then we make the mash to feed the family. When the day warms up, my love comes with us, bringing the little girl with her. We smile at each other, throwing snowballs at one another. Before going to sleep, I feed the boy, while my love feeds the girl. After feeding and putting the children to bed, she massages the young mother's belly. Her belly is becoming larger, and her breasts fuller as her child grows inside her. I watch my love's hands move along the young mother's body. She places my hands on the woman's stomach, teaching me how to massage her, rubbing her belly in circular motions. I feel the tiny kicks inside her belly.

At night when the young mother is unable to sleep, I watch my love as she sits on the young mother's lower back, massaging her upper back and neck. Through the soft orange glow of the coals, I see her slender body moving as she massages the young mother. Her slim bum moves up and down, her slender back stretching as her arms move. Her tiny breasts are firm, her pert nipples pointing down. Soon the young mother is sleeping again, and my love comes across the yurt to me, kissing me before crawling back into her robe. I yearn to touch her.

The full moon appears again. This is the snow moon, a sign of the deep snow before the days get longer. Father calls it the hunger moon. The days are getting longer, the temperature is warming up during the day, and more moisture is in the air, causing it to snow heavily. The horned beasts have a tougher time walking through the deep snow, and eating through the crust that accumulates on top of it.

I ration the mash, saving it for the young mother and her two children. I milk the long-haired beasts, feeding the milk to the children. After the young mother and her children are sleeping, my love and I crawl outside. We lie in our robes, watching the snow coming down. The night is bright, and whiteness is all around, creating large shadows behind us. We try to scare each other with ghost stories, creating pictures from the shadows, and listening to the wind howling through the trees. Jumping on me, she pushes me into the snow, rubbing snow down my neck. Laughing, I lift her shirt and toss snow inside. Soon we are throwing each other around, getting snow inside our clothes as we laugh and giggle. We crawl inside the yurt. Taking each other's wet clothes off, we hang them over the coals to dry. Then we jump into my sleeping robe, rubbing our hands over each other's bodies for warmth. I feel her small nipples between my fingers and her lips kissing me. Our arms wrap around one another as we absorb each other's warmth. We fall asleep together, dreaming.

Waking up to the smell of mash being cooked, I see the young mother preparing breakfast for us. She winks at us, then scoops each of us a bowl of mash with a spoonful of cream stirred in.

"It must have been a cold night for you two," she says as she wraps her arms around herself. "I remember the night when my love and I first lay under the stars together. It was a bright and starry night. We listened to the howling of the fanged creatures and watched the stars shoot through the dark sky. He used to tell me that one day we would become a star."

I tell her about my mother's grandmother, whose hair hung down to the ground, and how she laid down on the stone bench and became a star. It was the same night that my mother first felt the seed enter her.

I make a cup of tea for us; there is only enough for one cup, for the tea leaves are almost gone. We pass the cup around, telling stories of the past.

My love tells us that once in their village, there was a lady who could predict the future using tea leaves. The young mother smiles, then places the tea leaves in her hand. With a gentle breath, she blows them across her palm. After examining the placement of the leaves across her hand, she predicts that the ice queen will soon leave.

"To predict the future, we must look at the past. The ice queen always leaves soon after the snow moon comes," I say as I smile at her. "Once the ice queen leaves, the long necked feathered creatures will return."

"But who tells the long-necked feathered creatures to come?" my love asks.

"The lady who reads the leaves said my firstborn would be twin girls, but my oldest child is a boy," the young mother tells us.

"I can't wait until spring comes," she sighs. "All the flowers will bloom once more, and the fuzzy yellow insects will buzz around again, collecting nectar from the flowers."

"Yes," my love says as she touches the young mother's face. "This winter has been long."

The young mother winces, then puts her hands against her belly. "The child will come soon," she murmurs.

"Rest," my love says as she moves over to the young mother. "I will give you a massage."

I hand my love the special lotion, crushed from the golden flowers, and watch as her slender hands massage the young mother's naked body. When her skin is soft and shiny, my love lays the young mother on her robe, covering her.

"Sleep," she whispers, kissing her. "We must go and get the steeds ready. Every spring the village has a tournament. We will teach your boy how to ride."

"I will make him a bow from the seven woods," I tell the young mother, hugging her. "And your girl will learn how to ride the stallions with us." The young mother smiles, giving us each a hug.

My love and I go to the meadow, listening to the water flowing in the brook as the snow melts. We carry light ropes to lead the stallions.

Whistling at the herd, our two stallions lift their heads, then trot toward us. After slipping the ropes over their heads, we jump onto their backs, gripping them with our heels as they buck. Then we pull on the ropes, settling them down. The children watch us with excitement in their eyes. Once the stallions settle down, I take the boy with me, and my love takes the girl. At first the children are scared, but soon they are laughing and giggling with delight as we ride.

The fresh air makes them sleepy. Galloping up to their mother, we dismount from the stallions and bring the children into the yurt. Their cheeks are rosy as we place them in their robes for a nap. Their mother sips on a warm cup of milk while the children sleep.

My love and I practice with the stallions, galloping, trotting, and balancing on them. The days become a good routine. In the morning we look after the mother and her children, then we ride with the children until they are tired. In the evening, my love's mother and father feed us. They are delighted that we are improving with the stallions. It is a big thing to win the tournament.

After we have eaten, we sit around the fire, drinking tea. Then we wash the children, wrap them in their robes, and put them to sleep. When the children are sleeping, my love massages the young mother with circling motions on her belly. She also massages her breasts so her milk will come.

"Ah..." the young mother murmurs, closing her eyes. Soon she is sleeping soundly.

My love crawls beside me, her body tired. I massage her feet, kneading her arches. Then I spread lotion on her calves and thighs, working my fingers into her tight muscles. Her pleasant aroma drifts upward. My fingers caress the firmness of her bum, moving up her lower back and shoulders. Her neck is tight from holding her head high while balancing on the stallion.

"Mm..." She relaxes her body.

I turn her onto her back, massaging her neck. I brush my hands along her sides, from her slender waist to her shoulders, her nipples hardening as my fingers touch them. She whimpers, her body trembling. Then she exhales, letting out a deep breath as she falls asleep in my arms. I hold her tight, feeling the softness of her body against mine. I kiss her, listening to her soft moans as I touch her, feeling her body move as she dreams.

Moo! A long-haired beast bawls, its udder full of milk. The morning sun is just starting to rise. I get up, letting the young mother and my love sleep, then grab the empty bucket and go to milk the long-haired beast.

Moo! The long-haired beast shakes her head at me, wanting to be milked. Her horns are long and pointed, curving upward and inward. Her hair is long and shaggy, almost hanging to the ground. I rub her scalp between her horns. Her long curly tongue licks my face; I feel its roughness on my cheek. Smiling, I squat by her flank and place the pail under her udder. Grabbing the front two teats, I milk them until the pail is half full. Her calf nudges me, butting me aside. Laughing, I grab the pail and let the calf suckle from its mother. Its two short horns are just starting to grow from its head. I slap the calf on its flank, startling her. Like her mother, the calf has deep blue eyes, an apparent rarity among this herd.

"I brought some fresh milk," I say as I duck through the doorway, entering the yurt.

"Mm..." My love turns to me, stirring a pot steaming over the coals. "I just made a porridge from the grains; the milk will be delicious in it."

"Here, have some porridge with cream," I say to the young mother. "I separated the cream for you, so your baby will grow and be healthy inside you. Also, I have cream for your children."

I fill two small cups, one for the boy and one for the girl. They smile shyly at me, sipping from their cups. Fresh cream covers their lips, dribbling down their chins. My love spoons warm porridge into their mouths, and their tiny teeth chew it before they swallow.

The morning sun is warm. A light rain falls, causing a mist to fill the air. Water drips off the roof of the yurt. I collect some in a pot and heat it for tea. We sit in a circle as we sip our tea.

"I can't wait to be able to sit outside in the sun," the young mother says as she leans back. She lifts her knees and places her hands under her large belly. Her children sit beside her, wanting to feel the tiny kicks from their soon-to-be sibling.

"Come," I say to the young mother. "I will bring you outside." I put one arm under her bum and the other one around her waist. Her heavy breasts press against my cheek as I struggle to lift her. I move her into the ray of sunlight that shines through the door, letting her bask in its warmth.

My love washes the children. She rubs their bodies with tallow mixed with the whitest ash and the freshest oils from the flowers until their skin smells fresh. Both children have long black hair. The boy has two braids in his hair while the girl's hair is unbraided. Once they are clean and dry, and their skin is a rosy colour, she dresses them each in light trousers and a loose blouse. The girl's blouse is embroidered while the boy's blouse is pure white.

I wrap a light robe around the young mother, then settle her on soft pillows filled with the long-necked feathered creatures' tiny feathers. The soft downy feathers from under their breasts.

"Thank you," she murmurs, her grey eyes twinkling with a smile. She kisses me, her lips soft and warm. The front of her robe falls open as she leans back and lets the sun shine on her skin. Her ponderous breasts rest on her enlarged belly, her nipples large and fully extended.

"Rest," I say, kissing her. "We must check the herd of long-haired beasts."

I lift the boy on my shoulders while my love carries the girl in her arms. I grab a bag of dried berries mixed with the sweet nectar to take with us. We walk down the trail as a light rain falls. We laugh as the mud squishes between our toes.

Moo! a long-haired beast bawls. We look across the meadow and see a yearling lying on her side.

Moo! The long-haired beast lifts her head, her tongue hanging from her mouth. She is obviously straining hard.

Moo!

"What's wrong with her?" the little girl cries. "We must save her!"

"Look!" the boy yells. "Tiny feet are coming out of her!"

"It's okay," my love says as she pulls the children to her, kneeling with them. "She is having a little one. We will stay and watch to make sure things go well."

Moo! The long-haired beast strains, pushing hard.

I kneel beside the boy.

"There is a fanged creature over the hill watching us." The girl points.

"Steady," I say. "Everything will be fine."

"We will keep watch over the fanged creature and chase it away if it comes too close," my love says as she holds the girl in her arms.

I let the long-haired beast sniff me, letting her know that we will not harm her.

"Hold your hand out to her," I whisper to the boy. "Let her sniff your hand."

Moo! The long-haired beast bawls again. She lifts her head, reaching for the boy's hand. With her raspy tongue, she licks his fingers.

Moo! She pushes.

"Grab a leg," I say as I hold the boy's hand. "When she strains, pull hard."

We each grab a leg.

Moo!

"Pull!"

The boy strains, pulling with all his might.

Moo!

"Once more!"

A nose appears; we breathe hard.

"Pull!"

The long-haired beast strains, suddenly, the calf comes flying out of her mother, landing on top of us. We fall into the mud, soaking wet. The calf bleats, shaking its head as it struggles to rise.

"It's a boy," the girl giggles as she points at the small sac between its legs.

The new mother stands up and licks her newborn's nostrils, cleaning the membrane that covers its face.

"Ew...!" the boy sputters, wiping his face and scrambling backward.

I step back, letting the long-haired beast lick her newborn. She licks her calf's hide until its hair is soft and curly. She nudges it, pushing it up. The calf stands on wobbly legs, balancing precariously. The fanged creature slinks away, it has seen that everything is okay.

"Wow!" the little girl says, reaching for my hand.

The newborn calf stumbles to its mother. Sticking its nose under her flank, it latches onto its mother's teat, suckling hungrily. The long-haired beast sniffs her calf, then nudges it, her long tongue licking its back.

"Soon your mother will have a new baby like the long-haired beast," my love says as she pulls the children to her.

"Will she lick him clean?" the girl asks, giggling. "When I have a child, I will clean her like the long-haired beast licks her young."

I smile, then lift the girl into my lap. We sit and watch the calf bond with its mother. I pass a bag of dried berries to my love. She divides them between us, placing them in the palms of our hands.

"Can we milk the long-haired beast now?" the boy asks as he reaches for the pail. "The berries will taste good with her cream."

"We must wait, we will make sure she has enough milk for her calf," I reply, tousling his hair.

"Let's stay and watch the newborn and her mother for a while," my love says as she picks the girl up. "We must make sure that the fanged creature doesn't come back."

We climb to a large rock and sit together in the sun. The rain has almost stopped, and the air is warm and humid. Our clothes are sticky and wet from the long-haired beast giving birth.

"We must rinse off. Let's see if the stream is free of ice," I say as I stand, pulling my outer weather off me.

"The sun is warm, but the water will still be freezing. You go ahead, and we will watch you," my love laughs. We jump off the rock, searching out an ice-free hole in the stream.

"Listen!" The boy stops. "I hear water gurgling."

Ahead of us, rivulets of water run through the melting snow from an opening in the ice. Steam rises as the water gurgles upward, flowing against the ice.

"Let's light a fire first," my love says as she gathers fallen branches. "Then we can warm up when we come out."

We find a small cave near the hole, a hollow space within the blackened rock. A circle of rocks is placed within the cave.

"The perfect spot," my love says, placing the wood inside the circle. "An ancient site, used centuries ago." We set the children on a stone ledge, giving them the rest of the berries.

"Let's gather wood for the fire," she says as she kneels, searching for more wood.

The children gather dried twigs and moss, placing them in the centre of the stones. My love strikes the flints, blowing on the sparks. Soon she has a small fire going. I watch her throat muscles move as she blows into the flames. I throw some larger branches onto it, and soon we have a roaring fire.

"Okay." She grins, looking at us. "Time to get wet." She tugs my shirt and pulls it over my head. Then she pulls my trousers off, removing hers too.

"Come on. Let's go." She pushes me to the water's edge.

"Quick!" She picks up the two kids, stripping off their clothes, then grabs them in her arms and runs to the hole in the ice.

Splash!

"Eek!" all three of them sputter.

I leap into the water beside them, a sudden chill grips my bones. It seems that my brain will freeze. I sputter and gasp. The kids sink underwater, their long hair floating upward. My whole body contracts and my blood becomes like ice. I shiver uncontrollably. I grab the little girl and lift her onto the icy ledge. She slips on the ice, falls, and spins around. My love grabs the little boy and tosses him to me. I set him beside his sister. Then I grab my love by her waist and lift her up. I push beneath her legs, heaving her over the ledge. Her legs reach my shoulders as she pushes herself up. Goosebumps cover her backside. A small dimple appears under the crease of her bum. I clamber onto the ice, then scramble over to the fire. My love and the children sputter as they run, their bodies shivering with cold. Goosebumps appear across our bodies, our teeth chattering.

"Throw water on the rocks!" My love stutters, her lips blue.

She holds the children, all three of them cuddle together to absorb the heat from their bodies. I run back to the hole in the ice, scoop water into a pail, then pour it over the heated rocks.

Crack! A large rock splits open, and tiny shards go flying. Steam rises from the rocks, enveloping us with its moist heat. All four of us bask in the warm environment, absorbing the heat from the fire-warmed rocks and the heated air. Our goosebumps leave us, and our skin becomes wet and smooth.

"Why is your skin red?" the young girl asks.

"I am created from the red cliffs," I answer, smiling at her.

"I'll get water this time!" my love says as the steam dissipates. She grabs the pail and runs to the hole in the ice.

"Eek!" she yells as she leaps into the hole, her head disappearing under the water.

I gasp. She rises and throws her head back. Shivering, she runs back to the fire. Her lips are blue and her nipples hard, tiny bumps surround them. She throws water onto the rocks, splashing us and giggling as we scream. As she stands over the rising steam, her skin turns red, and her nipples become full and smooth once more. Sweat drips off her body.

"Jump in the water!" She laughs at me, pushing me toward it.

I lift the two children into her arms. Then I grab the pail, running to the stream. An electric current flows through me as I sink into the ice-cold water. Tiny air bubbles gurgle upward as I exhale. I pull myself up, feeling the cool breeze against my wet body. The tiny hairs on my arms stick straight out as I shiver. I pour the water over the heated rocks.

Crack! A rock splits in half. I bend over the steam, inhaling the moist air. My love laughs, her hands rubbing my skin until my body warms up. The children sit by the fire. Their teeth are no longer chattering and sweat glistens off their bodies. Our pores have opened, cleansing us. I spread our clothes over the heated rocks to dry. The fire becomes embers, yet it still retains its heat.

"Look at the yellow inside this rock," my love says as she holds a rock up to me. I touch the yellow vein flowing through the centre of it. It is smooth and soft, unlike the coarseness of the black rock surrounding it.

"It's the same colour as the sun," the boy says, reaching for it.

We lie with our bare backs against a smooth rock, absorbing the heat from it until the steam dissipates. I hold my love's hand as we lie together, the children beside us. I look above the rocky outcropping. A fanged creature is lying on its belly, its front feet extended as it basks in the sun and its piercing yellow eyes staring at us. I see the boy looking at it too. My love and the little girl lie side by side, their eyes are closed as they stretch out upon the rock, unaware of the fanged creature watching us. I close my eyes, dreaming.

A small hand touches my face, opening my eyes. "Wake up," the little girl whispers in my ear. I lift her into my arms and hold her above me.

"Fly like a feathered creature," I say as I swing her back and forth. Giggling, she stretches her arms and legs out, flapping her arms like a feathered creature.

"Swing me too!" Her brother laughs. I set the girl down, and then pick up the boy. I swing him up and down, turning him upside down. When he is dizzy, I set him on the ground, then pick up the girl again, swinging her until she can no longer stand. Both children laugh as they fall to the ground. Twirling, they try to stand, then fall again.

"Swing me too!" My love leaps into my arms. I smile, then toss her into the air, catching her as she falls. Her long hair covers my face. I hold her hands, swinging her around until we both fall to the ground, laughing and entangled in each other's arms.

"We must go back." She smiles. "The long-haired beast needs to be milked, and the children must be fed." I set her on the ground, playfully spanking her. She giggles, trying to slap me.

"We will spank you both." The children laugh as they try to spank us, jumping on us. A cloud passes over us, cooling the air.

"We must dress." I grab the boy's trousers, pull them over his legs, then drape his shirt over his head.

My love dresses the girl, then combs her hair with her fingers. We swing the children onto our shoulders and follow the path back to the village. I take the girl this time and my love takes the boy. Her knees clamp against my cheeks as we trod through the muddy parts of the trail. I tickle her feet until she is laughing so hard that she can barely stay on.

"Where did you guys go?" the young mother asks as we enter the yurt.

"We found a yellow metal, purer than any other metal." I smile at her, handing her the split rock.

"We found a hole in the ice." The girl giggles, hugging her mother. "We built a fire, then jumped into the icy water."

"The water was ice cold and we warmed ourselves over hot steam. Our skin contracted and then expanded; our pores opened." The boy laughs, holding his arms up.

The two children tell her all about their day, how the water was so cold, and the steam was so hot. I gather some dried meat and boil some edible roots for us to eat.

"You must be tired from your trip," the young mother says as she gathers her children into her arms.

We eat heartily, feeling sated, our bodies tired, but refreshed.

"We must wash. We are very tired." My love yawns. "The day has been beautiful but long."

The young mother removes her children's muddy clothing, laying their clothes beside the wash basin. Then she removes her robe and places it beside theirs.

"We will wash the clothes in the morning," my love says tiredly.

We remove our trousers and tops, cleaning some of the mud from them, then place our dirty clothes in a pile. My love passes me a soft cloth with the whitest soap spread on it. I scrub the boy while my love washes the girl. We wash them until their skin is almost white. I braid the boy's clean hair, one braid on each side of his head. My love washes the girl's hair, brushing it full and smooth. We tuck them into their robes, kissing them goodnight. They hug us, then soon they are fast asleep.

"The children are sleeping, and we must wash also," my love says as she pours warm water into the wash basin.

We wash ourselves with a soft cloth, enjoying the sensation of the warm water touching us while the air is cool. We sit on the soft blanket made from the fibres of the long-haired beast's hide, the softness of the blanket adding to the sensation. The young mother sits beside us, uncrossing her legs as she tries to wash her large belly.

"You will have twins." I tease her.

"Please, no!" She laughs, throwing her soft cloth at me.

I chuckle, grabbing the cloth. "Lie still," I murmur. "I will wash you."

The young mother lies on her back with her head resting in my love's lap. Her full breasts flatten on her chest, hanging down her sides. She lifts her knees and slightly spreads her legs. "I must be comfortable." She winks at me before closing her eyes.

I start with her belly, carefully washing her stretch marks. Then I lift her breasts and wash beneath them. Her nipples rise, turning a dark brown. A tiny amount of milk secretes from their tips. I squeeze them, laughing as her milk squirts into my face. "You will have lots of milk," I tease her. "Enough to feed us all!"

She giggles and her hands touch her breast, squeezing it. I close my mouth over her nipple, tasting the small amount of milk secreting from it, swirling my tongue around it until it becomes engorged in my mouth. The buds on my tongue taste the buds on her swollen nipples. I dip a cloth in the warm water. Once the cloth is thoroughly wet, I rub the mound between her legs, scrubbing the swollen folds of her outer flower. Then I spread her pink petals, exposing her slightly elongated stamen. I slip my finger inside, feeling the warmth and moistness of her flower, swollen and ready to give birth. She moans, wiggling her hips, forcing my finger to go deeper. I massage her tender pink petals, circling them, brushing against her stamen. Her nectar oozes from her; a musky sweet smell emits from her. I remove my finger, bringing it to my mouth to taste her sweetness.

I sink down, my body filling with desire. Her body trembles. I touch myself, shuddering. My love caresses us, rubbing the soft towel on our bodies, drying us. Its roughness is exhilarating on my skin. The young mother lifts one leg up, tucks it under her bum and fully exposes her swollen folds. I fall asleep in her arms, dreaming.

"Wake up!" my love whispers in my ear, kissing me. The smell of fresh tea fills the room, tea from the special leaves of the blue hills.

"I made a pot for the three of us," she says as she passes me a cup. Then she lifts a cup to the young mother. She drops a tinge of white powder into it. The young mother smiles, her eyes a shiny grey colour. They dilate as she sips from the cup. "Thank you," she murmurs.

My love and I prop her up against a soft pillow made from the tiny feathers of the long-necked feathered creature. She lies with only her robe wrapped around her. Lifting her robe, she places our hands on her belly, letting us feel the child move inside her womb. I kiss her belly, listening for the child.

"Sleep," my love whispers, kissing her on her lips. "You need your rest."

She removes the cup from her hand. The young mother smiles at us, her eyes glowing. Then she lays her head back, snoring lightly, her chest moving up and down. Her robe falls to her waist, and we watch the rise and fall of her breasts as she sleeps. The children awaken. My love mixes a small amount of milk with the mashed grains, adding the golden liquid to it, then gives them each a bowl.

"Your mother needs to sleep," I say.

"Come." My love grabs their hands. "We must feed the steeds."

The children smile excitedly, then get dressed to go outside. I give them a small amount of grain to feed the steeds.

"Let's ride." My love jumps onto her stallion. Reaching for the boy, she lifts him in front of her. I jump onto the red stallion, then lift the little girl up in front of me.

"We will ride to the meadow and watch the sun rise!" my love shouts, digging her heels into her stallion as she gallops away.

"Hurrah!" I yell, following her.

The children hang on, screaming as we soar ahead. The thunder of hooves follows us as the rest of the herd gallops behind. When we reach the edge of the ice where the wide-tailed creature lives, we come to a sudden stop.

Splash!

"The ice is melting!" the boy yells. "The wide-tailed creatures are swimming again." He loves watching them cut the trees down.

"One day I will make an axe to cut the trees down like they do," the girl declares.

We dismount, then sit and watch the wide-tailed creatures repair their homes and dams.

"There are six little pups swimming behind their mother." The girl points excitedly. "I hope our mother has three boys and three girls."

"I hope she has only one boy and one girl," her brother replies. "Then we will each have a playmate."

Crash! A tree falls to the ground.

"The father is building a new house for his family," the boy says. He points to a small dome. "I will build a home like that."

He gathers freshly chewed sticks and assembles them in a pile. The wide-tailed creature sits on its tail. Its short front paws are clasped around the trunk of the tree while its huge teeth remove chunks of wood from the tree, making smooth incision marks on it as it moves around the base, making a perfect cone.

Crash! Another tree falls.

The smaller of the wide-tailed creatures swims up. She waddles over to the fallen tree with her pups behind her. With her sharp teeth, she cuts the tree into sections, each one three times longer than the length of her body.

The pups' clamour around her, chewing on the smaller tree branches. I am amazed at the sight.

"I picked a flower for you," the little girl grins as she passes me a tiny pink flower.

"And one for me." She holds another one to her nose. "When I grow up, I will marry you." She climbs into my lap, holding the flower to my nose. I chuckle, then take a deep breath, absorbing the beautiful scent.

"Look at the flower." She touches each petal with her tiny fingers. "It has four pink petals with a white centre, and rising from the centre is a yellow stem with a tiny round tip on top."

She touches the tip, getting a small amount of yellow powder on her fingertip. "Mm…" She licks her fingertip. "Taste the flower." She lifts her finger to my mouth. I marvel at its sweetness.

"Soon a fuzzy yellow insect will land on the flower, spreading the male seed on it, and create a small white berry that will grow and turn bright red after the days shorten again," I explain as I pick another flower growing beside us, plucking its multiple yellow petals.

"I can't wait to taste it." She smiles, snuggling into my lap.

"I'm building us a dwelling like the wide-tailed creatures' home," the little boy says. He shows us the tiny home he is assembling.

"Let me help you." My love kneels beside him. "We will pick the perfect sticks for our home."

They run off into the bushes, gathering more sticks and twigs to build a domed hut like the wide-tailed creatures' home.

"But how will they chew the sticks?" the girl asks.

"Watch me. This is how the pups do it." I pick up a small branch and gnaw on its tender bark.

"Let me try." She grabs the branch in her pudgy hands, biting the bark.

"Ew…!" she sputters. "The taste of the flower is better than the taste of the tree's bark."

"Come, let us search the meadow for fresh flowers." I lift the girl onto my shoulders, and we walk through the meadow, searching for flowers.

The stallions chew on the fresh tufts of grass sticking through the melting snow, and a red-breasted avian pulls a worm from the ground as we traipse through the meadow in search of new flowers. My love and the girl's brother gather fresh sticks to build a dwelling for us. The wide-tailed creatures dig a canal with their teeth, hauling freshly cut saplings to the water's edge. The shadows grow longer as the sun begins its descent.

"Come," I say to them. "It's time to go back."

"Aww," the children say in unison.

"We will come back! But we must check on your mother," my love says as she hugs the children.

We leap onto our stallions, lifting the children up in front of us.

"Let's race!" the boy yells, kicking his heels into the stallion's flank.

The steed rears up, then leaps forward as they cling to his mane. The girl and I follow them, her hair blowing in my face. I smile, hanging onto her so she doesn't fall. We gallop through the gates of the village, to the stares of the villagers. Before going into the yurt, we brush the stallions down. I teach the girl how to brush its hair, and how to comb its mane. I let her sit on my shoulders, so she can reach the stallion's neck. The young mother rises as we enter the yurt.

The little girl runs up and climbs into her mother's lap. "I picked flowers for you. Smell them," she says as she lifts them to her mother.

"Thank you." Her mother smiles at her. "I had a good rest while you were gone." She reaches for the bouquet and lifts the flowers to her nose.

"Mm..., I love them. They are the most beautiful colour and best-smelling flowers I have ever been given," she says, holding her daughter in her arms.

"Let's put them in your mother's hair," my love says, holding a flower out to the little girl. The girl giggles, then places it in her mother's hair.

"We are building a new home in the meadow," her little boy says. He flexes his arms. "I will soon be a man."

The young mother grabs her children in her arms, then holds them close and places their hands on her growing belly. "Soon you two will have a new playmate," she says, smiling. My love and I smile at each other.

"We will milk the long-haired beast," I say as I grab the clay pot. We leave, holding hands as we search for the long-haired beast. It gives us fresh milk with loads of yellow cream on top. Spring is on the way. We both smile, kissing each other on the lips.

When the day warms up, my love and I practise riding the stallions. We place our hands on their necks, leaning forward. We kick our legs upward, balancing on our hands, our fingers gripping tightly, and our feet straight up in the air. We hold on, our toes pointing toward the sky. Letting go, we drop into a seating position, then we gallop side by side. We jump up and balance, standing on the stallions' back, holding onto each other's hands for balance. I reach my leg across and my love does the same. With a graceful side jump, we are on each other's stallions, dropping down again as we turn the stallions to the left, repeating what we did, and jumping back onto our stallions. My love jumps in front of me, standing on my stallion's neck. I grab her waist, throw her up and grab her ankles. She stands on my shoulders as I hold her, her arms outstretched, balancing on me.

The stallions are one with us, sharing our thoughts as we gallop through the meadow. Their spirit and our spirit have become one.

After practicing on the stallions, the three of us drink tea together. When the children are sleeping, I throw small logs on the fire, and we listen to the crackling of the flames.

"My father used to tell me that to master the bow, I had to become one with it," I say to the young mother. "The spirit of the bow would become one with me. Only then could I truly master the bow." I flex the bow, pulling on the string.

"The stallions are also becoming one with us," my love replies. "I feel it when I ride. No more thought, just their spirit guiding us."

"My late husband's spirit is with us tonight," the young mother whispers. "I feel him in the air. Lie still, I will massage you both."

She removes our robes, pulling them over our heads. The flames from the fire glow against our skin, its heat warming us. I feel her heavy breasts against the small of my back as she pushes me onto my stomach. Her large belly rests against me and her cool hands touch my shoulders. Her petals open as she straddles me. Her strong hands massage my lower and upper back. Feeling the tenseness leaving me, I close my eyes, enraptured by the feeling. My love watches us, then she moves toward my head. Her knees touch my cheeks, squeezing against them. My long hair tickles the insides of her thighs as she kneels against me. Her fingers massage the back of my neck, causing them to tingle gloriously. I feel the young mother slowly lift herself up. With a twist she turns me over onto my back, then she lowers herself down onto me, her folds touching me, and her stamen brushing against mine. Her calloused hands rub my lower belly. I feel the roughness of her palms against my smooth skin, arousing me.

My love leans over, her lips touching mine. I open my eyes, her pert nipples brush against my forehead. A drop of sweat drips into my mouth. I savour the taste of her sweat as my tongue touches her. She moans softly and reaches for the young mother, kissing her. My hands slide down the young mother's back, gently rubbing the erogenous area of her lower back, feeling the crevice of her large bum. Her engorged nipples brush against my chest. I am aroused, tingling.

My love lifts herself over me, straddling my face. She moans as I press my tongue inside her, licking her inner petals. Both girls arch their backs. Facing each other, they touch their tongues together, their nipples against each other's. I spread my hands under the young mother's bum, spreading her, pulling her petals into me. She growls, arching forward, her fluids gushing against my flesh. I lift my hips, pushing myself into her, feeling her open petals quivering against me as her nectar flows. I nibble on my love's inner petals, touching her sensitivity. She screams, pushing hard, her nipples erect, her bum moving rapidly. She clenches tight onto me, her body quivering. I tense; a feeling of bliss absorbs my entire body. I release, thrusting myself into the young mother.

All three of us are in ecstasy, wild, bucking, fluid flowing from us. We are three in one, becoming one in spirit. We lie together, gazing lovingly into each other's eyes, not wanting to sleep and lose the moment. We fall asleep in each other's arms.

I wake up before the cock crows. Both girls are beside me, one with child and one ready to be wed. I am a stranger here: red skin, one eye blue, and one eye green like my father's eyes. Their lips kiss me, I kiss them back, gazing into their eyes. Rising, I walk naked across the yurt, both girls watch me with desire. I stoke the fire, heaping the coals together. Then I heat a bowl of water, soaking a wet cloth in it, bringing the warm cloth for us to wash ourselves. I wash them, washing the stickiness of our love.

***

Today is the tournament. All morning my love and I brush the stallions, giving them treats and getting them ready for the day. The young mother makes us a large bowl of mash with extra cream. The whole village is getting ready for the event. Girls watch the boys practise riding. Men help their daughters with the steeds. Women cook food and watch the children. Some of the women ride the stallions with us. The sun is shining, the snow is gone, and the ground is dry. It's a perfect day for the tournament. Targets are set up for the archers and hurdles are set up for the jumpers. Bowls of warm water are set aside for washing injuries. Ice is stored in a cavern, ready for use in case of swelling. Dry strips of cloth are nearby for bandages. Everyone is excited and smiling.

My love and I oil our bows. We ensure our arrows are straight and true, putting new feathers on their ends. We shall bypass the targets and shoot the small white feathered creatures that are released, thirty at a time. The riders will gallop as fast as they can, shooting arrows at them. The older men will keep a tally of how many are shot. Roasted feathered creatures are a delicacy here and will be eaten after the tournament; roasted over hot coals, and copious amounts of salt spread on their skin.

With a thundering roll, twelve lads gallop through the meadow, starting the tournament. Behind them are seventy other riders, male and female, carrying flags. The colour and the noise are superb. The women have spent all year making these flags, using the softest cloth with the brightest colours. Once all the riders gallop through, the games begin.

A strong wiry lad enters on a wild stallion. One arm out for balance, he digs his heels in, spurring the steed on. One, two, three, four, and he is off, flying head over heels, landing on his head with his feet straight up in the air. With a loud crack from his neck, he rolls over, shaking himself as he gets back on his feet. Arms in the air to indicate he is okay; he walks subdued to the edge of the meadow.

Next is a young girl, racing a figure-eight pattern around six flags planted in the ground, only knocking one flag down. The crowd cheers.

My love enters the arena. She has the young mother's boy and girl with her. The girl in front and the boy behind her. The boy proudly carries the flag his mother has made. The sound of the flag flapping in the wind matches the sound of the pounding hooves. The young mother smiles as she watches her children. A young man is sitting beside her. He lost his wife the year before. Beside him is his young son, born three revolutions of the sun ago. My love gallops up to them, then stops and lowers the two children in front of their mother, their faces beaming.

Coming up in a row are seven men, sitting on their steeds as they gallop, shooting arrows at straw targets. One of the men misses all the targets. The crowd jeers.

My love and I enter from opposite ends of the meadow, galloping toward each other. We jump and somersault over one another, landing on each other's stallion, going the opposite way. The crowd is silent, hushed. Then they cheer. We jump up and stand on the stallions, turning around as we pass each other. We step across one another, back onto our own stallions, letting them prance as they gallop away.

Next is a group of young girls, trick riding. They release a flock of white feathered creatures. The crowd goes wild.

My love grabs her bow, takes seven arrows from her holder, and goes behind the large tree. Coming out with her knees pressed against her stallion, she gallops toward the meadow. The young mother is in the centre of the meadow. Her belly swollen with child; she releases seven plump feathered creatures. Jumping up, my love stands on her stallion. Her feet relaxed, she draws her bow and releases seven arrows, one after another. Seven plump feathered creatures fall to the ground in a circle around the young mother.

There is total silence, only the sound of the wind rustling through my love's hair, and the thundering sound of the stallion's hooves as they gallop away. Turning, she gallops back to the young mother. Grabbing under her shoulders, she lifts the woman onto her stallion. Then she prances proudly around the circle, the young mother in front of her. The crowd cheers, throwing their flags high into the air, indicating she has won the tournament.

I watch both women ride the stallion, the wind blowing through their hair. The one sits, and the other stands behind her, galloping around the circle. I hold the young mother's boy and girl, proudly watching them. The man with his young child is beside me.

More riders compete, but my love has won the show. Her parents wave their flags in the air, shouting excitedly. After the tournament is done, a huge bonfire is lit. The seven plump feathered creatures are roasted over it, and the young children pass one each to my love and I, her parents, the young mother, and her two children. There is too much meat for the little girl to eat by herself. She shares hers with the young man and his child. The plump feathered creatures are roasted with special spices, the best I have tasted yet.

I teach the young boys how to shoot the bow. My love teaches the young girls how to ride the steeds. The older boys and girls dance around the fire. The young mother sits beside the fire. Sitting beside her is the young father. Both are staring into the flames, their hands touching each other's. They look at each other, smiling and chatting; his hand is on her belly.

The older men and women keep an eye on the children, feeding them roasted nuts and dried fruit, and making sure they don't get too close to the fire. A big pot of fresh milk is heated over the fire, and a brown powder is stirred into it. Fresh golden liquid is added. My love gives me a cup to drink. It is the sweetest drink I have ever tasted, the taste of chocolate. Some nuts are roasted over a hot rock and sprinkled with a sweet syrup. A child passes the roasted nuts around to everyone. The older children place pieces of meat on a stick, then roast it over the fire. When the meat is perfectly brown, they dip it into a bowl of syrup, passing each person a piece. Everyone eats until they are full.

The days are getting longer, and the trees are budding, preparing for a new crop of fruits, nuts, and berries. The long-haired beasts have green grass to eat, and their milk gives lots of cream, rising to the top. Some have two calves by their sides, suckling on each teat. Their mothers lick the backs of their calves as they suckle. Occasionally, a calf will try to get more milk from another. The mother sniffs it, kicking it away when she realizes it is not her calf.

My love and I bring the children to a mare that will soon foal. In awe, we watch the whole birth, from the front feet sticking out, until the mother pushes the foal out of her. Standing up, the mother licks her foal clean with her tongue. The children laugh as the foal tries to stand on its long wobbly legs. The newborn foal is a male. Someday he will make a fine stallion. He is red like the stallion I ride. The children point to me and say that I am related to it because we have the same skin colour. I smile at them, telling them that my hair also matches its tail. As soon as the foal can stand, it wobbles over to its mother, reaches under her, and seeks out her teats to suckle on.

"How can the newborn foal know how to seek out its mother's teat right after being born?" a girl asks.

"It is in its memory," I reply as I hold her on my knee.

"But how can the foal have memory inside its mother?" a boy asks. "Does it possess its mother's memories from the womb, then create its own after it enters the world?"

"Some things are a mystery," I reply. "It's your job to seek out the mysteries as you go through life, communicating your answers to others."

***

The young mother's head is in my lap. Groaning, she pushes against me. I hold her arms tight. Her eyes are closed, her mouth grimacing in pain. She screams and pushes hard while lying on her back. I massage her shoulders, whispering for her to push at intervals. Fluid pours from between her legs. She lifts her knees up, her legs spread wide. My love faces her womanhood, placing two fingers inside her, feeling her dilation. I kiss the young mother's forehead, whispering to her, watching her swollen belly move, her large breasts heaving as she pushes. She screams again, pushing against me.

My love smiles at me, but she has a worried look as she kneels between the young mother's legs. Another push, and a crown of black hair appears. My love holds the newborn's head, pulling gently.

"Push," I whisper.

The young mother groans, pushing hard. The head appears, red faced, and eyes closed. She pushes again, and an arm appears. My love reaches inside for the other arm, straightening it, and pulling. One more push and the child is out. More fluid comes, mixed with blood. It's a boy. His face is wrinkled like the baby long-tailed creatures that look like us.

I hold the newborn, tickling his nose and spanking his bum. He cries and takes a breath. Fluid comes from his nose. His whole body is wet and wrinkled. The young mother relaxes, panting, and reaches for the child.

I place the child on her breast. She cuddles him as he latches onto her nipple. Suddenly, she pushes again, her face contorting in pain. My love kneels before her, spreading her swollen flower. A second child is coming. More fluid gushes from between her legs. She screams, grabbing my legs, and her nails digging into my flesh. Her head is tight in my lap, bent back. Her mouth is open, and her eyes closed. She moans as another crown of black hair appears, parting her pinkness.

A girl, pink in colour, comes out fast, her brother already loosening the muscles as he went through the birthing canal.

Twins, the tea reader was partly right. The young mother gave birth to twins, a boy and a girl. My love passes the second child to me. I tickle her nose and watch her sneeze. Then I place the newborn girl on the young mother's breast. Both children are suckling on her nipples now.

My love and I sit together with the young mother lying on our laps. We let her babies suckle until her breasts become flat. Then, using a bowl of warm water, we wash the twins. I also wash the young mother, cleaning her face, and rubbing her eyes. I feel the tiredness in her. I wash her neck and her breasts, gently cleansing her nipples to make sure all her milk is washed off.

My love puts another bowl of water over the fire, warming it. Then she hands me the warm cloth. I wipe the young mother's belly, massaging her newly acquired stretch marks. Dipping the cloth in clean water, I wash the folds of her womanhood, examining the tear on her. I wash the soft hairs surrounding her flower, cleaning all her fluids from them and wiping down her inner thighs. I massage her calves and rub the bottoms of her feet. When she is all clean, my love and I wrap her in her robe and place her twins beside her. She is so elated; she can not sleep. She coos to her twins, cuddling them, holding them in her arms and smiling at them. Looking up with a twinkle in her eye, she smiles at me.

In the distance a fanged creature howls. Another one answers it. I listen to the howl of the fanged creatures, thinking of how they howled when I first felt the young mother's stretch marks. The night I first laid with her. I hear small whimpers echoing the howling of the fanged creatures. The boy and girl are awake. I have no idea how long they have been awake. Time was lost during the birth of the twins. They crawl into the robes beside their mother and new siblings. We let them lie together and bring one of our robes to cover them. We wrap the twins in a dry cloth, knowing that in the morning the cloth will be wet. With the remaining water, my love and I wash each other. Once we are clean, we crawl under our robe and wrap our arms around each other, falling asleep, exhausted.

The sun shines bright, waking me. I make a mash for everyone, using the fresh milk from the long-haired beast. The long-haired beast is getting bigger around her belly. Soon I will have to quit milking her as she will need to prepare her body for the calf growing inside her.

My love washes the twins after they are nursed. Then she puts them in their mother's arms, helping them latch onto her nipples. I take the little boy and girl and teach them how to ride the stallion. I hold the girl in my lap while the boy rides behind me. At times I let the boy ride an old mare by himself. He loves it when he is on his own. The young father visits us quite often, helping with the newborn twins when we are out. He watches the young mother sleep when she is tired. We take his little boy with us, teaching him how to ride the steeds.

The whole village is excited about the birth of the twins, stopping by and giving food to the family. My love's parents are happy to see their girl improve with the steeds. She has become the best rider in the village. All the young men and boys are jealous of her riding abilities. I gather dead trees in my spare time, so the village will have enough wood for the coming winter. I stack wood near the yurt, so it will be close to the young family. The women and girls watch me work, sometimes stopping to chat. Smiling at me, they help me when they are able. The men and boys are more reserved around me. Some allow me to teach them the bow, others leave me alone.

I am happy here. In the evening, we all have tea together. After the young man and his child return to their yurt, and the young mother and her children are sleeping, my love and I talk about events that happened that day.

One night she asks me how we can have memories. "Why do we remember certain things more than others? And why do we forget some things we should remember?"

I tell her that we remember what we want to remember.

The days become longer, the grass grows, and the rivers begin flowing once more. The creatures with the wide tail are busy trying to stop the flow of water, building dams from twigs, mud, and branches. Their large teeth chop a tree down swiftly. Sometimes I take the tree after the wide-tailed creatures have cut it into pieces, bringing it to the yurt for firewood. A wide-tailed creature waddles to the water with its short legs, then slaps its tail on the water to warn the rest that I am there. I inspect its dam and am amazed at what it can do.

Someday I will build a dam like theirs, so I can have a pond beside my yurt. The time has come for us to take the herd back to their summer pastures. To where I first saw my love. We pack food and fresh water in leather skins, loading them onto the mares. We also pack extra pairs of loose-fitting trousers and shirts for the journey. The villagers feed us a great meal before we leave, including roasted feathered creatures, and the tail of a wide-tailed creature; piled high with fresh red berries and slavered with the sweet golden liquid.

The young mother kisses us, whispering that she will never forget the night that we became one in spirit. I tell her to look after the young man and his child. I hug the two, holding them tight.

"I will never forget the first time I laid next to you. The excitement I felt as your warm body laid against mine," I whisper in her ear.

I pick up her boy, then give him the bow I made for him. "Become one with the bow," I tell him. "Learn to shoot without thought."

I give the little girl a short ride on my stallion, telling her that when I return, I will teach her how to ride alone. With a wave, we leap onto the stallions, then gallop toward the rising sun. The herd of hoofed beasts gallop behind us, a cloud of dust following them. We ride all day toward the hills, setting up camp before the sun goes down. There are countless stars in the night sky. The only sound we hear is the neighing of the steeds. At times a shooting star flies across the horizon.

"Someday I will ride upon a star," my love says, smiling at me. "Travelling faster than the speed of light."

I pick a flower and place it in her hair. We smell the night air, and listen to the sounds in the dark, falling asleep in each others' arms. I feel her light breath on my neck. I dream of travelling through space, of the large winged creatures with black round feet my father used to tell me about. He saw their carcasses beyond the red cliffs, winged creatures without feathers.

Waking up to the smell of tea and the crackling of wood burning, I smile. My love has a fire going, boiling water for tea. After stirring a drop of the sweet nectar into the tea, she passes it to me. We sit naked together beneath our blanket woven from the fibres of the long-haired beasts, watching the rising sun.

"How can the sun travel over a flat earth?" she asks.

"Where would the water go if the earth was flat?" I ask. "My mother used to say we came from the water. 'A seed planted upon the water.'"

"Is that why water came out with the twins at birth?"

She plucks a red flower and places it in my hair. Then she moves the blanket away from us as she climbs into my lap. Sitting on me, she gazes into my eyes. I feel her slender bum rocking in my lap and the soft mound of her womanhood against me. I place my hands around her, pressing myself against her and rocking with her, our flesh rubbing together. With her arms around me, I rock in rhythm with her until our waters flow. I lick her tiny nipples as she arches her back, moaning.

We camp here for the day, letting the herd graze. Finding a stream, we wash in the water. Then we walk through the meadow hand in hand, picking fresh flowers but careful not to disturb the fuzzy yellow insects. She plucks the petals and feeds them into my mouth with her mouth. I taste the sweetness of the flowers, smelling their aroma, and tasting her lips.

"This is where we first met," she says with a grin, her eyes shining. "You were standing on that rock with your bow in your hand when I first saw you."

"I remember hearing the thundering hooves coming toward me. I saw your hair blowing in the wind as you rode your stallion. At first I thought you were a boy riding your steed. I was thirsty, and you jumped off your stallion, sharing your water with me. You were the most beautiful being I had ever beheld." I gaze into her eyes.

"I saw the red glow of the setting sun against your red skin, your long black hair shining in the sun, and your bow strung in your hand. My heart jumped when I saw you," she says, her eyes shining.

We walk hand in hand to the rock where we first lay naked together after washing in the stream. Disrobing, we climb onto a large rock jutting out above the stream. I watch my love dive into the water, her feet straight up, her toes pointing back, and her arms pointing down. She hardly makes a splash. I dive in after her, feeling the coolness of the water as I swim to her. I leap into her arms, splashing in the water with her. Soon we are shivering, and goosebumps cover us.

I watch as she climbs out of the water, her perfect form arching forward. Turning, she reaches for me and pulls me into her. We cling to each other, our bodies moulding together. Shivering, we lie down on the sun-warmed rock, rubbing our hands on each other's bodies to warm us up. Our teeth chatter, and our nipples become erect, pointing to the sky. We feel the warmth of the sun upon us. Beside us, a small flower is growing from a crag in the rock. The flower has seven red petals with twelve yellow stamens. Its stem is green. A fuzzy yellow insect crawls around its stamen, collecting pollen for her hive.

"You are my flower," my love says, smiling at me.

"And you are my fuzzy yellow insect," I smile back, looking deep into her grey eyes.

She pulls me off the rock, leading me to a mossy area covered in spring flowers. The fuzzy yellow insects fly from flower to flower. The smell is intense, the colours amazing. I lie in the moss, spreading my arms and legs like a flower. My love tickles me with her fingers, crawling over my body like a fuzzy yellow insect collecting pollen. I imagine the sensation of the flower as the fuzzy yellow insects' crawl on it. I lie still, feeling the wind on my body as my love touches me. I smell the aroma of her as she leans over me, mixed with the scent of the flowers. I listen to the buzz of the fuzzy yellow insects flying as she suckles on my nipples, feeling her lips over them; her tongue collecting my pollen, and her hair brushing against my face and neck. I feel her fingers crawl up my legs, moving my knees slightly. The feeling intensifies and I tingle all over, writhing. Her small breasts hang over me, her eyes half closed, her breathing hushed. She brushes her nipples against mine, her lips on my lips. I taste the sweetness of her lips. Her small stinger touches mine, rubbing against me. I arch, pushing tight against her.

I am the flower, wanting to reach out and touch her, lying in ecstasy as she crawls over my body. She turns her pink petals above my face, arching her back, her stinger against my mouth. As she moves her hips, I taste her nectar and smell the sweet aroma of her body. She places her fingers on the soft hairs around my rosy petals, spreading my inner lips and sliding her fingers around my folds. Her tongue touches me, enters me. I move, moaning, wanting to touch her scented flower as she moves her hips against me. She slips her finger inside me, massaging my sensitive nub. My arms and legs curl up as my body tightens, curving toward the sun.

I am the red flower. My skin is red, my one eye is green, and my other eye is blue. My hair is black and the soft hair surrounding the folds of my womanhood is dark brown.

I am a woman—strong, sensitive, loving, and loyal. I will stay with my love forever. I feel her body trembling, tasting her nectar as she tastes mine. I tremble, pushing my pelvis tight into her, feeling her flower brushing against my flower. We both tremble, moaning, and buck against each other. Turning, she faces me, and we lie in each other's arms, gazing into each other's eyes.

As we lie naked in the moss, we watch as a fuzzy yellow insect lands on a flower, wiggling its backside at us. My love laughs, imitating it as she wiggles her backside at me.

"The fuzzy yellow insect wants us to follow her," she says, giggling. Jumping up, she pretends to buzz around as she follows it from flower to flower.

Grinning, I buzz after her, smelling the flowers on the way. We come to a large grove of trees with a stream flowing through its centre. As we near a large log lying on its side, we watch as the fuzzy yellow insect lands before a tiny opening in it, wiggling her backside at the other fuzzy yellow insects at the entrance. After the dance, it crawls inside the opening while three others fly away in the direction that we came from.

"The fuzzy yellow insect just told the other ones where the flowers are," I say, smiling at my love. "We will stay here and learn from them. I will be your flower."

I wiggle my bum at her as I lean over a log. Laughing, she comes behind me, spanking my bare backside. Then she bends over, turns around, and rubs her bum against mine, our arms holding onto the log in front of us. With her flesh against my flesh, I dance for her, wiggling my body against hers. Soon we are in each other's laps, rubbing our soft mounds together as we build up in ecstasy, tasting each other's nectar.

We tremble, our hands clasping each other's bums and our tongues in each other's mouths. Our small breasts touch each other's. We turn on our backs, watching the fuzzy yellow insects land on us, sucking the stickiness from our love. We feel their tiny feet walking across our skin as they lick the sweat from us. We watch them fly away, letting others know that we are the flowers.

"Let's walk along the stream," my love says. She links her arm through mine. We walked naked along the stream, enjoying the sun on our bare skin. Coming out of a rock, we notice a small flow of water oozing from it. Steam rises as it flows into a pool of cool water. The water enters a small stream, gurgling down the rocky hillside. The water from the rock is hot to touch, and it smells like the rotten eggs of the large feathered creature. We dip our toes into the pool, feeling its heat. We sink into the water, relaxing, our faces turned to the sun. Once we are clean and our muscles are weak from the heat, we get out. Not bothering to dress, we set up our small yurt, which is just big enough for the two of us. After building a small fire, I sprinkle incense on it. A pink cloud floats above the fire, a sweet aroma coming from it. We sit there drinking our tea while smelling the sweet aroma.

We explore around us, discovering a cave in the hills. Inside the cave is a wall of ice. It is a short, but difficult climb to the top of the wall. On the other side is a gentle slide of ice with a shimmer of water on it. Below that, a small waterfall drops into another pool. This pool is hot and smells like rotten eggs. Giggling like kids, we slide on our bare bums down the slide, feeling the cold water hitting our sensitive areas, our whole bodies tingling as we enter the hot water with a splash.

A dim light comes through an opening at the top of the cave. Rodents with wings hang upside down from the cave walls, watching as we slide naked down the slide. Soon our backsides are red from the cold, and with our teeth chattering, we run back to the stream, jumping into the hot sulphur-smelling pool of water and feeling the healing water relaxing our muscles.

We gather chunks of ice and wrap them in hides. Then we load them onto the stallions and gallop as fast as we can to the village. My love's father and the young man dig a hole in the ground. We put the ice on the bottom and cover it with moss. With the ice, the village will be able to keep the long-haired beast's milk for an extended period of time, saving the lives of the small children whose mothers don't have enough milk in their breasts to feed them.

The twins have grown. The young mother runs to us, giving us a long hug and kissing us. We give her little boy and girl a ride on the stallions. My love's mother prepares a feast for all of us. Everyone is glad to see us. We stay the night, talking, laughing, and feasting. We tell them about the pools of hot water streaming from the rock. The rodents with wings, and the caverns of ice. They tell us how the village has grown. Wood for the fires and grass for the long-haired beasts is harder to find.

"You can feel the ribs of the stallions as you ride," her mother tells us.

Some of the villagers blame the young mother and my love's family for letting a stranger stay among them. They are jealous and scared of the red-skinned girl, with one green eye, and one blue eye. A girl who rides and shoots better than the men. It is decided that in the morning the young father will gather his yurt and belongings. He will bring his young child, and they will come with us. We will pack the young mother's yurt and belongings, and she and her four children will come too. My love's parents will stay in the village until her younger brother is of age.

Like the queen bee, we will set up another hive in the meadow, a land flowing with milk and honey. Over time, more families will join us.

THE TWELVE SHIPS

Rasp! Rasp! The sound of my rasp cuts through the air.

"What are you carving?" a sweet voice asks.

Looking up, I see the bright yellow eyes of a girl peering at me, the black slits of her pupils gazing at me.

"Snake Eyes!" some of the villagers call her. They are wary of her, scared of her intent gaze.

"I am designing a symbol of eternity to go over the door of the old priest's prayer house. He asked me to carve a special door frame for the people who stay."

"I love it," she says, tracing her fingers over the carving. "The slithering creatures twirl around the pole without touching each other. One twirls to the right, and one twirls to the left, encircling each other. Their bulbed heads face each other, exquisitely detailed. The two creatures are entwined, with no beginning and no end."

"Yes, it is the most exciting work that I have done yet," I reply, beaming at her. "The old priest comes every day to inspect my work. He picked the wood from a branch of the oldest tree in the village, the tree with the darkest and most finely grained wood. He says that those who enter through the door frame under the image of the slithering creatures will be healed."

"It's very beautiful. You are the best carver in the village. All the other lads are carving oars for the upcoming departure to the new land." She looks at me with her bright yellow eyes.

I love her eyes—intense, thoughtful, and hypnotizing.

"Some of the people in the village believe that the spirit of the slithering creature lives in you. They feel that you are the snake goddess. People are afraid of you."

"What do you believe?" she asks, her eyes twinkling.

She gives me a sly wink, raising her arms and entwining them around each other, clasping her hands together. Balancing on her toes, she circles her legs around each other. Then she arches her slim body backward, bending toward the ground. With her feet flat on the ground, her body is in a perfect arch, bent backward. With a fluid motion, like the slithering creature, she lifts her legs over herself, raising them high in the air. Her body is as straight as an arrow, with only her fingers holding herself up. I watch her muscles coil and tense as she raises herself, then curl around as she lowers herself to the ground. It is as if she coils her body around herself while sitting upon the sun warmed rock. She flicks her tongue in and out, her yellow eyes hypnotizing me. I shudder as her eyes bore deep into mine, unblinking.

"You are the slithering creature," I whisper in awe. "No wonder the villagers fear you." I want to touch her; my hands reach for her.

"Careful! My fangs will enter you," she hisses, baring her long pointed front teeth at me. Then she nuzzles my neck, drawing blood.

I grip her hands and wrap her fingers around mine. With a smooth grace, I lift her high into the air, her toes extending upward, reaching toward the blue sky. Standing on my toes, I watch her perfect form, rigid above me, only the tips of our fingers touching as she balances over me. I let go of her right arm. Her dress falls over my face, covering me as she stretches herself upward. I smell the aroma of her dress mixed with the scent of her body. She arches her back, bending her legs over herself, touching my shoulders with her toes. Letting go of my left arm, she stands on my shoulders, raising her hands. The strength and curvature of her body are amazing. No wonder the villagers fear her. I love her.

She looks down at me as she brushes her hair from my face. I glance up, seeing the sun glint on her smooth skin. She winks at me as she pulls her dress back over herself, dropping on the ground in front of me.

"Come," she whispers. "Let's finish the carving. The old priest needs it completed. The villagers are uneasy and need something to look up to. This year has been hard on everyone with the sickness and the fires."

She kisses my lips, her lips smeared red from my blood. Then she turns away, grabbing my hand and leading me to the forest.

"We must find the right shape and colour of branch for our carving. The pieces must be carefully selected, so all items mesh to make a oneness." She pulls my hand and leads me to the forested hills. We enter the midst of the trees, crossing the stream that goes through the centre of the meadow.

"I have never tasted fresher water," she says as she cups her hands in the stream, then lifts them to her mouth.

"Here. Drink the living water." She scoops more water up, lifting her hands to me. I slurp the water from her cupped hands.

"Mm…! It's the best water I have ever tasted." I smile at her, water dripping down my chin.

"But what is the taste of water?" she asks as she kisses me. "Is it the taste of me?"

She jumps up, running along the stream. Lifting her dress, she splashes through the water, the sunlight glinting through the droplets.

"Come, follow me. We will explore the beginning of this stream." She glances back at me, her face mischievous.

I lift my robe and follow her through the stream. Smooth pebbles, flat and round, cover the bottom.

"Look at the multitude of rocks scattered around, rocks of all colours." I say as I dip my hands into the water and pick up smooth stones. "On our way back, we will pick some. We will be able to use them for our carving."

"Let's skip rocks," the girl exclaims.

She bends over, picks up a flat rock, and tosses it across the water. It skips perfectly, seven times. "Beat that!" she cries.

I pick up a smooth black rock and skip it across the water.

"One, two, three, four, five. My rock beat yours." She laughs, then picks up another rock and skips it six times. "Now you have to race me up the tree." Running, she reaches the great tree, then swings through the branches to the top.

"This time I'll beat you!" I holler, running as fast as I can. Panting hard, I reach the tree behind her. Her dress flies in the wind as she leaps for the lowest branch. She slithers up the tree like the slithering creature, barely touching the branches as she swings up. Pulling hard, I grab tree limbs, swinging beneath her. I hear her heavy breathing as I near her. I reach for a branch, holding on tight and swinging my legs over the branch. We are even, face to face. Grinning, I hook my legs around her waist and swing her up, the supple branch I am holding, bends with our weight.

She somersaults up, grabbing the branch above her. Reaching down, she grabs my hand and pulls me up with her. Her dress catches on a knot, tearing. She kisses me before releasing my hand. Together we climb, side by side, swinging as we help each other up. The tree sways as we climb, and soon we are at the top, sitting together on the highest branch. I reach down and pull her torn dress back over her body, kissing the small scratch between her breasts. I taste the salt from the trickle of blood. We pant, our arms wrapped around each other as we look at the world below us, the breeze blowing our hair into each other's faces. I feel the softness of her hair against my cheek.

"Look at the craftsmen building the ships," I say as I point towards the bay. "They are almost done. I wish I could design the bulkhead."

"Don't worry," she replies. "You have a more important task. The villagers who stay will need the priest's prayer house completed. The old priest will stay and lead them in the way they should go."

"Not everyone believes in him. The fires have destroyed much of the forest. We are fortunate that some of the tall trees are left," I say.

"Many of our elders have also passed away from the sickness, dying like the trees that are burned. It is not just the older ones who die; the younger ones are getting caught up with the sickness and dying too. The sickness spreads like fire through the forests, taking everything it touches." She clenches my hand.

"I will ask the old priest why some are spared and many fall," I reply. "Some villagers say there is evil that must be stamped out. Be careful, they fear you. Let's climb down and find the sparkling rocks for the slithering creature's eyes."

I squeeze her hand as she pulls me to her, kissing me before leading me down. A faint smell of smoke drifts up, reaching our nostrils. We take our time climbing down, not wanting to leave our perch. The smell of smoke mixes with the smell of the great water.

"Do you think the whole earth will burn like the young priest says?" she asks as we walk through a patch of blackened earth. "The young priest says that where we are going there will be no more sickness or death. The trees will live forever, always producing fruit for us."

I reach down and pick up a piece of charcoal. "Stand still," I say, rubbing my fingers on the blackened wood. Touching her temple with my forefinger, I run a black line from her eyes to her cheeks.

"You are the warrior queen!" I declare.

The slits of her black pupils match the lines I have drawn. Giggling, she reaches for the charcoal, then draws two lines under my eyes. "I now name you the warrior king! Come, let's find the rock we're looking for."

She lifts her dress and runs toward the stream, clouds of black dust blow up as her bare feet hit the ground, her long black hair flying upwards. I run after her. Gritty dust enters our mouths as we run. When we reach the rock ledge overhanging the water, we leap, somersaulting into it. Its coolness refreshes our bodies as we wipe the black grime from us.

We swim to shore. I lift her onto the rock, her dress clings to her. Turning, she reaches for me, and pulls me up beside her. Her white linen dress is soaking wet, hiding nothing. The beauty of her body is fully exposed through the transparency of the fabric. The black lines from the charcoal have smudged across her cheeks. With my forefinger, I rub the charcoal along the ridge of her cheekbones. She smiles at me, the dark lines from the charcoal accenting her eyes. Her arms wrap around me, her body clings to me. Her lips touch mine, soft and sensual.

Crash! A loud boom comes from below. Looking down into the abyss, I see a large tree being chopped down. Another tree is lying on its side. Fourteen men are lopping off its branches, seven on each side.

"Where were you two? Everyone has been looking for you guys," our cousin shouts as we near the village. "The men have chopped the last tree down for the ships. The last mast will be raised tomorrow. You must stay and be a part of the celebration." The wide gap between our cousin's front teeth shows clearly as she speaks.

"You must help me make the special buns for the feast we will have after the last mast is raised," she pleads, her eyes imploring me. "Only you can knead the dough to make the bread come alive."

"I will help you prepare the dough," I reassure her. "We will let it rise slowly all night, and early in the morning, I will light the coals in the oven to bring it to the perfect temperature." She smiles at us, the wide gap between her teeth even more prominent.

"Yes, please help us prepare bread for tomorrow. Here are the grains." She passes me a small sack. "Mother reaped them from the fields today. The crops are scant, and everyone is excited to leave the village. The new land will flow with milk and honey."

"How is the carving for the prayer house door coming?" the old priest asks as he walks toward us, stopping to chat.

"Great! The red feathered creature has given us a stick we can use for carving the ornament," I reply. "Tomorrow we will look for the special rocks under the falls. We will use them for its eyes."

"Be careful as you travel there. The whole village is on edge. Some want to leave, and some want to stay. Everyone blames someone for the fires. Right now, we never know what will happen," the old priest warns us. "The people have chosen the young priest to lead them to the new land. I will stay here with the remaining villagers until my time is done."

"We will be careful," I assure the priest. "Here is the stick that we will be using for the carving." I pass the priest the stick. He runs his hands over it, admiring its shape and colour. Then a shadow covers us. We all look up, hearing the swish of the large feathered creature's wings as it soars above us, its body pure white. The old priest has a faraway look in his eyes.

"This is an omen. Take special care of the stick that the feathered creature has given you. I'm sure you will find the perfect stones for it. I must leave now to rest. I will see you three tomorrow."

"You are the wisest man in the village." Our cousin hugs him, kissing him on the cheek. "I will miss you. Take care of the people who will remain." We watch the old priest walk away from us, his shoulders stooped and a shuffle in his walk.

"I will get the mortar and pestle to pound the grains into flour," the carver's apprentice says, walking toward where they are kept. Sometimes I wonder why the apprentice chose to be a carver instead of a chef.

"Cluck, cluck!" The plump feathered creature ruffles in her nest.

"The feathered creature has just laid an egg," our cousin says as she walks toward the nest. She reaches under the feathered creature and retrieves three eggs. "Fresh eggs are what makes bread taste delicious." She turns and looks at us, her face beaming.

The carver's apprentice pounds the grain into flour, using the mortar and the pestle. In a carved wooden bowl, I mix some fresh milk with the flour, adding the right amount of water to make the batter.

"Here are the eggs!" our cousin yells, tossing us three of them to use.

"Eggs are three in one," I say as I crack one open, separating the yolk from the white. "The hard brown shell, the liquid white membrane, and the soft yellow yolk."

I crack two eggs into the batter, then toss the third one back to her. She catches the egg in her mouth, biting into it. The egg white, mixed with the yolk, drips down her chin. She throws another egg at me. I catch it, then crack it into the batter.

"This will be the best bread in all the village," I say as I dip my hands into the dough, pulling on it, then spreading it out.

All three of us knead the dough, pulling it this way and that, wrapping it back around itself, and stretching it out again. Soon our arms are covered in sticky dough. Giggling, we pull the dough off each other's arms. I place a finger full of dough into our cousin's mouth, feeling the wide gap in her teeth as she slides her mouth across my finger. She lifts her hand up to my mouth. I grab a finger and suck on it, savouring the taste of the dough mixed with sweat.

"We are done," our cousin giggles as she brings her hands to our faces, placing the sticky dough in our mouths. "We must let the dough rise. Let's go to the stream and wash while we wait."

"Yes, let's go." I grab their hands and lead them to the stream.

"Last one in the water has to wash the rest!" our cousin yells. She pulls her robe over her head, then tosses it onto the ledge as she leaps into the pool of hot water. The water comes from the ground, steaming hot. Farther down it cools off as another stream flows into it. Two streams flow into one, one ice cold and one steaming hot. The smell of rotten eggs wafts from the steaming water, softening as it mixes with the cold. I slip my robe off and leap in beside our cousin.

"Come on in!" we yell at the carver's apprentice.

The carver's apprentice stands shyly, hesitant to leap. Splash! The master carver leaps from the rocks above us, surprising us.

"Wow!" our cousin gasps at seeing him naked. His shoulders are broad, his chest ripples with muscles, and his thighs are strong and solid, like tree trunks. He smiles as he sees her awestruck face, posing for her as the sun shines behind him.

"If he's not yours, he's mine," she gushes, putting her arms around me, her large breasts pressing against my back. I smell the muskiness emitting from her body, her excitement.

"Come," I say, motioning to his apprentice. "Join us."

Unlike the master carver, the apprentice is always reserved and shy, barely speaking a word. The master carver leaps up in the water, splashing us. Our cousin giggles, swimming toward him. The water is soothing, rejuvenating our sore muscles as we soak in the it, absorbing its healing properties.

"Where did you go today?" our cousin asks.

I tell her about the trip toward the falls and how we climbed the large tree and watched the craftsmen fell the trees below us. I also tell her how I ached for the master carver to touch me as we sat against the tree branch, how my body felt as I sat on his shoulders with my legs wrapped around his neck, the tremors I felt as I jolted against him and the ecstasy flowing through me. She giggles as I tell her of my feelings for the master carver, her legs floating up as she sits on the submerged ledge.

"Let's rinse off in the river." She rises from the water, droplets dripping off her. She stands in front of us. Her breasts are large, her waist thick, and small rolls circle her belly.

"Hey!" she yells at the master carver and his apprentice. "We're going to the river to rinse off. Grab your robes and meet us there."

They clamber onto the rock ledge to get their robes and run to the river. We toss our robes in a heap on the rocks. Lifting our legs, we link arms and form a circle as we soar into the water, landing with a splash. Giggling, we push each other beneath the water, sputtering as we rise. I love the feel of the master carver's rough hands as they brush against my waist. His strong arms lift me up as he tosses me into the air. His apprentice smiles at us with a twinge of jealousy.

Our cousin jumps on the master carver's shoulders, wrapping her legs around his face and pushing him down. A pang of jealousy flows through me. I grab her under her arms and pull her off him. The sides of her breasts brush against the flesh of my inner arms. She falls, landing on top of me. Giggling, she puts her arms around me, wiggling her breasts in my face, and pushing her nipples into my mouth.

"Taste me," she murmurs, then kisses me. The tip of her tongue touches mine. She wraps her arms around my neck and her legs around my body. Her hair covers my face.

"We must put the dough in the oven," I say, my feelings mixed. "It will have risen."

She slips off me and sidles up to the master carver. "Are you risen?" she asks in her sultry voice. Her hands go under the water, reaching for him. She smiles coyly and throws her head back, thrusting her chest out, her nipples brushing against his chest.

I climb onto the rocks, the cool air giving me goosebumps. "Shall I help you?" someone asks. I feel smooth hands on my waist, gently lifting me. I pause, enjoying the touch.

***

The night is cool. In the distance, the dark sky glows red with the flickering fires. Smoke fills the air.

"The end of the world is near," the young priest whispers.

"Are you sure?" I ask.

He unrolls a piece of bark, coiled at both ends, and reads to me. His voice is strong and masculine. I smell his scent over the sweet smell of the smoke. Sometimes the smoke is strong and acrid. Other times it is almost calming, reminding me of when I was a child, suckling on my mother's breast as she cooked over the coals.

"In time, others will learn to read the words like I have." He rolls the bark back up, then seals it in a clay jar.

"Teach me to read," I beg him. "Let me read the words to you."

"When you are older and can understand. I will teach you." His hands touch mine. Smooth hands, not calloused like the master carver's hands, hands unscathed by work.

"Did you cut yourself today?" He runs his fingers along the tender wound on my finger. Then he draws my finger to his mouth, sucking on it like I used to suckle on my mother's breast. He loves it when I come with a fresh wound. Sometimes he will use his teeth to reopen it, drawing my blood into him.

"Blood is life," he whispers. "As your blood enters me, you will become part of me." He tastes my blood, and his phallus becomes raging hard.

"Taste me," he commands, drawing my head into his loins. I suckle on his phallus like he sucked on my finger. When he is ready, he instructs me to go on my hands and knees, facing away from him. During the darkest of the night, he lets loose with wild abandon, entering me, tearing me. I whimper, sobbing, feeling a sharp pain as he drives himself into me. When he is done, he soothes me with oils, then enters me again, this time slowly, and in his own way, lovingly. He never kisses me, and for that I am grateful.

"I must go," he says, touching my shoulder.

I recoil, moving back. I listen to him leave, making sure he is gone before I rise. Then I wash my tenderness in the cool stream. With clean moss, I wash his seed from me, watching the seed-laden moss float downstream after I am done. Tears well in my eyes. When the sun rises, I walk to the master carver's hut to learn from him.

"This is how you shape the wood," he says as he holds the branch that I peeled and sanded smooth. He holds it over the hot steam that rises from the heated water.

"Blow on the coals," he says softly, not harshly like the young priest's commands in the black of the night.

His hands are heavily scarred, his fingers long and slender. I want them to touch me. Sometimes I slide my hands along his to feel them. Although rough, his hands are tender, not like the smooth hands of the priest who handles me roughly.

"Tie the string," he says as he holds the ends of the wood, bending it in the shape of a U. He nods, indicating for me to tie the ends. I lean against him and tie the string around the ends, binding them together.

"This will dry nicely." His hands touch mine as he holds the wood. I smile, elated at the brief touch. He lays the wood atop the wet moss, then covers it with more moss.

"It needs to dry slowly, so it won't crack. We will fit it tomorrow." He grins at me. "You worked hard today. Your eyes are tired. Go home and rest."

"Thank you." I give him a shy look, thankful that he does not ask questions.

"Sleep in tomorrow. You can come to work later." He jabs me playfully, brushing the shavings from my arm.

"Let's wash first, though. You must be clean. A clean carver is a happy carver." He chuckles, then leads the way to the bathing ponds.

I watch him undress. His body is lean, strong, and muscular. His eyes glance at me, scanning my body. I flush, casting my eyes away. He turns and steps into the water, splashing it on himself as he washes away the sweat.

"Come on in," he reassures me. I look at him, then smile shyly before stepping into the water. He splashes me.

"Here." He tosses me a bar of fat mixed with the whitest ash. "This will make you as white as snow." I scrub myself, white suds dripping off me. Then I reach around, trying to scrub my back.

"I will wash you." He takes the soapy bar from me, then turns me away from him and scrubs my upper back. I lean forward as his strong hands press into my muscles, the ashy grit cleansing my skin. Does he know the effect he has on me when he washes me? His hands reach around my waist, touching me. I feel his phallus brushing against me. I ache for him. He steps back, his hands lingering on me.

"Can we join you?" Our cousin and the girl with yellow eyes stand on the ledge, the young priest is between them. I sink down into the water, watching them as they disrobe. The young priest looks at me, a glint in his eyes.

"Come on in." The master carver smiles as he sees them. His eyes glow when he sees the girl with yellow eyes. Her body is lithe and slender, almost like the slithering creature that wiggles along the ground. Instead of black round orbs in the centre of her eyes, she has black slits that expand and contract with the light and the darkness. Her tongue is long and thin, almost forked. Her two upper teeth are missing, but the two on either side are sharp and pointy, fanged like the slithering creature. Her stature is serious, unlike our cousin who is always frivolous.

Smiling mischievously, our cousin leaps into the water beside me. "Are you clean?" Her eyes twinkle, brown with green specks interspersed throughout. She grabs the bar of soap floating in the water. "Come, I will cleanse you." She grabs my waist, scrubbing my whole body with the bar. The young priest glares at her, not outwardly, but subtly, I see it in his stare.

"Are you sore?" she whispers when I flinch. Her fingers touch me, probing me. I close my eyes. Her hands are soothing and gentle. Her fingers press on me, massaging me, and entering me. Her large breasts brush against my body, not erotically, but lovingly and comfortingly. I sink into her soft flesh, my worries releasing from me. I close my eyes and relax against her body.

I open my eyes. The black feathered creatures fly across the moon, silent. The swish of their wings is the only sound as they fly above us. The young priest looks up, watching them fly. The girl with yellow eyes floats in the water, her tiny breasts upright, water splashes over them, her nipples hard and shiny.

"Is the carving done?" the young priest asks.

"Not yet," the master carver replies, his eyes bore into the young priest's eyes, as if warning him.

I look at the young priest and see him flinch.

"Why do you ask?" the girl with yellow eyes asks.

The young priest is wary of her. I see it in his posture. She stands facing him, her hands on her hips. The water comes up to her waist. I admire her. She stands up to the priest while others from the village waver before him.

"It will be done soon," my master says as he stands beside her.

I look at the three of them standing there. The priest and my master are tall, their shoulders broad. The carver's muscles ripples as he moves, his arms and chest strong from constantly carving the hardened wood. The priest's body is soft, but his voice is strong, and his eyes command the people's attention. The girl with yellow eyes is but a wisp beside the two. Her skin is pale, her body slender, and her hair long and black, hanging down her back. The sight of the three of them thrill me as they face each other. The girl has a tiny scar between her breasts.

"I will teach your apprentice to read tomorrow," the young priest says as he glances at me. I see the excitement and desire in his eyes as his phallus rises in the water. He discreetly turns aside.

"He likes you," our cousin whispers in my ear.

"I will come with him," she says cheerily to the priest. "You can teach us both to read."

"Sure," the master carver agrees. "Teach them both. I can work alone tomorrow."

"I will help you carve the emblem tomorrow," the girl with yellow eyes says. She puts her arm around the master carver's waist.

"Agreed." The master carver smiles. The young priest looks at them, his eyes downcast, but he nods in agreement.

"It will be fun," our cousin says as she puts her arm around me. "We will see you tomorrow." She swims up to the young priest and gives him a hug. She puts her legs around him, wiggling her bum up and down as her breasts splash in the water. He pushes her off him. She giggles, then kisses him on the cheek before she swims back to me.

"I felt him rise against me," she whispers in my ear. "I can't wait for tomorrow."

The young priest turns away and climbs up on the ledge. He stands strong and purposeful as he dries himself, his phallus risen with desire. He gazes at me as he pulls his robe over himself, a look of lust and desire in his eyes.

"We will be there before the feathered creature crows in the morning," our cousin says, her voice husky with desire. The girl with yellow eyes gives us a curious look.

"Come, let's go." Our cousin leads me to the ledge. She stands before me, drying herself, using the soft cloth to rub between her legs.

"Come." She motions to me, pulling me toward her. "Let me dry you."

Ever since I can remember, she has wanted to dry me after bathing. She rubs me down, patting me until my skin is red. I smell her scent emitting from the cloth as she dries me. It's invigorating and enticing, not like the foul smell of the priest after he penetrates me.

The girl with yellow eyes grabs the tiny shrubs growing along the ledge, pulling herself onto the rocks. Even though her body is lithe and small, she has superb strength.

"Here." Our cousin hands me the soft cloth. "Dry her." She pushes me toward the girl with yellow eyes. Then she sidles over to the master carver, holding her hand out to him. She pulls him up beside her, water dripping off his muscular body, his flesh a shiny glow.

"The cloth is wet. Good thing I'm small," the girl with yellow eyes says, smiling at me. She has always been kind to me. I envy her body, small and petite like mine but with incredible strength.

"Does the priest treat you well?" she asks. "It will be exciting for you to learn how to read." She holds my arm, looking at the cut from the knife. "Come by after you are done with the priest." She runs her finger along my wound. "I will put some lotion on it. It will heal without a mark."

"Thank you," I whisper, my eyes downcast.

"We should eat." The master carver pulls his robe over himself, much to the dismay of our cousin. I smile, knowing that she likes him immensely. The girl with yellow eyes also grins as she dresses. Our cousin reluctantly pulls her robe over her body, exaggerating her movements as she wiggles her hips, causing her breasts to jiggle, her nipples large and erect.

"Come, let's eat." The girl with yellow eyes unrolls the small pouch she carries, pulling out two pieces of dried meat from the finned creatures. She breaks them in half, sharing them with us. We sit on the grass, eating the pink flesh and listening to the creatures of the night. Tonight, the moon is large and luminous. It is almost as if I can touch it.

"You need your sleep." My master looks at me. "Rest." He puts a pillow under my head. I close my eyes, feeling his strong hands on me. I dream a peaceful dream, a dream of floating through the sky beside him.

I feel someone stir, waking me. The girl with yellow eyes is sitting up. Our cousin is draped over my master, drool dripping down her chin as she snores. His back is turned to her, his breathing steady as if he is in a deep sleep. A faint glow from the fires is across the hills. The girl with yellow eyes turns to us, making sure we are sleeping. I lie quietly, feigning sleep. Assured that we are all asleep, she slips her robe over her head, then gets up. I wait until she is at the edge of the camp before I rise and follow her. She treads quickly and quietly, walking to the fires. It's all I can do to keep up. A fanged creature howls in the distance, followed by a chorus of a multitude of fanged creatures. I shiver. She stops and kneels, holding her ear to the dirt, as if she is listening. They call her the slithering creature.

"Stay away from her!" the young priest always warns me.

The moon shines bright in the sky, a complete circle, round and full. It is during every full moon like this that the young priest calls me to his hut. In the silvery moonlight, he teaches me things. I breathe deeply, following the girl. She is a mystery to me. They say she controls the slithering creatures, wrapping them around poles for others to look at. The old priest is getting my master to carve an emblem of them over his doorway, an intricate carving. I follow the girl to the old priest's house, then wait outside as she enters, looking around to make sure no one is watching me. I hear muffled voices inside, then she comes out with a small vial of potion, barely discernible in her hand.

"Magic!" the young priest would say. "Evil magic!"

I look for the young priest, wondering where he is. The girl with yellow eyes walks toward the smouldering fires. I follow, not thinking she knows that I'm there. It occurs to me that I should be walking with her and not silently behind her, unknowingly.

"She is trouble!" the young priest always tells me when we see her.

Suddenly, she disappears. One second she was in front of me, then she vanished from sight. The fanged creatures howl beside me, close. I can't see them, but I hear their footsteps as they run past me. A horned beast runs ahead of them, fleeing from the burning bush. It bleats as the fanged creatures circle it, then tear into its abdomen, bringing it to the ground.

"What is more dangerous? The burning bush or the open meadow with the fanged creatures?" a voice hisses.

I jump in alarm. The girl with yellow eyes is beside me. Her eyes shine in the night, eyes like the slithering creatures.

"Don't be alarmed," she says as she holds up a small vial. "The old priest has given me the lotion; this will heal your wounds."

"Look ahead of us." She points toward a small body of water, the moonlight reflecting off it.

I squint my eyes to see better. Submerged in the water are three horned beasts, their nose and eyes just above the water.

"They are safe from the fires and the fanged creatures. The beast that ran was old and no longer able to hide," she whispers in my ear. "It was time for it to move to the next life, and in doing so, it fed the fanged creatures that remain."

"What will happen to the old priest? Will he go on the ships or stay in the village?" I ask.

"The old priest will stay; he has served his days."

"Will you stay? How about the master carver? Will he stay?"

"Will you go with him if he goes?" she asks as she looks at me, her eyes questioning. "What about your cousin? Will she go with him?"

"I don't know," I whisper.

We sit silently together, lost in thought.

"We better go back." I touch her hand. "Everyone will wake soon and wonder where we are."

"Here." She holds the vial up to my arm. "Let me put this on your wound."

I hold my arm out to her, watching as she puts a drop on her finger. She spreads the lotion along the length of my wound, rubbing it deep into my tissue. "It will feel better soon," she murmurs. Then she rubs the lotion on the scratch between her breasts.

"How did you get that wound?" I ask.

"We were climbing the great tree." She looks at me, a smile on her face, like she is reminiscing.

"With the master carver?" I look into her eyes, feeling slightly jealous.

"Yes," she sighs. "Let's go back before the others awaken."

We walk side by side back to the others, passing the old priest's dwelling. He waves at us.

"Tonight I will put the ointment on your other wound." She touches my arm. I look at her, wondering what she knows.

We walk past the tiny clearing where I was to meet the young priest. In the early morning light, he is sitting up, reading from his scroll. My heart flutters from fear and unknown dread.

"You will learn to read today." The girl with yellow eyes smiles at me, then runs her tongue between the gap in her upper teeth, her fanged teeth, sharp, and pointy.

"And you will help the master carver," I say, smiling at her, feeling anticipation and jealousy.

I look at the young priest as he sits, wondering if he sees us walking together. The sun is just starting to peak over the horizon, red streams flowing across the sky. A small crescent of a moon dips down on the other side. Six black feathered creatures fly over us, circling the horned beast that was slain. They land on a barren tree, each one sitting on a different branch, waiting for the fanged creatures to disappear.

The girl turns to me, her eyes glowing, the tiny black slits in the centre barely visible. She kisses me on my neck, biting the vein that pulses. I feel the twin pricks as her teeth break my skin. Her tongue laps the blood pulsing from my neck.

"You and I are the same," she whispers, her voice husky. I bend my neck to her, my breasts tighten, and my nipples become hard. I let her suckle on me, bite me, probe me. I see the young priest watching us. I close my eyes, surrendering to the sensation. She breathes heavily. I feel the cool lotion from the vial touch my skin.

"This will not leave a mark," she hisses, rubbing the lotion on the twin pricks.

Her lips are red like the rising sun. She kisses me with her wet lips. I take her hand and lead her back to the others. She closes her eyes, letting me lead her. Coming back to the others, I see our cousin's plump body riding up and down on my master. His stiff phallus is inside her, her heavy breasts swaying over his face. I am envious. The girl with yellow eyes keeps her eyes closed, oblivious to our cousin's antics. I see that my master is sound asleep, rigid and hard but asleep, dreaming. Does he know what she is doing to him?

Our cousin rises off him, his seed dripping from her open folds. Without seeing us, she walks to the stream and washes herself, making sure his seed does not leave her. She wants his child. The master carver stirs and awakens, realizing his loins are wet.

"I must have dreamed." He gives us a sheepish look, covering himself. "Where were you two?"

"Watching the fires," the girl with yellow eyes says.

"Are they spreading?" our cousin asks as she returns from the stream, her face smug. "We must sail soon. Our children must not be raised in a barren wasteland."

Her face is flushed, her breasts full and upright, her body warm and desirable. I look at my master. He cannot contain the desire in his eyes as he looks at her. I smell her aroma emitting from his loins.

"We will learn to read today." She gives me an excited look. "Then we can teach our children to read."

"But we have no children." The girl with yellow eyes corrects her.

"Not yet," she replies. "When we reach the new land, we will." She puts her hands over her belly, smiling smugly as she slowly pulls her robe over herself, flaunting her body in front of us. She looks down at my master's loins, her eyes full of anticipation and fulfilment. I look at the girl with yellow eyes. Her eyes are downcast, yet she smiles as she looks at my neck. I remember her hot breath as her teeth punctured me.

"Teach me to read," she mouths to me.

"I had a strange dream," my master says to her.

"It was no dream," our cousin twitters to me. She grabs my hand, leading me to the small grove where the young priest stores the vases containing the grey paper with symbols on them.

"We have arrived," she says as we enter the grove. The young priest is sitting alone, reading from the scrolls. As usual, his hair is long and uncombed, cascading down his back. His feet are bare and dusty, the bottoms covered in calluses. He wears a white robe made from the fibres of the plant with three leaves on its stems. Tied around his waist is a light cord, knotted in the centre with three loops. When he sees us, he holds out a smouldering bundle in his fingers. He smiles, his eyes leering at me.

"Your minds will be enlightened," he says as he passes our cousin the thin bundle. She breathes from the end until the tip is glowing red. Inhaling deeply, she holds her breath before blowing the smoke out of her mouth, her lips pursed. She blows it into my face. Then she holds the bundle to my lips.

"Suck it all in," she whispers.

I inhale deeply, feeling the burning in my lungs. My head spins. I giggle as I exhale. Then I look at the young priest, strangely desiring him. We sit in a circle, and he traces his fingers in the sand, creating signs and symbols, explaining what they mean. I copy him.

"But I can change the symbols to change the stories." Our cousin draws with her fingers in the sand, changing our symbols.

"Here you are as a man." She draws an image of the priest with his phallus hard and erect. "And here you are as a woman." She rubs her fingers over the phallus, evening out the sand and drawing breasts like hers on the image of the priest.

I sit in the sand, drawing pictures of men and women, changing them with a stroke of my hand.

"How do you draw time?" I ask, looking at the priest. He draws a line in the sand, the length of his arm. Along the line he draws twelve divisions, evenly apart.

"But time is continuous," our cousin says, looking at the line the priest drew. "Yours has a beginning and an end."

She draws a circle, dividing it in twelve. "Time has no beginning and no end." She traces her hand around the circle. "Time is a circle, like life."

We inhale once more from the bundle, breathing deeply and blowing the smoke into each other's face.

"But you had a beginning," I remind her. "And your child to be born will have a beginning."

The priest gives her a look. "Your child to be?"

Our cousin looks at me. "If and when I have a child, he or she will have a beginning in body, but the mind and spirit will be continuous."

"But how can two people joining together create another body and spirit?" I ask. "And where does the spirit come from? Can another spirit be created from within the first one?"

"Yes," our cousin replies, looking at the priest for reassurance.

"If the emblem of the body comes from the master carver, can the spirit come from you?" I ask the priest. "Can your spirit enter me as your body enters me?"

"There can only be one in the centre," our cousin answers. Then she looks at both of us, saying, "If I have twelve children, I will be in the centre, and my children will surround me in twelve divisions." She leans over and makes a mark in the centre of the circle.

"But what about the father?" I ask.

The young priest is quiet, contemplating my cousin's words.

"What does it say in the book?" she asks him.

He relights the small bundle of the mood-enhancing weed, drawing its incense deep into his lungs. He passes the bundle to our cousin, holding it as she inhales. She giggles as she exhales. Then she rolls in the sand, her hands digging into it.

"An image!" she squeals, lifting an object. "A phallic image!" In her hands she holds a carving, carved from marble. It's black with white swirls through it.

I bring the burning bundle to my lips, inhaling the aromatic smoke. I hold it in before exhaling, smoke rings exiting from my mouth.

She holds the marble image up to the sun. The sun's glow enhances its warm colours. She looks at me, her eyes mischievous, then passes the carving to me. The carving is hard, yet smooth to the touch. I can almost feel life in it. I rub my hands along the small ridges around its glans. The two round orbs at the base are small and tight, fitting into the palm of my hand.

I draw another breath from the diminishing bundle, then blow the smoke onto the carving. It is obscured until the smoke dissipates; I pass the carving back to her. She places the phallic image in the centre of the circle she has drawn. A shadow stops at the first mark she has made. "This is the firstborn," she says, holding her belly.

"But what about the night?" the young priest asks. "Will the moon shine like the sun, circling the marks as the sun circles them in the day?"

"We shall see." Our cousin draws from the bundle, blowing the smoke into the young priest's face, then passes the bundle back to him. He brings it to his lips, drawing deeply.

"During the day, I am the sun." She stands up, drawing her robe around her waist. "And during the night you are the moon." She motions to me.

"You are the centre." She kneels in front of the young priest, untying the three knots on the cord that hold his robe together. "The shadow of the sun will land on each of the twelve divisions as it circles the earth."

She pushes him into the sand, her hands stroking him until his phallus points to the sky. I watch as she lowers herself on him, the same as she did with my master. I think of the phallic image, black with white swirls on it. Can she conceive twice, once from my master and once from the young priest?

I look at the sun, red in the sky, lowering itself beneath the horizon. As the sun goes down, her plump bum settles over his glistening phallus, clenching him, and drawing his seed into her. Opposite the sun going down, the moon rises.

"You are the moon," she says, motioning for me to come. She passes me the phallic image as she rolls off the priest. She lies on her back with her knees up and her head extended back. Her breasts are large and firm, pointing up. I touch the tip of the phallic image to her shiny lips, lubricated by the priest's seed. It slides easily into her depths, the carved orbs resting on her outer petals. I feel the priest's hands touch me as he kneels behind me. My head is light from the aromatic properties of the smouldering bundle, my senses nullified. I no longer feel the pain as he enters me. Our cousin's soft groans fill the air as she writhes with the movement of the phallic image inside her.

Howl! The fanged creatures circle us.

Hiss! The slithering creatures dart past us.

I feel his phallus twitch as his seed shoots inside me. I slip away from him, watching as our cousin straps the phallic image around her loins. The young priest goes on his hands and knees in front of her. Like the drawings in the sand, he becomes the woman, and she becomes the man.

***

"Did you learn to read?" the girl with yellow eyes asks.

I give her a sheepish look. "If you change the symbols, you change the stories."

"What do you mean?" She looks at me. The black slits in her eyes are broad, her interest piqued. "But how can changing the symbols change the stories? Aren't the stories the same regardless of the symbols?"

"It's like us as carvers. We can change the image of the creature by carving it in a different way," I say.

"But the creature does not change."

"No, but the image in the beholder's mind does."

"What is your image of me?" she asks, her voice luring.

"I will carve your image as I see you."

"But you can only carve me as I am, not as you want me to be," she says.

Our cousin walks toward us; the marble image is in her hand. The young priest walks beside her. He gives us a wary look as they stop in front of us.

"Did you learn to carve?" our cousin asks the girl with yellow eyes.

She shows us a delicate carving, a slithering creature with a forked tongue, wrapped around a pole.

"It's beautiful," I murmur to her. "Did the master carve it?"

"No, I did."

"Where is the master carver?"

"I don't know."

"Usually, he's never away." I touch her hand, comforting her.

"I wonder where he is." Our cousin looks worried, her hands touch her belly. "I will look for him."

"I'll go with you," the young priest says.

"Let's go to the old priest's house." The girl with yellow eyes touches my arm. "Maybe he is there."

"Okay," I agree, nodding. "I'll pack some bedding and bring some food." I gather a small roll and a satchel of bread and dried berries. In another satchel I place two of the dried finned creatures from the salt water.

"Do you think that he's okay?" she asks when I return. I look at her. The small dimple on her cheek is pronounced as her face creases with worry.

"He will be fine." I encourage her.

I adjust my pack, then wing it onto my back. I grab her hand and lead her toward the burning forest. Her slender fingers fit perfectly into mine. We walk silently together, searching for any signs of the master carver.

"There's the old priest's dwelling." She points to a small hut in a charred clearing. "The fires have surrounded the hut but not touched it."

We walk toward the old priest's hut, admiring the wooden carving on the door.

"Come inside," the old priest says as he emerges from his hut. His shoulders are stooped, and his gnarled hands are wrapped around the hook of his cane. I have never been inside his hut before. It's filled with all kinds of ointments and vials. Some are on shelves, and some hang in satchels from the ceiling.

"Something for everyone," he says with a chuckle in response to my wide eyes.

A slithering creature with fangs is wrapped around a pole. It raises its head, swaying back and forth, as if trying to hypnotize me.

"It is safe." The girl with yellow eyes picks it up, letting it twirl around her arm. The slithering creature raises its triangular head, flicking its forked tongue in and out as it circles the girl's neck. I see faint pinpoint marks matching the slithering creature's fangs over the veins that pulse in her neck, two tiny red dots on each side of her blue veins. I raise my hand to my neck, touching the tiny marks from the girl's bite.

"We must understand the poison." She looks at me as she places the slithering creature back onto its pole. "If we understand the poison, we will not be harmed."

The slithering creature circles the pole, not moving, appearing the same as the branch it is entwined about. I lean toward it, peering at the slithering creature and the pole it is wrapped around. The two are the same, one is a branch, and the other is a slithering creature.

"Some people are camouflaged like the slithering creature," the old priest says, looking at me with his cloudy eyes. "You think they are part of the same branch, but they are not even part of the same tree." He touches the slithering creature, rubbing his finger under its throat. I step backward, his eyes following me. Although his eyes are opaque and almost sightless, he senses things around him, and his acute memory recalls things as they are.

"How do they camouflage themselves?" I whisper, goosebumps appearing on my arms.

"Some as priests, some as carvers, others as saviours."

"How can you tell if a person is real or a mirage?" the girl with yellow eyes asks as she looks at the slithering creature on the pole.

"You must learn to recognize the signs," the old priest answers as he clutches the curve of his walking stick. It is then that I notice that what looks like an extension of the hook is a sixth digit on his hand. He smiles at me, holding his hand up and spreading his fingers.

"Six?" I gasp. I touch his fingers, five fingers and one thumb, shrivelled yet still long and slender. He grabs my hand, his grip powerful.

"Is the young priest a camouflage?" the girl asks, not batting an eye about the sixth digit on the old priest's hand. "He doesn't like me."

I look at the girl's eyes. From a distance I thought they were yellow, but up close they are teal, the colour that blue and green make when I mix the dyes together. I look again at the old priest's eyes. Even though they are opaque I see that the one is blue, and the other is green. I remember the pages of the book that the young priest read to me, a story from long ago. The old priest chuckles, then grabs an aged leather satchel hanging from one of the branches that the slithering creature is wrapped around. He pulls dried leaves from it, then sprinkles them in the bottom of three goblets.

I recoil, thinking about the smouldering bundle the young priest shared with our cousin and I when he taught us to read. The old priest heats water over the hot coals until it is steaming. Then he pours it over the dried leaves in the goblets. He drops a dollop of a sweet, sticky nectar into each cup, stirring it with a dried twig.

"Drink," he says, passing each of us a goblet. I take the goblet and lift it to my mouth. The drink is sweet, aromatic, and blue in colour.

"Where did you get these leaves?" I ask in awe.

"From the blue hills," he replies. "Far from here."

"But the hills were never blue," the girl says.

"No, they were never blue," the old priest agrees. "Only from a distance did they appear blue, but up close the hills were full of colour."

I look at the two of them. "Where are the hills? Have you been there? Do people know if they are camouflaged? Do they believe they portray the image that people see?"

"Not always." The old priest raises the goblet of steaming liquid to my mouth, peering at me. I sip the hot drink, tasting its sweetness, its aroma tantalizing. The girl's lips purse as she drinks from her goblet. I love the dimple on her cheek.

"It's late. Stay here tonight." The old priest leans back, resting against his cane. "The master carver is safe."

I look at him, wondering what to say. Then I look at the girl. *-Is it safe to stay*? I wonder.

She nods in response to my silent question. "Yes, we will stay here tonight."

I unroll my bedding, spreading it out in the corner away from the slithering creature. The girl opens the satchel containing the bread and the dried finned creatures. We sit cross legged in a circle as we eat, washing the food down with the hot, sweet liquid. I have never tasted anything so flavourful, so sweet. After we have eaten, the old priest pulls out a red vase with white parchment inside. He pulls the parchment out, then spreads it in front of us. The parchment is torn and almost illegible. His gnarled finger points to the symbols, reading them as his sixth finger hovers over them. He shows us how to read the symbols.

"When written with the black ink of the eight-legged creature that swims in the great water, the symbols do not change," he says, giving me a knowing look.

I look at the white parchment with the black symbols written across it. I touch the parchment. It is easily torn, not like the image our cousin found in the sand, the hard image, black with white swirls throughout it. The old priest reads the symbols, telling us stories of long ago, of fires burning, floods, sickness, and happiness amongst it all.

"But that's the same story as today," the girl whispers.

"Yesterday, today, and tomorrow," the old priest replies. "The stories never change. Only the names change."

"But you can erase the stories written in the sand," I tell them, "Or change their shapes."

I think of the young priest kneeling in front of our cousin, the phallic image strapped to her loins.

The old priest takes two stone tablets from the wall and shows us the etchings in the stone. "The symbols written in the stone will not change. They will last for all eternity." His fingers trace the etchings. He passes us each a tablet, letting us run our fingers along it. "What is written in the sand will wash away, but what is written in the stone will last for generations."

The girl yawns, and the dimple in her cheek stands out. I want to tell her how beautiful she is, but I do not dare.

"You two will need your sleep in the coming days," the old priest says. He lays his robe in the centre of the hut. "You will be safe here."

The girl kisses him on the cheek, then hugs him. "Thank you," she whispers.

I see a faint resemblance between the two. I touch the girl's cheek, feeling her dimple. Then I cover her with a light robe, kissing her lips. She smiles, her eyes closing as she falls asleep. I look at the slithering creature wrapped around the pole, then back at the girl. Her breathing is shallow.

"Can I carve?" I ask the old priest.

He grins, his face old and wrinkled, a permanent smile in it.

"Yes, you can sit there." He motions to his table, full of vials and potions. In a wooden box covered in webs from the eight-legged insect he pulls out an assortment of shiny tools.

"I keep these well-oiled." He passes them to me with his gnarled hands. Beside his bed is a walking stick, ivory in colour. He passes it to me as well.

"It was her mother's," he says grinning, his two front upper teeth missing, just like hers. I thank him, then lay the tools on the table, spreading them out in a fan shape, eight tools in all. I rub my finger along the edges, drawing blood. The old priest passes me another goblet of the hot liquid, sweetened with the golden nectar.

"Don't stay up all night," he admonishes me. Then he lies down on his cot, pulling a light robe over himself.

The girl and the old priest sleep in the same position, one arm and one leg outstretched as if they are curled around a tree branch. I look at the girl as I whittle, carving her in a supine position, wrapped around a pole. When I am done, I lay the finished carving beside the girl.

"It's beautiful." I awaken to her voice. "Did you make it?" Her eyes shine. She has the rod in her hand, turning it this way and that. "How did you make the eyes?"

"They are from the sparkling rocks I found among the soft black rock, a tiny, hard, sparkling rock, hidden within the mounds of the soft black rock."

The figurine is of the girl. Below her waist she is a slithering creature, and above her waist she is the girl, with ivory skin, pert breasts, a strong neck, and shiny teal eyes.

"How did you carve the hair?" she asks, stroking the figurine's hair. The hair is fine and intricately carved, individual strands hanging down to her lower back.

"And it's black like mine." She combs her fingers through her hair, running them through its length. It is as if she makes the rod come alive.

"You carved my dimple." She smiles shyly, touching the figurine's cheek. Her eyes twinkle as she feels the tiny dimple on the figurine's bum just before it turns into a slithering creature. "You carved both." She gives me a coy look.

I smile, thinking of how she laid last night, trying to impose the shape of her body in my mind, to carve it perfectly. I almost missed the tiny dimple on her bum, its shape and texture, the same as the dimple on her cheek.

"It is the shape of your mother." The old priest twirls the figurine around, admiring it, a twinkle in his eyes.

"You two must eat." He cooks us a bowl of pottage made from the red grains collected during the last full moon before the cold moons came. During that time the sky was littered with falling stars, falling from the sky like leaves falling from the great tree. He spoons in a dollop of the golden nectar collected from the six-sided combs of the fuzzy yellow insects.

"Six is an important number," he tells us, showing us a piece of the comb. "The earth was created in six days."

"Is the earth six-sided?" I ask.

"Are we the centre of the world?" the girl adds.

The old priest smiles. "So many questions. Go and explore the world." He sends us out the door. "Come back tonight and tell me what you have seen."

The feeling I have with the girl is different than with the master carver and the young priest. It is hard to explain. I love my master, and I want to be with him. I admire the young priest's quietness and his resilience.

"You should be a priest instead of a carver," the young priest told me in the quiet of the night after he read me the stories from long ago.

"But the carvings last forever," I replied. "And the stories change over time."

"Not if they are written down," he said.

Whoever reads the stories can change the words," I reminded him. He put his smooth hands on me, turning me over.

"The stories are true," he whispered as he entered me.

"Should we explore the cliffs?" The girl with yellow eyes touches my hand, bringing me back to the present.

"The rod is beautiful." She gives me a shy look, her eyes the colour of the slithering creature's eyes. She twirls the rod in her hands.

"Did you carve this also?" She points to the carving over the priest's door.

"I carved the slithering creatures, and my master carved the totems."

She runs her hands along the carvings. "I helped him carve the totems the day we went looking for the wood."

"I know." I feel a pang of jealousy when she gets that faraway look, remembering that day. The two of them went looking for the exotic wood while I stayed behind to carve the figurine for the young priest's ship.

"Let's go." She grabs my hand, leading me away from the old priest's dwelling. I walk beside her, our footsteps matching each other's.

"Do you want to be a priest?" she asks as we walk. "You're so calm and collected. You would make an excellent priest."

"But I'm learning to carve." I smile at her.

"You can be both," she replies, grinning. "The villagers need a person like you."

"Maybe, but I'm learning to carve pictures to tell the stories. I'll show you when we get to the cliffs." I am excited to show her what I've been working on, the pictures carved into the cavern's walls. We walk toward the red cliffs that overhang the water. In the distance are the hills that overshadow our village.

"The hills sure are red today, the reddest I've ever seen, is it an omen?" She stops and gazes at the hills.

"Red seems to be a distant colour, one we see in the distance," I say as I glance at them as well.

"And up close." She kneels in front of a red flower growing on a green stem.

"Smell it." She puts her nose up to the flower, sniffing its petals. A yellow stem rises from the centre of the bud, crowning at the top with multiple tiny stems.

I lean down beside her, sniffing the flower. "Red like your blood and yellow like your eyes."

She touches the tiny bulb on top of the stem. A yellow powder remains on her fingertip. She blows on her finger, sending the powder billowing into the air.

"The flower's seed," she murmurs, watching the tiny wisp of a cloud floating through the air. "They will find other flowers and propagate each other."

I touch the stem with my fingertip, depositing the yellow powder onto the stem of another flower.

"This flower has an ivory stem like yours," she says, giggling. She leans over it, touching the stem with her nose. Then she wrinkles her nose at me. A small yellow dusting covers the tip.

"I'm allergic to you!" She sneezes, her water droplets landing on me. I laugh as I put my finger on the end of her nose, wiping the pollen away.

"Taste me." I put my finger in her mouth and feel the space between her sharp, pointed teeth. Teeth like the slithering creatures.

We watch one of the fuzzy yellow insects as it lands on a flower. A stem protrudes from its mouth, and it sucks the nectar from the pollen-laden stamen. On its furry legs, it collects the yellow pollen, depositing it on the pistil of another flower as it lands on it.

"We are the flower," she says, giggling. "Male and female alike."

She touches the flower with her lips, her upturned nose wrinkling as she sniffs it. Her eyes sparkle in the light, the tiny black slits barely visible. Her face is beautiful. I think of my master—his solid looks, chiselled features, and strong hands. The girl is like me, slender, wiry, and strong. We are both female but different. Is she part male also, like my master? We lie in the tiny meadow, untouched so far by the fires.

"Do you think our cousin is with your master, learning to carve while we are away?"

"She adores him." I lie closer to her, our bodies touching. "She always comes by when we're carving."

"Does she say anything about him to you?"

"She wants the young priest to teach her how to read." I pluck a tiny flower hidden in between two rocks, putting it in her hair.

"I'm a flower between the rocks." She grins, her eyes mischievous. "The master and the priest." She lies on the ground, turning over. Her robe rises to her waist, her small bum lifts up.

I look at her. "What does the young priest say to you?"

"He wants me to stay," she laughs. "I think he wants me to burn in the fires with the slithering creatures."

"He incites the people to believe that they must leave this place. He tells them it will be destroyed by the fires." I gaze into her eyes.

"What do you believe?" she asks as she turns over, lying on her back. She lays her head in my lap and looks up at me, her hair flowing over me, soft and silky.

"I don't know," I whisper. "I found some drawings from long ago carved into the walls of a cave."

"The caves with the slithering creatures inside?" She looks at me in awe. "The ones we're never to enter?"

I gaze back at her. "You've been inside them?"

She gives me a wary look, followed by a shy smile. "You're like a priest, always knowing. Don't tell a soul." She pleads. "The young priest will incite the people to burn me along with the slithering creatures."

"I won't," I promise her.

I remember the time the villager's gathered straw and piled it over the slithering creatures' nest. The straw caught fire so fast, and the slithering creatures came out from under it, only to be stomped on by the howling villagers, men and women alike. I recall the terrifying smell as the slithering creatures burned, their bodies twisting around each other.

"No one will know," I say as I put my arm around her. "No one will harm you."

We enter some thick shrubs that cover the hills. The thickness of the shrubs hides us from prying eyes. All the same, I glance back, glimpsing the young priest searching for us. I duck, pulling her down with me. We crawl through the underbrush until we reach an obscure opening hidden by a flat stone. I move the stone aside.

"Hurry!" I whisper.

I help her over the hole, lifting her arms up. Her robe catches on a small branch, staying in place as I lower her. She dangles below me, holding onto my hand, her other hand searching for a handhold. I drop her, watching as her robe flutters down, falling over her. I slide over the opening and drop down beside her. The cave is dark. The girl gasps, her hands gripping my wrists.

"You knew," she whispers. "Who else knows?"

"No one as far as I know," I reply.

As our eyes become accustomed to the darkness, I lead her across the damp floor, careful not to slip. Water drips down from above, splashing us.

"Careful." I hold onto her arm.

A slithering creature slithers in front of us, pale from the lack of sunlight.

"This one doesn't bite," the girl says, picking it up. It wraps around her arm, raising its head, its eyes opaque like the old priest's eyes. She passes the slithering creature to me. It drapes around my arm before dropping to the ground. A ray of light shines through a tiny hole above us, illuminating the wall across from us.

"Feel this." I place the girl's hand onto the rock wall.

"Feel the indentations along its face." I slide her hand along the wall, letting her feel the grooves.

"The pictures are etched into the wall," she whispers. "It is in the shape of a ship."

"There are eight people on the ship," I say as I trace her fingers along the carving.

"Wow!" she whispers, goosebumps appearing on her forearms. "How old are these carvings?"

"Ancient," I reply. "The etchings are worn and smooth, not rough like a new carving."

As our eyes continue to adjust to the darkness, we see more carvings and designs.

"Who did this?"

"They were done over multiple years and eras," I reply. Then show her the different shapes and styles of carvings. "They were all carved by different tools. Some are rough, and others are smooth. That, and the amount of erosion in each one indicates its age."

"Is this yours?" She points to an unfinished carving, its edges still rough.

"Yes," I whisper.

A shadow covers the ray of light.

"Hide!" she exclaims. "The young priest is outside! At times I smell his aroma on you." She wrinkles her nose, smelling the stale air. I step back, surprised.

"He won't find us," she assures me. "The priest is scared of this place, the birthplace of the slithering creatures." She pauses. "You're not afraid of me. Why not? The others are."

"The old priest isn't afraid of you either, nor is the master carver."

"No, they're not," she agrees.

"Is the old priest your father's father?"

She remains quiet for a time. "He is my mother's father. We must stay hidden until the young priest leaves."

I think of the many hours I have spent with the young priest. "What will he do to us if he finds us?"

"He will do nothing to you." She reaches for my face, brushing her hands against my cheek. "He loves you like a child."

"But I am no longer a child."

"He thinks of you as a child."

I think of the young priest and the girl I am with. She challenges me, questions me.

"Do you think of me as a child?" I ask. "It is the young priest who showed me the way of all creatures."

"Not the way of all creatures," she replies sadly. "Only his way with you. Come, let's explore deeper in the cave." She grabs my hand. She uses the rod I carved for her as a guide, sweeping it across the ground, searching for crevices and crannies that might hinder us. We crawl through tunnels and wet streams inside the cavern, sometimes in total blackness, and sometimes a faint light appears.

"We are twins in the womb," she says as she leads me through the earth's depths.

"Do I trust you?" I touch her feet, making sure she doesn't get too far ahead of me. She chuckles under her breath.

Suddenly we come to a cavern filled with light. The cavern faces the great water, the sunlight shining through an oval opening. The way the rocks are situated, one cannot discern the opening from the outside. I crawl to the opening and look down in awe, kneeling at the edge of the crevice.

"Where are we?" I ask. "How did you find this place?"

"I am from the depths of the earth."

I look at her in amazement. Her cheeks are smudged with black dirt, her elbows and knees scuffed from crawling, and her robe is dirty and torn.

"You are the same as me." She giggles as I stare at her, then I look at myself. My arms and legs are also streaked with the blackness of the earth, my robe tangled around my waist. I laugh.

"There are the ships." She kneels beside me, pointing across the water.

I look in the distance. I gasp, pulling back. "There is my master." I point. "And our cousin."

"Don't worry. No one will see us or know where we are." She puts her fingers in her mouth, blowing sharply. A shrill, piercing sound emits from her, another one echoes it. I hear the swish of wings, then a feathered creature, red in colour, lands on the cave floor. It has a scaled creature with fins in its curved beak. The girl takes the finned creature and splits it in two. Ravenous, we eat it raw like the feathered creatures do. I chew the delicate meat, spitting out the scales as my stomach growls. I didn't realize how hungry I was.

The red feathered creature hops around, eyeing me. Then it turns back to the water, soaring through the air with its wings outstretched. It dives into the water and brings up another finned creature in its talons. I hold out my arm, and the red feathered creature lands on it, dropping the finned creature into my palm. The girl looks at me in awe. I wink at her.

"Here." I pass her the finned creature with scales. She divides it with me, then with a sharp stone, she cuts off its head, giving it to the red feathered creature. The red feathered creature tosses the head in the air, then swallows it as it lands in its beak. It cocks its head at us, then lifts off my arm and soars into the hazy atmosphere, hazy from the burning fires.

We sit in the shadows of the cave, hidden from prying eyes. The only thing they will see if they look at the cliffs is the scat of the red feathered creature on the rocks below. The only entrance to the cavern is a long maze of dark tunnels through the abyss of the earth or a climb up the smooth walls of the rock face, which is wet from the waves pounding against its base.

"We will spend the night here," the girl whispers. She spreads her robe out in the light shining through the opening.

"The young priest will be looking for us, and my master will worry."

"Let him look." She looks at the red hills across the water, the colour of flames. "He won't find us."

"Why does the young priest hate you?"

"Come, let's rest." The girl pulls me beside her, not answering me.

We lie down together, staring through the opening.

***

"Let's use this one." I rub my hands along the length of a stalwart log.

"The fires have marred it." He scratches off a piece of singed bark.

"The burning has enhanced it, not marred it. It has blackened it like my skin." I stand tall in front of him, my hands on my hips. My body is stout, my breasts large and upright.

"The wood is the colour of my skin," I say, my voice soft and seductive as I turn to him. He smiles at me, averting his eyes. He is taller than me, even though I am tall for a woman.

"The wood is hard." He presses his fingernails into it. "It will be difficult to carve."

"Hard like you." I touch his arm and run my fingers along its length. "We will be on the first ship. We need to be the strongest and the hardest."

He shrugs. I know he is worried for his apprentice who has been gone for two days, as has the girl with yellow eyes. The ships will leave in the morning, regardless of who is on them. The young priest has been looking frantically for them.

"Okay, grab an end," he mumbles. "Let's take this to the ship."

"We will carve it here and assemble it in the morning."

"Why?" he asks, surprised.

"I cannot say."

Ever since the fires, the village has been divided. Some want to leave, and others want to stay. I will be on the first ship with the village's newly elected leader. It has been decided that I will help with his young family. My mother has nursed his children since they were born. They suckled on her breasts until they could walk. It was during the last full moon that my mother passed away during the famine. Food has been scarce for seven years now, and she sacrificed her own food for the children, only to have her body wear down, unable to resist the sickness that followed the famine.

"You must stay with the children," she had pleaded with me before she passed.

"I will." I had promised her as I clutched her hand. My eyes were wet with tears.

"Why did you stay with the new leader and his family?" the master carver asks as he lifts his end of the log.

"For the children." I smile as I think of the youngest. All her questions, and her excitement to sail on the new ship.

Their father is wary of me because of the colour of my skin, but he knows that his wife is frail and will need my help on the journey. I pick up my end of the blackened log. We haul it to a small clearing at the edge of the charred brush. I see the scratches on his broad back as he carries the log, his shirt stripped down to his waist. I am wearing only a soft white skirt, made from the softest silk. Sweat drips down my back.

"We will do our carving here," he says as he lowers his end to the ground. "I must get my tools."

"I will stay here," I reply as I lower my end down. I watch him leave, his shoulders slightly hunched, his steps weary. I pick up a sharp stone and scrape the singed bark off the log. The sun beats down on me and sweat drips down my brow, falling on the log. I remove my skirt and drape it over a dried branch. A slithering creature lifts its bulbed head before it slithers from the rock I am about to pick up. The stone is rough, perfect for sanding the log. I straddle the log, rubbing the stone along its length, smoothing it until I can rub my hand along it without feeling any roughness.

Sensing someone near, I glance up. The young priest is standing beside the newly elected leader. They are hidden in the bushes, thinking I can't see them. I smile, thinking of the young priest's desire for the master carver's apprentice. Pretending to teach his apprentice to read, the two spend many hours together.

"You're back," I say as I hear light footsteps behind me. I sit on the log and turn to face him. The master carver looks at me, astonished.

"It's too hot to carve with my skirt on, and I don't want it getting blackened." I grin at the look of surprise in his eyes as I stand up. The log is wet from my sweat, an imprint of my bum and inner thighs on the blackened wood. I giggle as I think of how the black won't show on me. Then I turn around, my back facing him as I lift my leg over the log. He looks around nervously.

"Don't worry." I turn to face him. "No one will see us." His eyes roam over my body. A welcoming breeze blows across me, cooling my sweat-soaked skin. I walk over to where I hung my skirt, lifting my legs up one at a time as I balance on my feet, stepping into my skirt. I pull the skirt up my darkened legs, dark like the burnt wood.

"The wood is beautiful," he says as he rubs his hands along it, looking at the colour it has turned into from me rubbing it. "The colour is perfect, not a deep black but more subtle and more exotic."

"Like me?" I smile mischievously, lifting my right leg onto the log as I face him. His eyes glance between my legs. I look down, pretending not to notice. Then I flex my knees, spreading them, accenting my inner flesh. He adjusts his stance. I see his phallus stiffen under his robe.

"The perfect colour," I say, feigning innocence. "We better start carving. The newly elected leader wants it completed soon. I saw him and the young priest watching us when you went to get your tools."

He glances into the bushes, a worried look on his face. "The old priest wants his carving completed also," he mumbles. "How can I do both with my apprentice gone?"

"I will help you." I hold the end of the log as he removes his tool belt, laying his chisels and knives in a row beside him. "I will hold the log steady for you."

Once again, I straddle the end of the log, holding it firmly as he carves. My inner thighs press tight against the wood, releasing as I rise to turn the log when he needs me to. Soon he no longer needs to tell me when to rotate the log. I watch him closely, turning it when his chisels reach the sides. He constantly looks up at me, scanning my body as he carves. I know it is not out of lust or adoration but so his hands can carve what his eyes see.

He starts with my head, my hair flowing down my back. He carves the log so my head is raised up, looking forward. My arms are by my sides, not resting, but ready for flight, or fight. I marvel as the chips fly from the log. He rubs his hands across his bow. Without thought he removes his shirt, tossing it into the grass. His forearms bulge as he uses his knife to shape my breasts.

He looks up at me, eyeing my breasts. "Chest out," he murmurs. I almost ache as I watch him carve my nipples, wishing his hands were on me. His tongue curls as he concentrates. He leans back, looking at the carving, then looking at me, carving a little more to make the nipples erect, capturing the tiny bumps that surround them. A shadow crosses over us. We look up, seeing a small cloud form.

"Not now," he mutters, resuming his work.

I lift my skirt as he gets closer to me, my folds pressing into the wood, my inner thighs chafing as they grip the log. Soon he has carved my back in an arched position. The bones in my back are prominent.

He looks at me. "Skirt or no skirt," he murmurs to himself. Then his knife slips, cutting his finger. I reach for his hand, sucking the blood from his finger. A small red dot drips onto my nipple as he moves his hand across my breast.

"A skirt," he decides, "Sliding down to indicate speed." His hand touches the hem of my skirt, pulling it down. He carves the top of my bum, my hips flared. Below the crevice of my bum, he starts carving my skirt. His gaze is intense. He motions for me to remove my skirt while he continues to carve. I smile as I watch him adjust himself on the log, his arms guiding the chisel into the wood. His excitement grows, his stiff phallus peering through his loincloth, which is soaked with his sweat.

I remove my skirt slowly and seductively, giving it to him. He picks it up and drapes it over the log. He peers at it, then back at the log. He carves a spitting image of the skirt onto the image of me. He smiles as he nears completion, his entire body covered in sweat. His eyes glow in anticipation of seeing the finished product. My body tingles with excitement as the carving reaches completion.

"Almost done." He looks up at me, grinning. I smile, then sit back on the log and open my legs to release the tightness in them from gripping the log. A smell of desire emits from me. His nose wrinkles as he sniffs unconsciously. He kneels at the end of the log.

"It must join," he murmurs. He eyes the folds between my legs. His fingers touch my petals, spreading me. He carves an exact image of my inner chamber into the end of the log.

"Why?" I ask. Fluid oozes from me, my inner thighs once again clenching the log.

"So it is together forever." He grins at me, his body flushed with excitement. He sinks down on the log. Straddling the carving, he faces me. His eyes gaze at me. He is unable to contain his excitement as he completes the work he is creating.

"Will it fit?" I murmur, moving forward on the log, sliding up to him, careful not to touch him, not wanting to break the spell. His tongue curls, and his eyes glaze as he slides forward, his phallus erect, moisture oozes from the small opening at the tip. I lean back, watching as his bulb touches my moist petals. I adjust myself, letting him push at my entrance, my inner folds wet from the excitement of watching him work and the thrill of him about to enter me. The glans of his pink phallus slips inside my black petals, the only part of our bodies touching.

He stops, our emotions electrifying, the thrill intensifying. Then he releases, his white nectar spilling inside me. I moan, closing my eyes. His hands grip my bum, pulling me toward him. The shock I feel as he touches me, his length gliding inside my inner flower. The sensation, the ecstasy, the long wait, I spasm, locking my inner muscles around his rigid phallus, milking him as he pulses inside me. I open my eyes and gaze into his eyes. He squeezes my flesh, pulling me toward him, our loins rubbing against each other. My hardened nipples touch his chest, rubbing against his skin. I put my arms around him, clinging to him.

A red feathered creature screeches in the distance. Another screeches in reply. The red feathered creature soars to the cliff walls, carrying a finned creature with scales in its talons. An arm reaches out, and the feathered creature lands on it. Moments later it swoops down into the water, scooping up another finned creature. Another arm reaches out, the feathered creature landing on its wrist. I smile. The two are safe.

I gaze into the master carver's eyes. He gazes into mine with wonderment, adoration, and bewilderment. The log is wet from our love. I tighten against him, rocking back and forth, feeling him rise once more within me. I throw my head back, screeching like the red feathered creature as his seed pulses inside me. Three times he fills me.

A shadow darts from the bushes. One of the slithering creatures drops from a branch, circling the shadow's neck. It grips it, biting into the tender flesh. A tiny cry ensues. We are safe.

"We must go back," I whisper, kissing his lips. We help each other dress, then pick up the newly carved beam and carry it toward the ships.

"Can I help you carry it?" a sweet voice asks.

I look down, chuckling. The youngest girl is running toward us, her hands holding up her white skirt. "I'm wearing your skirt," she giggles.

Her small fingers are hooked into the helm, pulling it forward. Her waist is narrow, her tiny ribs prominent. Behind her is her younger brother, struggling to keep up.

"Look what I made," he says, holding up a replica of a ship.

"Cute," I reply, smiling at him.

"Do you like it?" He holds it up to the master carver. "Will it float?"

"It will sink," his sister teases him.

"No, it won't!" the boy yells at her.

"Let's try it," the master carver says. He lowers his end of the wooden figurine to the ground. "We need a rest."

Although he is tired, his face is happy, and his eyes sparkling.

"Agreed." I lower my end, grinning back at him, my arms aching.

"What did you two carve?" The boy clutches his toy ship as he looks at our carving.

"It's a carving of you," the little girl says in awe, her large eyes looking at me.

"When I get big, I want to be just like you." She twirls around, releasing her skirt. It twirls down to her ankles.

Laughing, I reach down and pull it back up, tightening it around her waist. "It's too big for you. Where is your skirt?" I give her a quick hug.

"You have to grow up to be like her," her brother retorts. "I'm big now. I'm going to be a carver." He hands the tiny ship to the master carver.

I smile as the master carver bends down beside the boy, examining the ship. "It's beautiful."

The boy grins from ear to ear. "Let's bring it to the water!" He jumps up and down with excitement, clapping his hands.

I smile at the two children. They are the youngest children of the newly elected leader and his wife. For days they have been talking excitedly about travelling to a new land.

"When we get there, I will be a princess," the girl had said. "We will have all the food we can eat, and mother will no longer be sick."

"And I will be a carver!" the little boy had declared, flexing his arms.

I am to go on the first ship with them. Their father, the newly elected leader, has chosen me to look after the children after my mother passed away from the sickness. He and the young priest have commanded the master carver to carve an image of me to install on the bow of the first ship.

"A symbol of strength," he had said as he leered at me. He ignored his wife; I think secretly hoping that she would pass from the sickness before the ships sailed. The young priest always confided in him, saying his wife would become a liability on the ships, slowing us down. If she were to pass before we set sail, it would be lawful for him to take me as his new wife when we reached the new land.

"Can I touch it?" The young girl reaches for the carving.

"Her skirt is sliding off." The boy giggles, trying to pull up the skirt on the figurine.

"When I get big, you can carve an image of me, carve me like this." The girl puts her hands on her hips. She looks adoringly at the master carver, striking the same pose as mine.

"I will go on your ship," she teases her brother.

"No, I will put him on my ship." He points to the master carver.

"But women are stronger. They must lead the ships. Carve me," she pleads. "Put me on your ship."

The master carver chuckles.

"Stand still," he commands her. He pulls out his small whittling knife, then carves a tiny branch in the shape of her body. He does a brilliant job.

"Let's mount it." She holds the image to the bow of her brother's ship.

"How will it stay?" she asks as the tiny figurine falls off the bow.

"Here." He cuts a stem on the bow, then whittles a hole on the end of the image.

She guides the image onto the stem. "I am your guide through the rough seas."

"Will you carve me when we get to the new land?" she asks as she climbs into the master carver's lap. "I will be fully grown then."

"But he will stay." The boy eyes his newly carved ship. "His apprentice will come with the young priest, and the master carver will stay with the old priest."

I look at the boy in surprise. "Who told you that?"

"Father." He looks at me, his face sad. "I wish the master carver was coming with us."

"Let's sail your boat." I lift him into my arms and snuggle him against my chest, trying to cheer him up. He presses his face against me. The carver lifts the girl and tosses her on his shoulders. She giggles as we walk to the small pond in the middle of the meadow.

"It is safe here," I say as I lower the boy beside me. "The water isn't deep."

"Throw me in!" the girl says, laughing.

The master carver lifts the girl over his head, then tosses her into the water. She leaps up and splashes us, her skirt floating in the water. The master carver smiles mischievously at me.

"Careful! I'll throw you in." I say as I grab him and push him into the water beside the girl. Her brother giggles, then pushes me into the water. I purposely fall backward as he laughs with delight.

"Here! I will rescue you." He sets the ship he built on the water. Then he blows on the small craft. Its tiny sails, made from leaves, billow out as the ship scoots across the water straight toward me. He jumps up and down, clapping his hands and smiling. I kneel in the water and purse my lips, blowing the tiny ship toward his sister.

"Jump in!" the girl yells to her brother, pushing the ship toward the master carver.

"Father will be mad if we come home with dirty clothes again," the boy says as he removes his clothes and jumps in beside us.

"Mine are clean at home." The girl laughs, then picks up my skirt, which she wore today, and tosses it onto the bank to dry.

"Is it true that you are staying?" I ask the master carver, leaning into his arms. "I thought you were coming with us."

He puts his arms around me. "It has been decided that I will stay with the old priest."

"I will stay with you then."

"The children need you."

I look at the boy and girl playing in the water, sailing their tiny boat. They are so young, untouched by the division of the people.

"I will come back for you," I say as I hold his strong arms.

A black feathered creature caws as it flies over us. Another one joins it.

"We better go back. The children's mother will be worried."

"Come, let's go!" I holler at the children.

"Aww!" the boy yells.

"Race you!" his sister challenges him. They scramble up the bank, water dripping off their bodies. I laugh as I pick up the boy's clothes and the skirt which the girl was wearing. I carry them in my arms. As the children race off, the girl turns and waves at us, skipping as she runs.

"I will miss you." Tears glimmer in my eyes as I put my arms around him. He picks me up and lifts me on the bank. We walk back to the figurine we carved. The children are waiting for us.

"I'll miss you too," he says, kissing me on the lips.

"Hey!" The girl glares at me. "He's mine." She stamps her foot. We chuckle together.

"They adore you," I say, smiling at him. "You should come with us. The villagers need you."

"So do the ones who will stay."

"I know." I reply. "I want to stay with you. I'm not afraid of the fires or the slithering creatures."

"The newly elected leader needs you," he says, squeezing my hand.

"No, he doesn't, and neither does the young priest!" I reply. "The children and their mother need me for a short time, then I will come back to you."

"Can we carry it?" the children ask. Each one is on an end, trying to lift the carving.

"You're heavy!" The boy grunts, his small arms trembling as he struggles to lift the image.

"Lift it like this." The master carver squats beside him, flexing his knees as he bends down. "Keep your back straight."

I grin at the two. The master carver looks up at me and winks.

"Lift!" I tell the boy. He clenches his teeth as he lifts the carving a tiny bit off the ground.

"Help me too!" The girl pleads with the master carver, struggling to lift her end.

"I'll help you," I say as I kneel beside her.

"No! I want him!" she replies, pouting.

He laughs, then walks over and kneels behind her, putting his strong hands on hers. Together they lift the end of the carving off the ground.

"We did it!" the girl cheers.

"Can we ride on the figurine?" The boy clambers onto it, straddling it.

"I want a ride too!" The girl climbs onto the figurine's back, putting her hands under the carving, and gripping its breasts. The boy sits atop the smooth skirt the carver has carved, his hands clasping onto the carving's bare waist.

I smile at the innocence of the children, their legs clenched around the carving, their thighs pressed against the wood. From behind they are the same. The girl has two braids in her long hair, and the boy has one braid the length of his back.

I pick up the tail end of the image as the master carver picks up the head. It's as if the image of me is alive, my hair flowing as we walk. He turns to me, smiling, then turns back and walks toward the ships. I look down to where he first entered me. My hands touch the area where he pierced me. A slight discolouration in the wood will be there forever, the spot where my blood mixed with the seed that entered me. I sigh, knowing that even if we are separated, his seed is growing inside me. As we walk toward the open water, we hear the villagers' nervous laughter. Some are excited to leave, and others want to stay. The smell of fresh bread and the finned creatures baking over hot coals fills the air.

"Where is the newly elected leader?" someone asks.

"And the carver's apprentice?" another person says.

"And the girl with yellow eyes?" asks a third.

A group of children run up to us, the girls wearing skirts, and the boys wearing shorts. "Where were you?" The children surround the young boy and girl, chattering excitedly as they eat fresh bread and baked finned creatures.

"I made a ship!" the boy announces, showing it to his friends.

"And the master carver made an image of me!" The young girl shows the other girls the small carving of herself.

"Wow!" they exclaim. "Can you carve me?" they ask in unison, tugging at the master carver's hands.

"Hold on," I reply, laughing. "First we must eat."

The children pass us bits of finned creatures and bread with their grubby hands.

"Freshly baked!" they say in unison.

"The baker just made the bread this morning," a young girl says as she holds a piece to my mouth.

"And the cook ate a whole loaf herself!" a boy adds with a giggle. He holds his arms out, indicating the cook's size. We eat small bits of food, some of it already chewed.

"I want to be carved as a warrior," one of the boys says, striking a fighting pose. "So, when the sea monsters come, they will be afraid of me."

"Carve me like this!" Another girl stands with her arms raised. "Let my hair flow in the breeze." She tilts her head back, facing the sun, her skirt billowing around her waist. I smile. The children are laughing once more, excited to sail.

"But I'm staying!" A little boy lowers his head in dejection. "Who will carve me when you leave?"

"I'm staying also," the master carver says as he picks the boy up. "When the others leave, I will carve you."

"Okay." The boy sobs quietly, lifting his hands to his face.

A little girl reaches for him. "I am staying too," she says, seeking to comfort him.

"Carve us both!" She tugs on the master carver's hand. "You can carve us together." She leaps onto the boy's back, her arms around his neck and her legs around his waist.

The children strike poses and push each other around, deciding what they want to be. Most of the boys want to have a fierce face while the girls want to soar with their arms spread out. One of the boys wants to soar like the black feathered creature, the one with the white head, and sharp talons. We chuckle as we watch the children play.

"We better mount the figurine on the ship soon," I say as our stomachs rumble.

"Yes, let's erect the figurine of you first, then we can eat," the master carver replies.

We pick up the figurine and admire it once more. The children run their hands along it, giggling.

"Did you get your clothes dirty again?" an older girl asks as she comes behind us. She is the oldest sister of the two children who went with us. "Father will be mad if your clothes are soiled."

"I'm clean!" the boy says, turning to show his sister.

"Where's your skirt?" she asks her younger sister, lifting it up around her waist.

"I wore hers," the younger sister says, pointing at me. She picks up the hem of the skirt she is wearing and runs behind her brother.

"It's too large for you," her older sister says in a tired voice. "It's always falling down."

I feel sorry for her. Whenever I am gone, she must look after her mother and the rest of the children. Her father is hard on her.

"I will wash their clothes," I say to her.

She gives me a tired smile. We leave the children laughing and playing as we walk to the first ship in the flotilla.

"Careful!" The master carver cautions as we climb over the rocks. The ship is moored facing a large flat rock, the helm reaches over it. We lay the figurine on the rock. The shaft protruding from the front of the ship is higher than I can reach.

"I will sit on your shoulders," I say as I look up at the shaft, reaching for it.

"Here." He passes me a vial of oil.

"Where did you get this?" I ask in surprise.

"From the small glands behind the fangs of the slithering creatures."

"But the poison is deadly," I reply, remembering a young boy who succumbed to a slithering creature's bite. It would not release its fangs until the boy's body was stiff.

"This is the oil, not the poison," he assures me.

I pour some of the oil in the palm of my hand. It feels light, yet my fingers easily glide against each other from its properties. I give him a shy look, wanting to put the oil on the glans of his phallus instead. He bends down, letting me climb on his shoulders. I pull my skirt up so as not to hinder him as he rises.

"Lube the end." He motions to the shaft he has carved on the ship's bow.

I balance one hand on his head as I reach for the shaft with the other hand. I squeeze my knees against his neck. His shoulders push against my bum as he raises his hands, holding my knees in place. A thrill flows through me as my sensitive nub rubs against the muscles in his neck, exhilarating me. I touch the shaft, spreading a small amount of oil along its length where the figurine will mount to. I grasp it firmly, rubbing my hand along it. My face flushes as I realize that the shaft is an image of his hardened phallus.

"When did you carve this?" I ask in surprise.

"Guide it in," he says, chuckling as he lifts his end of the figurine up to me.

I grip it with both hands as I lift it over my head, my knees clenching tighter around his neck. His fingers dig into my flesh. I guide the figurine onto the phallus he has carved. Now I realize why he was gazing intently at my inner flower as I sat facing him. He was carving the insides of my flower on the end of the figurine. The tiny petals of my flower will lock firmly around the ridges on the image of his hardened phallus. I smile as the two pieces slide together with the help of the oil, perfectly mated, bottoming out at the right length.

"Tug on it," he urges.

I tug on it, unable to uncouple it.

"We are together forever," he says with a grin.

I look down at him, unsure whether to cry or laugh. Suddenly, I start laughing and crying at the same time, falling into his arms.

"Let's eat." I look at him as he holds me, my eyes brimming with tears. He kisses me before lowering me to the ground. We walk back to the others, our arms around each other. The villagers separate as we walk through them. Some scowl at us; others smile discreetly.

"Eat some bread," an old lady says, giving us a loaf. "I just baked it this morning."

She scowls at the others. "I'm staying here. The new leader is nothing but trouble. Look at how he treats his eldest daughter."

"Thank you." I take the loaf from her, breaking it in half and sharing it with the master carver.

An old man smiles at us, then shares a finned creature with us, baked over hot coals. "I'm staying too," he says with a toothless lisp. "They don't want us old people on the ships, only the young."

He glances at the master carver. "I heard that you're staying, and your apprentice is going."

"Yes, I am staying." The master carver nods.

"Good, the old priest needs you," he says, then he looks at me and asks, "Are you staying?"

"No, I'm to go on the first ship with the newly elected leader and his family," I reply. "We just installed the figurine on it."

I squeeze the master carver's hand, giving him a loving look.

"Take a look at the figurine the young priest installed on his ship." The old man points to the ship that the young priest will go on.

"Where is your apprentice, and the girl with yellow eyes?" a young woman asks the master carver. "Will they be back before the ships sail?"

He shrugs. "I don't know."

"The young priest says that everyone must be ready, or they will stay." The young woman glares at me.

"I suspect that the new leader has caused them harm," another woman says. "He's missing too."

"Shh…" I warn her. "Not everyone thinks like we do. We must be careful."

I turn to the master carver and grab his hand as a crowd gathers around us. "We should go; let's walk to the ships." I tug on his hand, leading him to the flotilla. We walk past the people. The young priest is standing at the edge of the crowd.

"Who else is missing?" He glares at me as we walk past him. I stare at him until he averts his gaze.

"Your skirt is soiled and torn," he says, giving me a sour look. "Be ready to sail in the morning."

"When our leader returns, he will deal with you," he whispers so only I hear him.

"I'll be ready," I reply as I stare into his eyes.

We stop in surprise as we near the ships. The young priest's ship is first in the flotilla. Extending from its bow is an image of an angelic being. It appears to be an image of the young carver.

"Why?" the master carver asks in surprise. "Who carved this?" He touches the figurine, running his hands along it.

"It is my apprentice's trademark," he mumbles.

I stand before the figurine, examining it. A red feathered creature soars above us, circling. From its wings a feather flutters to the ground. I watch the feather swirl through the air, drifting toward us.

"It's white," he exclaims as I catch the feather in my hand. "A white feather from the red feathered creature? How can that be?"

"It's a sign that your apprentice is safe."

"Do you believe in signs?" He takes the feather from my hand, twirling it in his fingers.

"Signs are tough to decipher at times," I say as he puts the feather in my hair.

"White against the blackness." I smile at him. "Let's look at the other ships' figurines."

I grip his hand, leading him to the flotilla. We walk along the rocky shore inspecting the ships. The ship I am to go on is second in line behind the young priest's ship. Only two ships have a figurine on them, the first ship with the image of the angelic being, and the second with the figurine in the image of me.

"Why do the other ships not have figurines on them?" I ask as I look down at the twelve ships, one for each family. "You should carve one for each of them. They should have figurines too."

"There is not enough time before they leave."

"One more," I encourage him. "I'll help you. We can carve them." I point to a couple sitting on the rocks. "Look how they sit together."

The girl is sitting on a stone, her legs folded beneath her and extended behind her. She leans to one side, her hands on her knees. Like me she is wearing only a skirt, draped around her waist. The young lad kneels in front of her, his hands on her knees, his eyes pleading. I watch his lips move. He is saying that he must leave with his family. His father is sick, and he is the oldest.

"I will leave with you," she says.

"Your mother needs you," he replies.

The girl's father died of the sickness. Like the young lad, she is the oldest, and she must stay with her family.

"Let's walk along the shore," I say, taking the master carver's hand. "We will look for the perfect log."

We find a log washed up on shore, half under the water and the other half sitting on the rocks along the edge.

"We will use this. It will stay on the rocks as a reminder that she is always here, waiting for him to return." I say as I pull the log up onto the rocks, wiping away the tiny sea urchins that cling to its bottom.

We carve the image of the girl and the young lad kneeling before her, his eyes imploring her. She sits staring at the red hills, her legs beneath her, one arm touching the ground; and the other arm on the boy's head as he sits on his left knee, his other knee up. We carve them as they are sitting there. The setting sun shines on them. The girl's budding breasts casts tiny shadows on the boy's face. Her slim waist shows that she has endured hunger. Her belly button is a small thin line; her hair falls across his hand. His eyes are pleading, large, and luminous. We carve them as if they are naked. His body is strong and muscular, her body slender and resilient. Masculine and feminine we create them. I look at the two as they sit there, not knowing we are carving them. The girl is beautiful, and the boy handsome. It pains me to see the two of them together, knowing that they must separate.

"Is your apprentice male or female?" I ask the master carver. "It is an angelic being that is carved on the young priest's ship?"

The couple get up and walk to the village. Her waist is narrow and her hips wide. His shoulders are broad and his bum slim. He touches her hand; their fingers intertwine. We erect the carving on the rocks, securing it for all time.

"It will be a sign," I say as I intertwine my fingers around his. "For those who stay and those who return for their loved ones."

"Shh . . ." The master carver squeezes my hand, pulling me toward him.

I hear a shuffling noise behind us. I grab a stick, ready to charge. Two shadowy creatures are scurrying up the ship, running to the freshly carved figurehead. A hearty guffaw comes from the deck, followed by a laugh.

"Quick!" a hushed voice says as the two make their way toward the front of the ship.

I draw my arm back, ready to hurl the stick.

"Not yet," the master carver whispers.

The one in front removes her robe, tossing it behind her. Now I see it is the village cook, followed by the baker. He is a young lad, small and lithe. Both his legs together are thinner than one of the cook's legs. The cook chuckles as she climbs onto the figurine, her ponderous breasts hanging over the beam, and the fleshy rolls of her bum jiggling in the air. The young lad climbs behind her; his fingers clinging to her thick waist.

I chuckle as the moonlight glows on them. It seems like his skinny bum will be sucked between her wide cheeks as he attempts to mount her from behind. She coos, her voice throaty. His skinny arms reach around her. Her nipples are large and dark, covering the mounds of her breasts. She squeals with delight when his fingers touch them, howling when he squeezes them. I glimpse his phallus, long and hard, disappearing between her enormous cheeks. I glance at the master carver. His grey eyes are laughing.

"This will test the figurine's strength," he says, chuckling.

The cook howls with delight as the young lad enters her. Her fingers reach behind her, dipping inside her enormous flower, her petals open and wet. The lithe lad rocks back and forth, his compact bum thrusting above her glistening folds, his tiny hips slapping against her large cheeks. The comical sight and sounds entice me. I lower my hand to the master carver's loins. His phallus is erect and throbbing. I cup my hands around his phallus, feeling his veins, my fingers touching the ridges along his glans.

The young lad stiffens, pounding deep between the cook's cheeks. He throws his head back, pulling on her nipples. She thrusts her hand inside her flower as he deposits his seed inside her rectum. Fluid gushes from her sprouted petals. I feel the master carver stiffen, and his phallus jerks as his seed spills into my palms. I lower my mouth to him, engulfing him, sucking on his phallus until he releases once more. I swallow everything he has, tasting his nectar, sucking hard for more.

A shadow passes under the moon, and the two beings scurry off the figurine, gathering their robes. They pass us unknowingly, the lad's phallus dripping and still half erect. On the rocks beside us, she turns, opening her heavy legs for him. This time he enters her flower, thrusting between her shiny folds. Her ponderous breasts roll across her chest. We sit quietly, not daring to move, watching as they couple together, sweat dripping down their bodies.

***

"Did you make the image for him?" the girl with yellow eyes asks.

I nod.

"It's okay," she touches my knee. "It's what he wanted."

We sit inside the cavern, watching the workers across the water. At the edge of the woods, the master carver is whittling a log.

"Do you miss him?" She gives me a pensive look.

"Sometimes." I glance at her. "But the dark-skinned girl is with him."

We watch as she sits on the log, posing for him as he carves, her skirt draped on the branch behind her.

"It's her image that he is carving."

"Yes," I reply. "It's an image of her."

The two carve the log at the edge of the clearing, not knowing that anyone is watching them.

"She looks after the family of the newly elected leader. Some say his wife will not live long enough to sail to the new land."

"Will the family stay?" I ask.

"The master carver will stay, and the dark-skinned girl will go on the first ship with the newly elected leader and his family."

"But why do they not carve the image of the village leader's wife instead of the dark-skinned girl?"

"I saw the leader following us. I believe he is searching for the slithering creatures."

I look at her in surprise. The fangs in her mouth are prominent as she speaks of the newly elected leader.

"Why would he look for the slithering creatures?"

"He wants the poison."

"But why? What will he do with the poison?"

She sits quietly, her arms around her knees. Then she stands up, flexing. "Let's explore the rest of the cavern while the sun shines inside." She glances at me without answering.

I look at her lithe body, envious of her shape, then we move to the back of the cavern. The opening facing the great water seems small, no bigger than the red feathered creature's nest, but the inside stretches into the depths of the earth, twisting and turning like an ancient river.

"Water flowed through these tunnels ages ago," I remark. "Once the water below us was as high as these caverns."

"Where did the water disappear to?"

"I don't know." I love her curious mind, always questioning.

We crawl through openings and tunnels with our hands in front of us, feeling the way, careful that we can back up if we can't continue ahead. One at a time we go through the tunnels, warning each other of any dangers. Winged creatures with the heads like those of rodents fly ahead of us, and unseen water runs through gullies and cracks beside us.

"What if we never make it back?" she asks. "Who will help the master carver and the old priest?"

"We'll be careful," I assure her. "We'll make it back."

A pale slithering creature darts past us, its head large and blunt. We come to a small opening, almost like a throat going down into the abyss of the earth.

"We better not go inside. The earth will swallow us." I stick my hand through the opening. The dim light that shines through has all but disappeared.

"Feel it." She puts her hand inside the opening. "It's warm and moist, like a birthing canal. We can only come out this way. We cannot go back in."

I crawl backward, sliding against the walls. My robe covers my face, slipping over my head.

"It's a good thing I have small breasts, or I would get stuck," I say with a giggle as my chest scrapes against the rocks.

"Mine are small like yours." She laughs, slipping from her robe also. "Naked we came from the earth and naked we will return."

We roll our robes into a ball, using them to push against the ground as we propel ourselves backward. Slowly we crawl backward to the main cavern inside the edge of the cliffs.

"We made it!" the girl exclaims. Then she screeches, making the sound of the red feathered creature, curling her fingers like its large talons.

Screech! The red feathered creature answers her, flying toward us. In its talons it holds a plump white feathered creature. It lands before us, cocking its head and dropping the feathered creature in front of us.

"I wish we could light a fire," I say as I reach for the plump feathered creature. "This would taste wonderful roasted over the coals."

"Soon," the girl replies. "In a bit they will be tired of looking for us, then we can light a fire."

"But we need wood." I point out.

I hold the creature as she strips the feathers from it. Then she uses her sharp nails to open the feathered creature's cavity, pulling out its insides. She drops the entrails in front of the red feathered creature, thanking it for giving the plump feathered creature to us. The red feathered creature devours the remains. The girl uses her fanged teeth to strip the tender meat from the bones, sharing them with me. Our stomachs growling, we devour the strips of meat, chewing it quickly to overcome the thought of eating it raw.

"This is for the finned creatures in the water." She pushes the carcass over the edge. A small finned creature without scales, and a triangular fin, swims toward it, nudging it.

"Should we warn the master carver?" I say as I look into the distance as he and the dark-skinned girl walk back to camp, carrying the freshly carved figurine, the image of the dark-skinned girl.

"They will not enter the water yet. The children of the village are surrounding them." She picks up a long white feather lying on the cave floor. She coos to the red feathered creature, speaking softly to it. The red feathered creature grabs the white feather in its beak, then flies away.

"The dark-skinned girl will recognize it as a sign."

I look at her in awe. "You have the spirits of the creatures' within you and are able to transform from one creature to another!"

"We are all one spirit," she replies. "Only our bodies are different."

"Can you fly?" I ask.

She chuckles, then stands up, waving her arms like the feathered creatures flap their wings. The sun filters through the opening, casting her shadow over the cavern's walls. A trickle of water seeps from a ledge, collecting in a small pool before it exits out the opening, dripping down the cliff. I will use the wet wall to find the opening if we need to access the caverns from the water. She leans forward on her knees, putting her hands on my upper thighs and kissing me on the lips. I feel a tiny shock and exhilaration as our lips touch. She holds her palms under the small stream coming from the rock face, then lifts her hands to me. I purse my lips and swallow the cold water, feeling it run down my throat. I do the same for her. I almost sense the young priest's anger, as if he knows that two of the same flesh are kissing each other.

"Do you love my master?" I ask the girl as she gazes longingly at him.

"The dark-skinned girl is with him. It is her image he has used as a figurine for the newly elected leader's ship."

"Yes, but he is staying, and she is leaving." I want to hold her. "And I am to leave, and you will stay here with the old priest."

She sits against the cave wall.

"I am going on the young priest's ship," I say with a sigh. "I want to stay here with you and the old priest."

"You are staying." She pulls me to her. I sit between her legs, our feet outstretched as we face the opening of the cavern. "We will stay together." She wraps her legs over mine; I lean back in her arms.

"What will the young priest and the newly elected leader say if I don't show up tomorrow?" I ask. "I'm supposed to be the master carver when we reach the new land."

"Everything will be alright," she whispers. "Look at the master carver and the dark-skinned girl. They are creating another image."

"Only you and I can see afar like the red feathered creature," I say as I look through the opening. In the distance we see a young couple kneeling on the rocks. The master carver and the dark-skinned girl are carving an image of them. "The others cannot see like us. Only the old priest could see that far before his eyes became glazed."

"He still sees without the full vision of his eyes," the girl replies. "He senses things around him."

I think of when we stayed there last night. I felt that he knew where I was even though I doubt he could see me with his eyes.

"He uses his senses to see and his hearing," she says. "He has taught me to do the same."

"What controls his thoughts? His thoughts are not the same as the young priest's thoughts. Are your thoughts the same as his?"

"Everyone's thoughts are different." She leans forward. "My thoughts are different from yours."

I lean back against her as she puts her hands around my stomach. The young priest would hold me like this after he read to me. Words from the book of truth, he would say to me.

"Do you believe in the truth?" I ask, looking into her eyes.

"Truth is a perception." Her breath is soft and warm on the back of my neck. "The truth someone speaks may be different than another speaks, but both believe they are speaking the truth. The old priest says that our village will survive the fires while the young priest tells the villagers that the village will be razed by the fires."

"But that is only speculation by observation and not the truth. The old priest has seen many things survive in his lifetime and many things die," I reply, enjoying her touch.

We sit and watch the sun set, shining red over the water. The moon rises opposite it, large and luminous, a single eye amid the myriad of stars against the blackness.

"The sun and the moon are the truth, always rising and setting in a pattern." She rubs her hands over my stomach, a soft touch as her hair falls over my face. She kisses the back of my neck, nibbling on it. Her hands are soft like the young priest's hands, but gentler. We are alone in the cave. No one knows where we are. I let her touch me, craving her.

"The priest said to stay away from you," I say as I feel her lips on my neck.

"Then why didn't you?" She pricks my neck with her fangs, drawing blood. "Our blood is the same," she murmurs, her tongue presses against my neck, feeling the pulse of my veins as my heart throbs.

Water drips down from the stone, a constant drip, keeping time, a steady beat like my pulse. Her tiny breasts push against my back. She lowers her hands to my lap, caressing me. I hear the young priest's voice, strong and resonating, echoing inside the cave walls. The moon rises higher, its silvery light glowing on us. Her hands touch between my legs.

Never let another touch you. The voice of the young priest rings in my ears. I gently push her hands away. She sits still behind me, her body against mine, warm and gentle. I squirm against her, desiring her, wanting her touch.

"Touch me," I whisper, pulling her hands to me. I sit with my legs spread, letting her fondle me, soft moans coming from her. Her fingers pry me, lifting my flesh, squeezing me. My nub becomes hard and elongated.

"You are a woman!" the young priest would tell me.

"It is what he wanted you to believe," the girl whispers, reading my thoughts.

I give myself to the girl, realizing that the truth is mixed with lies. I never was a female, only the young priest's girl. I believed the lies he read to me, the stories of valiant men with younger men. I close my eyes, forgetting about him. She moves around me, sitting on my lap, facing me. A new feeling rises inside me. I slide my hands under her bum, my finger touching the small dimple on her right cheek. She leans forward, kissing me, then biting me.

I open my eyes to the silvery glow of the moon on us. Her eyes look into mine, the black slits large. The cave floor trembles as I lift myself up, releasing into her. A large crack appears above her, the length of the cave to the small tunnel leading into the earth. The tunnel collapses, and she screams in ecstasy, clinging to me, convulsing on me, drawing my seed into her.

"We are here forever," she whispers. Our bodies are wet, glimmering in the silvery light.

Screech! The red feathered creature alights on the edge of the cavern opening, the morning sun glowing orange behind it. We chuckle, feeling elated as we let the sun warm our naked bodies.

"It was wonderful." The girl with yellow eyes smiles at me, her eyes glowing.

"Beautiful." I snuggle beside her, feeling her body against mine, a feminine touch.

She reaches for the finned creature that the red feathered creature holds in its beak. Her fingers are slender and the feathered creature's claws are as long as her fingers. They both have long pointed nails.

"Let's eat." She shares the finned creature with me. Its flesh is raw and oily. As we eat, we look around us. Rocks are scattered around the opening into the earth, blocking our exit. The only way out is the tiny opening facing the great water.

"We should have wings." She grins, then stands up, waving her arms up and down.

"Or fins." I stand beside her, pretending to swim like the finned creatures. I hear the young priest call out, searching for me. I no longer fear him or crave his body against mine. The cliff wall is sheer, impossible to climb down. Below it is the great expanse of water. In the distance are the red hills.

"Do you think we can climb down?" I look down, seeing the tiny waves lap against the cliff walls.

We look again at the opening, which is barely discernible, covered in rocks and grit.

"We are children inside the earth." She grins at me. "When the time is right to leave, the earth will open for us."

I wish I had her confidence—and her fearlessness.

"What do you think caused the earth to tremble last night?"

"You!" She winks at me.

I smile, thinking about the ecstasy I felt. She stands before me, her face warm and loving, a tiny scar between her breasts. Her arms touch my shoulders as she pushes me to the ground. The slit on the end of her tongue is barely visible. She lowers herself on me, her moist flower enveloping my erect phallus, her bare feet against my sides. The sun shines on us, smiling it seems, its glow warm and comforting. I bask in her warmth, her subtle movements, the sway of her body over mine, her tiny moans echoing off the cave walls.

"The ships are leaving." She raises her arm, pointing. We sit on the edge of the opening, our legs dangling, splaying our toes. "You are with me." She grins, snuggling up to me.

I put my arm around her, feeling the tiny dimple on her bum cheek. The red feathered creature flies over us, screeching.

"Look at her." She points to the feathered creature. I look up at the feathered creature, watching her circle, as if warning us.

I gasp.

"What's wrong?" she asks.

A large creature without scales and a triangular fin swim below us. Three lines are behind its jaws.

"It breathes through those slits," the girl says. The triangular finned creature swims toward the ships. Three more are following it.

The young priest's voice echoes through the cavern's opening, one last call, looking for me. I see him standing by the angelic figure of myself on the first ship, the carving I carved for him. In the distance my phallus looks small, its rigid erection pointing ahead. The young priest's eyes turn to us. They glint as they sweep across the cliffs, searching for us.

"Do not fear," the girl says, comforting me. "He will soon be gone."

"Ahoy the sails!" a gruff voice shouts.

We watch as the sails lift in unison, and oars dip into the water as the vessels surge ahead, each one carrying a family, and their servants. A tear drips from my eye as I think of the young priest leaving. Who will teach me to read?

"We will teach ourselves," the girl says, once more reading my thoughts as if she is one with me. I hold her hand, our bodies pressed together. The morning sun is rising in the sky, and a haze of smoke drifts across the water.

"No more fires!" a young lad shouts with glee.

"A land flowing with bread laden with the golden nectar!" an old lady cheers as she bites into a crusty loaf, her upper teeth missing.

Crumbs fall to the ground as the feathered creatures dance around her, gathering them up, then flying away after they have swallowed a morsel. An old man lifts a flask to his face, red liquid streaming down his chin. He burps, then raises the flask up to his mate, pouring it down his throat.

"They're going to the same place they are leaving," the girl with yellow eyes says sadly.

"Yes," I agree, "A complete circle, only on another land. They will find themselves the same."

We look across the water. A huge crest of a wave is surging toward the first ship, smashing into it. I gasp as the young priest hurtles through the air, his hands gripping the figurine's phallus.

"Come!" The girl bends over the ledge, grabbing my hand. We leap headfirst, diving toward the water, our arms extended and our feet straight out. Our robes lie on the rocks behind us. We fall forever before we hit the water, our hands cutting through the surface like a knife.

Screech! The red feathered creature swoops down, diving beside us, its wings tucked in and its legs pointing outward.

Splash! We hit the water, our breath leaving us and our ears succumbing to the pressure. The girl moves her arms and legs, slithering forward and upward like the slithering creature. I follow her, my chest constricting as I hold my breath. We surface, gasping for breath. Then we swim with all our might toward the ships.

A triangular finned creature swims beside us, black in colour, its underbelly is white, and its mouth filled with rows of teeth. It snatches the old man in its jaws, the flask dangling from his arm and red liquid flows from it. The water churns, becoming redder as the triangular finned creature clamps down on the old man. I watch in horror as the arm floats, the red liquid from the flask mixing with the red liquid spewing from the end of his arm. A white bone protrudes from the centre. One of the three triangular finned creatures swimming behind the first grabs the arm, clamping down on it, and spitting the flask out. The other two swirl around the first, butting against it, trying to dislodge the corpse from its mouth. The body has become a decoy, saving the rest from certain demise as the triangular finned creatures thrash around it, intoxicated from the red liquid. Our arms tiring, we surge ahead, fear spurring us on.

The young priest is clutching the figurine's phallus, his own phallus is rigid as a slithering creature dangles from his neck. Its fangs are locked into his tender flesh, its poison causing him to become rigid. Unable to let go of the figurine, the priest bobs up and down in the water, his eyes bleary. He stares at me until his eyes become wide, open, and sightless. A shudder flows through me. Even in death the young priest's phallus is rigid. The slithering creature encircles him, wrapping its body around him.

We come to a large body floating in the water, her ponderous breasts bobbing up and down. It is the village cook, her eyes pleading with us. Without saying a word, we grab her, pulling her with us as we swim. Her pudgy fingers barely fit into our hands. The figurine of the dark-skinned girl floats past us. She clings to it, her arms wrapped around it.

"She will be okay," the girl with yellow eyes mouths to me.

I look once more at the cook wrapped around the figurine, her ponderous breasts covering the small breasts of the figurine of the dark-skinned girl. Her enormous bum is up in the air, her velvet folds large and open. The girl with yellow eyes nudges me, her eyes twinkling. Another raft floats beside us. It has four bodies lashed to it. I recognize the old priest's door frame. One of the persons floating on the raft is the baker, a lithe, young lad with wiry arms and legs. He smiles when he sees the cook, then he reaches for her, his strong hands grabbing her pudgy fingers. He draws her to him. The other three sleep, exhausted from the ordeal. The lithe young lad sits on the edge of the door frame, pulling the cook up into his arms. Her breasts drape around his shoulders, her large bum covers his small loins. The door frame rocks dangerously, almost tipping over as the cook rocks on the lithe lad, moaning.

Seeing that they are safe, we push the figurine of the dark-skinned girl in front of us. The dark-skinned girl is treading water, holding onto the newly elected leader's children. Her body is tired, her breasts sagging, and her white skirt is nowhere to be seen. We help her and the children onto the figurine. Ironically it is the figurine of herself that saves her and the children from drowning. The figurine is still coupled to the broken helm of the ship. Even with the strongest waves, it did not uncouple.

The newly elected leader's wife floats past us, her arms and legs splayed out and her clothing in tatters. I swim to her, lifting her head up. I feel a faint pulse in her neck. The girl with yellow eyes lifts her onto the wooden figurine of the dark-skinned girl, behind her children. Her husband is nowhere to be seen. We lash both pieces of floating debris together. The slithering creature is wrapped around the pole, fastened to the centre of the door frame.

"We must gather more debris." The girl with yellow eyes looks at me, her fanged teeth appearing shiny and sharp, a trickle of blood dripping from her mouth.

"I let out the poison." She touches the neck of the children's mother, showing me the tiny pinpoints breaking her skin. I feel the mother's pulse. It is growing stronger. The newly elected leader's wife opens her eyes and looks into mine.

"They must see the slithering creature wrapped around the pole," she whispers. "They will swim to it and be saved."

"We will gather more debris," I reply as I kiss her neck, feeling her pulse.

I push away from her, swimming behind the girl with yellow eyes, collecting floating debris for the living to climb on. A wave crests above us. The young priest is still mounted to the wooden carving of myself, my phallus embedded in him. He turns one final time before the figurine sinks to the depths, carrying him with it. The slithering creature releases its fangs from his neck, then swims away from him.

"He's gone!" the girl with yellow eyes whispers.

***

"Come." I feel a tug on my hand. "Let's climb the mast and watch from above."

"Yes, let's go." I leap up. "Race you!"

"One, two, three, go!" he yells.

The ship lurches, and our bare feet slip on the deck as we take off running. A wave crashes over the side, knocking my feet from under me. Sliding on the deck, I scramble up, but not before he reaches for the mast.

Using his hands and feet, he shimmies up the mast. I am right below him, watching him climb, his strong toes gripping the mast right above my fingers. Mischievously, I touch his arches, ducking as he kicks at my head.

"That tickles," he giggles.

His muscles are strong and supple, flowing the length of his body. He digs his toes into the mast, pushing himself up. Soon we are sitting on the crossbeam high above the ship, feeling the breeze on our faces.

"It's so peaceful up here," I say, hugging him. "I love it. Remember the day we climbed the tree? We watched the building of the ships from our perch. Look in the distance. Our tree is still there."

Splat. A large white feathered creature flies over us, dropping its offal on the beam beside him.

"Yuck!" He laughs, sliding over to me. "I wish we could fly. Then we would soar to our tree and back to the mast. The village is but a speck in the distance. The old priest's house looks like a dot among the other houses from here."

"Do you think the old priest will stay in the village?" I ask. "A lot of the villagers think he's to blame for the fires. They also say that the young priest tried to poison him. Do you think it's true?"

"I don't know." He gives me an innocent look. "It seems the village is divided in what they say and believe."

I nod in agreement. "Yes, they are!"

I stand up, balancing on the beam, and point toward the old priest's dwelling. "Look, I can barely see the door frame over the priest's dwelling. Do you see the twinkle in the slithering creature's eyes glow, as the sun shines through it?"

I look at the eyes, wondering how they can twinkle, it is as if they are alive.

"The eyes are gorgeous," he replies. "Dead but alive."

I look at the water below us. Its calm, yet a wave swept over us.

"The water is as smooth as ice. I wonder where the wave came from," he says, looking perplexed.

"Do you think the omen of the old lady is correct?" I ask. "That the ships will sink, and all who leave on them will perish?"

"The master builder says these ships can sail through any storm. Talented craftsmen built them from the strongest of trees, able to withstand strong winds."

"But the fires have ravaged the forests, and most of the trees have felt the effects of the fires." I look at the blackened forest. "What if some of the wood used for the ships comes from those trees?"

"Hopefully, the wood will be strong and true," he replies. "The young priest blessed the logs before they were hewn."

"True. He did bless them." I look at his strong face, my heart fluttering. "I'm excited to go on this voyage with you by my side." I put my arm around him.

Our village has been building these twelve ships for seven years, preparing for the clan to divide and explore new lands. The last seven years have provided scant rain, and the ground is barren. Fires ravage every day; it seems that the whole earth is burning. Twelve families will leave the village, each family on its own ship. This way the tribe will multiply, and our bloodlines will stay pure.

The elders picked the twelve families who will separate from the clan and sail to the new lands. All the rest will remain. Strong men hewed large trees that were not destroyed by fire, delimbing them. Masts were carved from the trunks, strong enough to bear sails and withstand sudden wind gusts. The young lads carved oars from the branches. The oars are strong and supple, able to propel the ship quickly through the water. Young women wove and sewed cloth together for the huge sails. Talented dyers collected pigments and mixed colours, painting the families' emblems on the sails.

The young priest's ship has a freshly carved figurine on it. His ship will lead the flotilla.

"A child will lead the way," the young priest has told the clan.

I look at the figurine on his ship, pointing straight ahead, a small child standing as a man. One arm hangs on the lead rope, and the other motions for others to follow him. The young priest is standing beside the figurine, a scowl on his face as he searches for the young carver, who is missing. It is said that the young carver carved the figurine, a carving of himself, his phallus erect.

***

It was in the third moon of the seventh year that everyone was to assemble and prepare for the departure. We had a great feast the night before. Blessings and prayers were said, and tears were shed as loved ones said goodbye. The morning was bustling with excitement and dread. The air was still while only a slight hue of smoke filled the sky.

"I'm going to climb to the very top," I say as I scurry to the top of the mast, my toes curling around the ropes as I balance standing up. "Look at the expanse of blue water in the distance." I look down, spreading my arms. "This will be the adventure of our lives."

He beams at me. "You are the lady of the mast. When we get to our new land, I will make a carving of you. I will place it on the front of the ship pointing forward, with your arms stretching outward. You will guide the way."

"Like the great white feathered creature." I flap my arms as if I'm flying. "Seeking new lands and adventures."

"We will sail on the water like the finned creatures, scaled and unscaled alike." I look across the vast expanse of water. "Look, the finned creatures without scales are swimming with us. They will keep us safe, and the large winged creature will lead us to land if we follow her."

"Come stand with me on the top." I reach for his hand, pulling him up beside me. His hands are large and calloused, but his grip is gentle. Balancing together, we stand side by side. I turn to him, reach for his lips, and kiss him.

"Hey!" someone shouts from below. "Down here!"

Below us, on the next ship, I see our cousin waving gleefully, her feet wide apart as she stands on the deck.

"Hey!" she hollers. "I wish I was on your ship. You two are free to do as you wish. I must help with the chores."

"I was up before sunrise loading the ship with food!" I yell at her. "You were still sleeping in your cot."

"No one should be up before the sun!" she replies, laughing. "I was still dreaming beautiful dreams."

"You miss the gorgeous sunrises. This morning the sunrise was a brilliant red spreading across the whole sky. I wish you would have seen it with us."

"I will be up early with you tomorrow. I would love to climb the mast with you, but you know I'm terrified of heights. The ground is where we belong, standing on the flat earth, so we dare not fall off the edge. Have you two not listened to your father's teachings? We must be careful when we sail that we don't drop over the edge of the world like the others who left before us, and never returned."

I chuckle, remembering our father's tales of whirlpools in the water and land with no end.

"The old priest tells us that the world is round!" I holler at her. "He says we will sail all the way around the world and come back to this fire-ravaged island. No one believes what he says because they can't see that far ahead of themselves. It's the same sun that rises over the red hills as the sun that sets over the great water. Only one comes up on one side, and the other goes down on the other side. It proves the earth is round, like a ball."

"Heretic!" a shrill voice screeches at me.

"Don't sail over the edge! You'll all perish!" another voice cries from shore.

"Silly old woman," one of the men below us mutters. "She thinks only those left in the village will survive. Little does she know that the earth is parched, and all those who remain in the village will soon be burnt to a crisp."

"Yes!" another man grunts. "Let's get away from this certain death." He swings his oar into the water, propelling the ship away from land. I feel the ship sway as it surges ahead.

"Do you think those who stay will perish?" I ask the lad beside me as we steady ourselves on the top beam.

"Soon the rain will come, and those who are left will renew their life," he says as he puts his arm around me.

"We have only enough food for forty days and forty nights," I remind him. "If we don't find new land before then, we will die."

"Hush." He squeezes me tight. "The gods who created us will protect us. We will survive."

A shadow covers us. We look up, hearing the swish of wings, the large winged creature circles, as if warning us. I gasp, and my muscles tighten as I stare ahead in awe. A wall of water is coming toward us, higher than the mast of the first ship in the flotilla. Everything happens so fast. There is no wind and not a cloud in the sky. The water is as smooth as ice. Everything is calm, yet the wall of water comes. The women are preparing for the first meal on the ship. Fresh bread is being buttered, and soup laden with meat from the woollen creatures is being poured into wooden bowls.

"Come down!" someone yells. "Dinner is ready."

Winged creatures circle the ships, shrieking and searching for crumbs. Sea creatures swim around us, scaled and unscaled alike, some with triangular fins. I watch in horror as the wall of water hits the first boat, snapping it in half, and turning it over end for end. I remember the tremor I felt last night. I thought that it was just a dream. I see the young priest holding onto the figurine's erect phallus, both of them hurtling through the air.

The wave hits the second boat, breaking it in half, shattering it. Only the figurine of the dark-skinned girl is intact, withstanding the sudden surge. Bodies fly through the air, splashing into the water. Distant screams match the screeching of the gulls. The next two boats overturn, splintering into thousands of pieces, bodies floating everywhere.

"Help!" someone screams. Our cousin is standing by the rail on the boat beside us.

"Jump!" we yell.

Seconds before the wave hits her boat, she leaps overboard.

"Jump!" the lad says, gripping my hand.

Without hesitation, we leap high into the air, the mast bending backward as the waves crash over the boat. It seems like we soar forever, weightless, the large winged creatures circling above us. The wind whistles in my ears, drowning out the screams as I fall toward the water.

Splash! The air is knocked out of me, and everything turns black. This must be the prelude to death. Something soft brushes against me, and long whiskers rub against my face. I am being pushed upward. My head surfaces. Choking, coughing, sputtering, I gasp for air. The lad clings to me, water spewing from his mouth and his lips turning blue.

A wave hits us, lifting us up. I look around us; everything is chaos. A sea creature without scales and with a blunt nose swims away from us. It lifts a body from the water, tossing it onto a floating piece of debris. In a split second the crest of the wave drops, and we are surrounded by water, only to be lifted again, bobbing up and down. I hang onto the lad, keeping his head above the water. As we ride the crest, I see the remnants of our ship crashing onto the shore, rolling over, bodies spilling out as it turns. The wave drops, and we are surrounded by water once again, a black abyss. We catch another wave, which lifts us up. I see the mast from our ship smashing into the door frame of the old priest's home. His hut is floating into the sea, a wall of water surging back is carrying it with it. Bodies float past us, and an arm reaches out.

"Help! Please! Help me!" A shrill scream splits the air.

I turn and grab the arm, pulling the body toward us. Her mouth is open as she screams in agony. Her face is bruised, and her wide gapped teeth snap shut on her tongue. Blood trickles from her mouth. I recognize the face of our cousin.

"Help," she moans.

The door of the old priest's house nudges me. I cling to it, pushing the lad onto it. Then I reach for our cousin and pull her onto our tiny raft. Her clothes are in tatters. A wave rolls over us and the remnants of her clothing wash away. I remove my robe, using it to lash us onto the raft. The cold water splashes against our naked bodies, numbing us. A wave returns from shore, pushing us back out. Our cousin is turning blue. I press hard against her chest, forcing a stream of water out of her mouth. Someone clambers onto the door frame, pulling himself up. I reach for him. It is the young baker.

"Help!" I plead.

The young lad lifts our cousin's head and blows into her mouth, breathing his breath into her lungs. The old priest's door frame floats toward us, bobbing in the water. I grab it, and we lash it to our raft, making it bigger. The rope from the sails touches my arm. I secure it around the door and the frame. The entwined slithering creatures look as if they are alive. I gasp as one slips into the water, swimming away from us.

The four of us cling to the tiny raft. As fast as the waves come toward us, they retreat from the land, carrying bodies and broken dwellings from the village into the sea. Debris from the ships intermingle with debris from the village. The bodies of the villagers who stayed, float with the bodies of the villagers who sailed toward a new life.

Steam rises from the land as the waves crash over the smouldering ashes of the fires, quenching the flames. Clouds roll across the sky, created from the steam rising from the ground. A light rain falls. Thankful, we open our parched mouths, trying to collect the fresh water. The waves slow down as the sun sets, its redness shining across the horizon, creating an eerie glow across the water. I raise the emblem of the slithering creatures around the pole in the middle of the raft. Huddled around our symbol, we succumb to sleep, our bodies huddled together for warmth.

"Caw! Caw! Caw!" The black feathered creatures awaken us.

"Everyone is gone." Our cousin sobs, her eyes red from crying and the brackish water. "We were supposed to start a new life. The old lady was right. 'You will surely perish if you sail away.' She warned us."

"Hush," I whisper, holding her tight.

"We are alive, and we will survive. We must be strong and stand together," I tell the lad and our cousin. "The village is destroyed, but we will look for survivors. We must have hope."

The black feathered creatures band together on the trees, cawing raucously.

EPILOGUE

"The stories are the same but different."
"Stories are based on the perceptions and memories of the individuals telling the tales."
"Will there be other stories?"
"Yes, there will be other stories!"
I smile dreamily, putting my head in my love's lap, listening to the sound of the waves.

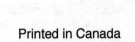